CHILL OF FEAR

KAY HOOPER

CHILL OF FEAR

RANDOM HOUSE
LARGE PRINT

fic

Copyright © 2005 by Kay Hooper

Published in the United States of America by Random House Large Print in association with Bantam Book, New York.
Distributed by Random House, Inc., New York.

Library of Congress Cataloging-in-Publication Data

Hooper, Kay.
Chill of fear/Kay Hooper.
p.   cm.
ISBN 0-375-43516-6 (lg. print)
1. Government investigators—Fiction.
2. Tennessee—Fiction. 3. Psychics—Fiction.
4. Large type books. I. Title.

www.randomlargeprint.com

FIRST LARGE PRINT EDITION

10 9 8 7 6 5 4 3 2 1

This Large print edition published in accord with the standards of the N.A.V.H.

CHILL OF FEAR

PROLOGUE

Leisure, Tennessee
Twenty-five years ago

The little girl huddled, shivering, in the back corner of the closet. She didn't like the darkness, and shut her eyes tightly so she wouldn't see it. She held her hands over her ears, pressing hard, to shut out the sound.

Tha–thum.
Tha–thum.
Tha–thum.

But she couldn't close it out, no matter how hard she tried, and had the frightened notion that it was inside herself. Sometimes, if she put her hand over her chest, she could feel her heart beating, and thought it would sound like that.

Tha–thum.

But this sound was in her head, thrumming, beating like tiny wings as though something tried desperately to escape.

"Go away," she whispered.

Tha–thum.

Look.

Tha–thum.

Listen.

She couldn't read very well, it had always been difficult for her, but she could see these words as though they were etched in her mind in bright, flowing script. They were always like that, the weird, shiny letters spelling words she understood.

Hurry. Look.

She couldn't not look. Had never been able to ignore or withstand those commands.

Hands still covering her ears, she reluctantly opened her eyes. The closet was dark, as she'd feared, but light seeped underneath the door. And even as she focused on that sliver of brightness, she felt the slow, heavy vibrations in the floor underneath her.

Hide.

"I am," she whispered, trembling. Her gaze was fixed on that sliver of light, and the dread inside her was swelling, huge, filling her.

It's coming.

Her breath caught on a silent sob as a bit of darkness crossed the sliver of light, and the vibrations beneath her ceased.

Then the bit of darkness swallowed the light, and she heard the closet door rattle.

Tha–thum!
Tha–thum!
Tha–thum!
Oh. No.
It's here.

Five years ago

"You're a hard man to find."

Without taking his eyes from the papers spread out on the table before him, Quentin Hayes said, "But not impossible, obviously. Who was looking for me?"

"Noah Bishop."

Quentin did look up then, his brows rising. "Of the Spooky Crimes Unit?"

Bishop smiled faintly. "I've heard the nickname."

"Telepathically? That is supposed to be your psychic ability, right?"

"It is. But I didn't need telepathy to pick up on the ridicule." He shrugged. "We'll probably always hear variations of that. But respect will come with success. Eventually."

Quentin studied the other man, noting the curiously light gray eyes and scarred but striking face that spoke of strength and danger, and undoubtedly prevented all but the bravest souls from expressing open ridicule. That, plus his extraordinarily high success rate as a profiler, had earned Noah Bishop quite a lot of respect within the Bureau, even if this new unit of his **was** earning just as much mockery.

Still, Quentin had earned his own considerable reputation as a solid investigator who preferred to work alone, and wasn't at all eager to join a team—or go public with abilities he had been at some pains to conceal.

"So why're you telling me?" he asked.

"Thought you might be interested."

"Oh, yeah? I can't imagine why."

"Of course you can." Bishop came into the room and sat down on the other side of the table, still wearing that faint, amused smile. "You saw me coming. Months ago? Years ago?"

Refusing to reply to those dry questions, Quentin said, "I'm not on the clock, in case nobody told you that."

"What I was told was that you've spent at least two previous vacations here in Tennessee. In this same small town. Probably sitting in this same seldom-used conference room of a police department that hasn't had to deal with much except traffic tickets, domestic disputes, and the odd bootlegger or meth lab in the last twenty years or so. Here you sit, going over the same old dusty files while the local cops shrug and keep the betting pool going."

"I hear the odds are tipping in my favor," Quentin said.

"They admire sheer persistence."

"Most cops do."

Bishop nodded. "And most cops dislike mysteries and unsolved cases. So, is that why you're here?"

"You mean you don't know?"

The mockery didn't appear to disturb Bishop in the least. Matter-of-factly, he said, "I'm not clairvoyant. Not a seer, like you. And I'm a touch-telepath, not an open one. Not that touching you would necessarily help me to read you; virtually every psychic I've known has developed a shield to guard themselves."

"Then you just assume I'm psychic, is that it?" Quentin had to ask, even though Bishop's specific reference to "seer" meant he was doing more than assuming.

"No. I know you're psychic. The same way you know I am, because we tend to recognize each other. Not always, but most of the time."

"So when do we exchange the secret hand-shake?"

"That would be just before I give you your de-coder ring."

It surprised a laugh out of Quentin; he hadn't marked Bishop as a man with a sense of humor. "Sorry. But you have to admit, an FBI unit made up of psychics is pretty off the wall. Almost comic book."

"It won't be one day."

"You really do believe that, don't you?"

"Science is understanding more every day about the human brain. Sooner or later, psychic abilities will be correctly classified as just an-other set of senses, like sight or hearing, just as normal and just as human."

"And you won't be head of the Spooky Crimes Unit anymore?"

"Let's just say that it's only a matter of time before the doubts and disbelief are proven wrong. We only have to be successful."

"Ah, gee, is that all?" Quentin shook his head. "The closed-case-to-open ratio in the FBI is running—what?—about forty percent right now?"

"The SCU will do considerably better than that."

Quentin wasn't sure what he would have

replied to the other man's optimism, but an interruption presented itself when a member of the Leisure Police Department appeared in the doorway.

"Quentin, I know you're supposed to be on vacation," Lieutenant Nathan McDaniel said with only a glance toward Bishop, "but I thought you might be interested in this—and the chief okayed telling you."

"What's up, Nate?"

"We just got a call. A little girl's gone missing."

Quentin was on his feet immediately. "At The Lodge?"

"At The Lodge."

When the sprawling hotel had been built back around the turn of the twentieth century, it had been christened with some grand-sounding name, now long forgotten. For more years than anybody remembered, it had been called simply The Lodge, and somewhere along the way the owners had given up and accepted that name.

It had been a favored vacation spot of the rich and reclusive fairly consistently throughout its history, for both its grandeur and its isolation; far from any major city and reached only by a single winding, two-lane blacktop ascending miles from the small town of Leisure, it was about as far from civilization as one could get, especially in these modern days of instant or near-instant communication.

But for all its isolation, The Lodge had more than its fair share of amenities to tempt guests to make the journey to its doors. Its large main building and numerous cottages all boasted spectacular views of the surrounding mountains, and among its other attractions were miles of winding trails for hiking or horseback riding, beautiful gardens, a huge clubhouse holding both an Olympic-size swimming pool and indoor tennis courts, and a very nice eighteen-hole golf course.

Add to all that a highly trained and discreet staff ready to pander to a guest's every whim, lovely rooms and cottages with luxurious beds and bedding that guests had been known to purchase after a visit, and first-rate spa facilities, and you had a hotel that had put Leisure, Tennessee, on the map. Or at least on the map of deluxe vacation spots.

"The only problem," Quentin told Bishop as they got out of Quentin's rental in the circular driveway in front of the main building, "is that the place has a nasty habit of losing people—and they're almost always children."

"I don't imagine they include that in the brochures," Bishop said.

"No." Quentin shook his head. "To be fair, there isn't really a pattern to the thing unless you have the sort of suspicious mind I have. And from what I've been able to piece together over the years, the dead and missing, though usually connected to the hotel in some way, are almost never guests. Kids of people who work here, or in the general area, mostly. Locals. And people in this part of the country don't open up to outsiders, or want anyone meddling in their business."

"Even when that business is missing children?"

"They're the self-reliant sort, believe me. They get their dogs and their shotguns and go looking for themselves. In the old days, nobody even bothered to report any kind of problem to the police, and as far as I've been able to make out, it's just as often true in recent years."

"What sort of time frame are you talking about?"

"I've gone back twenty years, at least. And found half a dozen suspicious accidents or illnesses, as well as one unquestionable murder. Not statistically significant for a hotel with as many people passing through as The Lodge can claim, according to the books. But I'm not buying it. And—"

Bishop waited a moment, then prompted, "And?"

"And there have been at least five unsolved disappearances connected with this place, most but not all kids."

It didn't take psychic ability to know that Quentin had changed his mind about what he'd been about to say, but Bishop didn't press him. He merely said, "I think if I were a parent, I'd hesitate to bring my child here."

"Yeah. Me too." Quentin was frowning as he watched Nate McDaniel and another of the local cops speaking to a clearly distraught man near the hotel's front steps.

"And you keep coming back here to find out why this place seems to be . . . cursed?"

Quentin didn't argue with the terminology. "As you said—most cops dislike mysteries."

"Especially the ones that touch them personally."

Quentin's frown became a scowl, but he didn't reply to that since McDaniel turned and moved toward them, indicating with a jerk of his head that they should join him.

"According to the girl's father," he told them, "she's not the type to wander off. The mother was having a day at the spa, so he and his daughter were spending the day together. Horseback riding this morning, then a picnic lunch out in the rose garden. But the hamper The Lodge provided didn't have the girl's favorite drink, so he went in to get it. Says he wasn't gone five minutes, though it was probably closer to ten. When he got back to their blanket on the grass, she was gone."

McDaniel sighed. "Half the staff's out looking for her, but they didn't call us for at least an hour."

Bishop said, "They've covered the grounds nearest the buildings, then?"

"So they tell me." McDaniel eyed him. "I know why Quentin turns up here every so often, but what about you, Bishop? The chief said you were here to talk to Quentin, but might be willing to help us out with this."

"I'm always willing to help search for a child," Bishop said. "Did anybody see her after the father left her in the garden?"

"Nobody we've talked to so far. And there were other picnics going on in other parts of the garden; it's a Lodge tradition, especially in summer, like now. But all the others were couples, and my guess is they were too wrapped up in each other to pay attention if a child wandered by."

"What about if she was dragged or carried past?" Quentin demanded.

Bishop glanced at him. "People notice what's out of the ordinary. If the child had been resisting or protesting, someone would have taken note. Assuming she was seen at all."

McDaniel said, "And there's no sign of a struggle of any kind, Quentin. We won't find footprints in a garden that's mostly grass and flagstone paths, though we are checking the planting beds. The only thing the girl left behind was the sweater she was wearing earlier. I've called in one of the local search-and-rescue canine teams; they should be here within the next half hour."

"What's her name, Nate?"

"Belinda. Her father says she's never answered to a nickname. She's eight."

Quentin turned without another word and headed in the direction of the rose garden out behind the main building.

"There goes a man with demons riding him," McDaniel said almost absently.

"What sort of demons, Lieutenant?"

"You'd have to ask him. All I know is what I've observed the last couple times he's been here. And all that tells me is that he's haunted by a crime nobody's been able to solve in twenty years of trying. The difference is, Quentin just can't let it go."

Bishop nodded slightly, but all he said was,

"We all have that one case, don't we? The one that haunts us. The one we dream about at night."

"Yeah. But there's another difference for Quentin. The case that haunts him is right out of his nightmares. And his own childhood."

"I know," Bishop said.

It was, everyone agreed, creepy enough that a child had vanished right out of a bright rose garden on a sunny summer afternoon; what was even more chilling was when the search-and-rescue bloodhound, after sniffing Belinda's little pink sweater, merely sat down and howled mournfully.

"Has he ever done that before?" Bishop asked the handler, who shook his head adamantly.

"Never. Cosmo knows his job, and he's the best tracker I've ever had. I don't understand it." He bent to his dog, murmuring reassuringly to the trembling animal.

McDaniel shook his head as well, baffled, and told those of his people that had been standing by to continue searching without the aid of a dog. To Bishop, he said, "If you have any special expertise to offer, now would be the time."

"Yes," Quentin agreed, staring at Bishop challengingly. "Now would be the time."

"I don't know the terrain here as well as the rest of you," Bishop said, "but I'll do my best. Quentin, perhaps you could show me the layout of these gardens?"

"And I'll go talk to the father again," McDaniel said with a sigh.

Quentin watched the cop stride back toward the main building, then said to Bishop in a low-ered voice, "Okay, so no dog-and-pony show for the locals. I get that. But whatever abilities I may have aren't telling me a damned thing, and I'm hoping yours can be a lot more help in finding this little girl."

"Telepathy won't help," Bishop said, his own voice low. "But there's another little knack I have that might."

"What is it?"

Without answering that specifically, Bishop said, "I need a high place, somewhere I can see as much of the surrounding area as possible."

"The main building has an observation tower. Will that do?"

"Lead the way."

The "tower" was little more than a cupola jut-ting up from the roof on one side of the Victorian-style building and housing a twenty-five-foot circular room whose shutters were left wide open in summer. Since The Lodge was centered in a sprawling valley, it was possible to see for miles from this vantage point.

Bishop was silent until they reached the top of the stairs and the tower, then said, "I've always believed animals are sensitive to things most people are oblivious to, things beyond even their own keenest senses."

"Unfortunately, they can't tell us what's upset them. Or are you telepathic with animals as well as people?"

"People only, I'm afraid. And not much more than half of them. You know these extra senses of ours are as limited as the usual five."

"I don't know a whole hell of a lot about the subject, if you want the truth," Quentin said, moving to the side of the tower that overlooked the garden area. "Not much science on it, at least that I could find, and I wasn't very interested in most of the cockeyed theories masquerading as science."

"Join the SCU, and I can guarantee you'll learn everything science and experience can tell us about psychic abilities. Your own and others'."

"I'm not what you'd call a team player."

"That I can live with," Bishop said, joining him and gazing out over the gardens. "I need a seer, Quentin, and they're rare."

"I don't **see** anything. I just know things

sometimes," Quentin finally admitted. "Stupid, useless stuff, mostly. That the phone is about to ring. That it's going to rain. That I'll find the keys I lost in some unlikely spot."

"But sometimes," Bishop said, "you know where an important piece of evidence will be found. Or precisely which questions to ask of which suspects. Or which line of an investigation is going to be a dead end."

"You've been reading my file," Quentin said after a moment.

"Of course. You're one of the few psychics I've been able to find already in law enforcement—and the only one already within the FBI."

Quentin glanced at him, then shrugged. "I've never been able to use my ability as an investigative tool. It's never been under my control in any sense."

"We'll teach you how to exert whatever control is possible. Teach you how to focus and channel your abilities. How to use them to aid an investigation."

"Will you? Can **you** do it?"

Bishop smiled faintly at the direct challenge, but rather than answering looked out over the valley and put all his concentration into opening up and strengthening his "normal" five senses. It was like having a blurry image snap suddenly into focus, while in the background faint sounds became louder, clearer, and he could smell the roses far below.

He wasn't about to admit to Quentin that the term coined for what he was doing was using his "spider sense," not after the other man's mocking reference to comic books.

"Bishop—"

"Wait." He reached out farther, and heard bits of conversation from the searching officers and hotel employees, words and phrases, disjointed and unimportant. Beneath the scents of roses and other flowers and freshly mown grass, he caught the savory odors of cooking from the hotel's kitchen, and someone's tangy perfume or aftershave, and the warm, dusty scents of horses and hay and leather. The razor-sharpness of what he saw blurred as though a zoom lens sought distant objects and struggled to bring them into focus.

Bishop pushed harder, reached farther.

The colors washed into one another, the scents blended unpleasantly into a thick miasma that caused his stomach to churn, and the sounds and voices he heard were a cacophony pounding inside his head—

"—or we could check down by the creek—"

"—of course I wasn't flirting with him—"

"—the guest in the Orchid Room needs—"

"—empty stables she might have—"

"—only a matter of time before we have to drag the streams and lake—"

"Daddy? Where are you? I'm afraid—"

It's coming.

"Bishop!"

He looked down at Quentin's hand on his arm, then at the other man's face, his vision blurry for a heartbeat or two before it cleared. And he could hear only the distant sounds that were normally audible from this height. Smell only the distant, pleasant scents of a summer afternoon.

He didn't have to ask to know that he had been too still and too silent for too long, and had to mentally shrug off the lingering chill he felt. He wondered if he had been able to tune in to his surroundings with such unusual strength because there was, as Quentin believed, something different about this place. The coldness Bishop had sensed was at least an indication that he might be right.

But there was little time to ponder that.

"Can you ride?" he asked, unsurprised by the slightly hoarse sound of his own voice.

Frowning, Quentin said, "Yeah, I can. What the hell did you just do?"

"I . . . tuned in to this place. Let's go."

Quentin followed, still frowning, and within ten minutes they were aboard two of the hotel's horses and following one of the trails that wound up into the mountains. Bishop led the way, not saying much but intent, concentrating, as though listening to some inner voice that was guiding him.

Quentin wasn't really surprised to see that Bishop rode well; he had a strong hunch that the other man was the sort who would master whatever he chose to no matter how much effort or time was involved.

Which, Quentin knew, undoubtedly included his psychic abilities.

But what **had** he done back in the tower? Whatever it was, it had been an actual, physical effort; his eyes had dilated so much that for an instant, gazing into them, Quentin had thought of ice rimming a deep, black pool. Unsettling, to say the least. And what had Bishop said—that he had tuned in to this place? What the hell was that supposed to mean?

He urged his horse up beside the other man's despite the narrowness of the trail, and said, "Do you know where she is, or are we just out for a nice afternoon ride?"

"I know where she is," Bishop replied calmly.

"How?"

"I heard her."

Quentin digested that for a moment. "From the tower? You heard her way up there?"

"Yes."

Quentin glanced back at the considerable distance they had already covered, then said almost involuntarily, "Bullshit."

"The mind," Bishop said, "is a remarkable tool. And so are the senses. The usual five, plus whatever extra ones we're lucky enough to have."

"Bishop, you're out of your mind—and **all** your senses."

"We'll see."

Quentin dropped back but continued to follow Bishop, telling himself that he was just humoring a lunatic. But the quiet voice in his own mind that had so often told him where to look or what to ask or what would happen next was telling him that little Belinda was going to be found, and that it would be because Bishop had, somehow, heard her.

"Belinda?"

"Go away," she mumbled, blinking in the brightness of Quentin's flashlight. She was squeezed back into a corner near the old rock fireplace, but seemed to do her best to make herself draw even farther away, to make herself smaller. "Don't hurt me." Her voice was thin and shaky, the plea ending in a hiccuping sob.

"It's okay, Belinda, you're safe now. We're going to take you back to your parents." Quentin tried to make his own voice soothing, but the child's terror was palpable and he dared not reach out for her.

"Let me try," Bishop said.

Quentin gave way willingly; there was very little space inside the ramshackle building that might once have been a house of sorts, and between them he and Bishop were probably looming over the sobbing child, he thought. She was obviously dazed and confused, though appeared unhurt barring a small cut on her forehead.

What Quentin couldn't understand was how she had managed to get way up here, much farther from The Lodge than a child her age should have been able to travel in the time allowed. Under her own power, at least.

"It's okay, Belinda," Bishop said, softly repeating Quentin's assurances. But he didn't hesitate to reach out and gather the child into his arms.

To Quentin's surprise, the little girl not only didn't resist or protest, but actually visibly relaxed, and stopped crying. She even looked a little sleepy, as if exhaustion had caught up with her.

"Let's get her out of here," Bishop said.

Quentin radioed the other search teams that Belinda had been safely found, and Bishop handled her slight weight easily as he carried her before him on his horse back down the mountain.

As relieved as he was that the child had been safely found, and impressed though he was with the way Bishop had been able to do that, what interested Quentin the most was Belinda's response to the other man. With those pale eyes and the angry scar down his left cheek, his didn't seem a face that would inspire confidence in a terrified little girl, yet from the moment he had touched her, she had seemed perfectly trusting and content in his arms.

"You're good with kids," Quentin noted as they rode the last half mile back to The Lodge. "Any of your own?"

Bishop glanced down at the dark-haired girl nestled against him, and Quentin saw a flicker of pain, quickly gone.

"No," Bishop replied, "none of my own."

"I guess some people just have the knack. I never did. I like kids okay and all, but they don't warm up to me quickly."

"She's been through a lot," Bishop said.

Quentin didn't bother to say that it wouldn't have made much difference in how she reacted to him. Instead, he glanced at Belinda's drowsy face and lowered his voice to say, "You heard her all the way up there; I assume you can hear her now. What happened to her?"

"She doesn't remember." Bishop's voice was low as well.

"What, nothing?"

"Nothing after waking up this morning. She doesn't remember the earlier ride with her father or the beginning of the picnic." Bishop paused, then added, "Not so uncommon after a head injury."

"No, but . . . how did she get that injury? And how the hell did she travel miles across a valley and up into the mountains in hardly more than a couple of hours?"

"I don't know."

"No hoofprints around that old shack, except for those our horses made. No tire tracks. Hell, no footprints that I saw—not even hers."

"Yeah, I noticed that."

Since they had nearly reached The Lodge, Quentin dropped the subject for the time being. But after Belinda had been safely returned to her overjoyed parents and all the questions and exclamations and thanks had been dealt with—with amazing discretion and creative evasiveness on Bishop's part—he brought it up again.

The two men sat at a fairly isolated table in a shady section of one of the verandas with a couple of cold beers—compliments of The Lodge.

"You noticed there were no footprints up there. I think we both believe she couldn't have gotten all that way on her own. So what do you think happened to Belinda?"

"I don't know. Without evidence of any kind, there's no way **to** know."

"I'm not asking what you know. I'm asking what you think. What you feel. I saw your face when we got to that old shack up there, and it didn't take a telepath to know you were picking up something you didn't like."

After a moment, Bishop said, "It was an old building, and like most old buildings it held a lot of . . . echoes. Unfortunately, there's no way I know of to separate layers of time, to distinguish the psychic echo of something that happened a century ago from something that happened yesterday. Or today. Or twenty years ago."

There was another pause as Quentin stared at him, and then he said quietly, "It didn't happen up there. What happened twenty years ago."

"I know."

"You know a hell of a lot, don't you." It wasn't really a question.

Bishop smiled. "You think I'd try to recruit a new team member without knowing everything I could about him first? There won't be many secrets in the SCU, Quentin, that goes without saying. We're a unit of psychics. And from the telepaths who can pick up thoughts to the empaths who can pick up pain, we're going to eventually know pretty much everything there is to know about each other."

"If that's your recruitment speech, it's likely to scare away more potentials than it entices," Quentin muttered.

"Is it scaring you away?"

"Answer something for me first," Quentin said. "What **did** you feel or sense at that shack?"

"The same thing I felt, for a split second, up in the observation tower. Something old, and dark, and cold. Something evil."

"What is it?"

"I don't know. Never felt anything like it before. But I can tell you that it's been here a long time. That we frustrated it today by finding Belinda when we did. And I can tell you that it's what touched your life twenty years ago."

"How could you possibly know that?" Quentin demanded roughly.

"You grabbed my arm in the tower, remember? I felt it then. That whatever's happening here is something you're connected to. It's why you keep coming back here, because you're tied, bound, to this place, and not just by your memories. By something else as well. And you'll come back again and again until you've found the answers you need."

"You can't offer those to me?"

Bishop shook his head. "No. And you won't find them this trip, I'm sure of that. It isn't yet time."

"You said you weren't a seer."

"I'm not. But one thing I've learned is that there's a kind of rhythm to most things. To the universe. A sequence of events, a pattern, a proper order. I feel that sometimes. And what I'm feeling here is that the time isn't right, that the darkness here will stay hidden a while longer."

With a stab at humor, Quentin said, "You're just saying that so I'll leave and join your unit."

"No. If I could help you settle with your past here and now, I would, believe me." Bishop's mouth twisted slightly. "I know what it is to spend too much time looking back instead of ahead. But that hasn't crippled me, and it won't cripple you."

"You sound very sure of that."

"I am sure. Just as I'm sure of what I said to you a few hours ago. You **did** see me coming, didn't you, Quentin? You knew I'd ask you to join the SCU."

Quentin laughed ruefully. "Oh, hell, I saw you coming years ago."

"It's why you joined the FBI."

"Yeah. I had a law degree I didn't know what to do with, and was actually thinking of becoming some kind of cop. And then one day I... knew the SCU was something that would happen. I knew I'd be part of it."

Dryly, Bishop said, "And still made me come to you."

"Well, a man wants to be valued."

"I think," Bishop said, "you undoubtedly earned your reputation for reckless independence."

"I think you're right. I also think we've wandered a bit from the subject. I'm not willing to give up here, Bishop."

"I wouldn't ask you to. I'm just asking you to look ahead rather than back. For a while. Your past will always be there, trust me on that."

"The girl in my past died," Quentin heard himself say.

"I know. And the girl—the woman in my past is out of my reach almost as surely as if she were dead. At least until the universe is ready to pick that thread back up again."

"And weave it back into the pattern?" Quentin shook his head. "What if it's a lost thread?"

"It isn't. She isn't. And neither is your Missy, Quentin."

It was the first time anybody had said that name to him in a long time, but Quentin felt himself flinch inside. "She's dead. All I can do for her now is find out why she died."

"I'll help all I can. You have my word on that."

"But not until the time is right?"

"Some things have to happen just the way they happen."

Quentin looked at him curiously. "Your mantra?"

"Something like that. Believing it keeps me sane."

"Then maybe you can convince me. In the meantime...what the hell. It seems we both knew this was inevitable." He held out his hand to the other man. "You've got yourself a seer, Bishop."

And as they shook hands, he almost told Bishop about the little voice in his head that was whispering, **He'll find Miranda. But not yet. Not just yet.**

Then he saw the flicker in Bishop's pale eyes, and realized that the telepath had read him and his little voice. But he hadn't needed a seer to tell him what he was utterly convinced of. He would find his Miranda. Sooner or later.

Quentin wondered if he would be so lucky with the end of his own troubled quest.

Present day

Nightmares again?"

Diana Brisco slipped her cold hands into the front pockets of her smock and frowned at him. "What makes you ask?"

"That." He nodded at the canvas on its easel in front of her, a canvas with a dark background and bright, harsh slashes of color in the foreground.

She joined him in staring at the canvas, and finally shrugged. "No, no nightmares." For once, at least. "Just in a mood, I guess."

"A dark mood."

"You told us to paint what we felt," she said defensively. "I did that."

He smiled, the expression lending his already angelic features such beauty that she unconsciously caught her breath.

"Yes, you did. And quite powerfully. I'm not worried about your work, Diana. It's superb, as usual. I'm concerned about you."

She mentally shook off the almost mesmerizing effect of his physical presence and ignored what she suspected was a pat-the-pupil-on-the-head compliment, saying, "I'm fine. I didn't sleep well, but not because of nightmares. Just because..." She shrugged again, unwilling to admit that she had been up half the night staring through her bedroom window, out over the dark valley. She had spent far too many nights that way since arriving in Leisure.

Looking for...something. God only knew what, because she certainly didn't.

Gently, but also matter-of-factly, he said, "Even if this workshop was designed for self-expression rather than therapy, I'd be offering the same advice, Diana. Once we're done here, get out of The Lodge for a while. Go for a walk, or a ride, or a swim. Sit out in one of the gardens with a book."

"In other words, stop thinking about myself so much."

"Stop **thinking**. For a while."

"Okay. Sure. Thanks." Diana knew she sounded brusque and wanted to apologize for it. He was only doing what he was supposed to do, after all, and probably had no idea that she'd heard it all before. But before she could form the words, he merely smiled and moved on to the next of his dozen or so "students" here in the bright, open space of the hotel's conservatory.

Diana kept her hands in the pockets of the paint-stained smock and frowned at her painting. **Superb,** huh? Yeah, right. To her eye, it looked more like the finger painting of a highly untalented six-year-old.

But, of course, quality was hardly the point. Talent was hardly the point.

Figuring out what was going on in her screwed-up mind was the point.

She took her gaze off the painting and watched as Beau Rafferty moved among his students. An artist of his caliber teaching this sort of workshop had struck her as extremely odd at first, but after a week of classes she had come to realize that he had a genuine gift not only for teaching, but also for reaching and helping troubled people.

Other people, at least. She could already see changes in most of the others participating in this workshop. Strained faces had begun to relax, smiles had appeared to replace frowns or haunted anxiety. She had even seen a few of them out enjoying some of the activities The Lodge had to offer.

But not Diana. Oh, no. Diana was still having nightmares when she could sleep at all, she couldn't remember the last time she had felt relaxed, and none of the myriad sports or recreational facilities here held the least appeal for her. And despite Rafferty's undoubted genius and ability to teach, she didn't believe that her rudimentary artistic skills had improved either.

In fact, this whole thing was probably just one more waste of her time and her father's money.

Diana looked back at her painting and hesitated for a moment before picking up her brush and adding one small streak of scarlet near the lower left corner. That finished it, she decided. She had no idea what it was or what it was supposed to represent to her, but it was finished.

She began cleaning her brushes automatically, trying to concentrate on the task and not think.

But, of course, that was part of her problem, the short attention span, these scattered, random thoughts and ideas flitting constantly through her mind, usually so fast they left her confused and disoriented at least half the time. Like bits and pieces of overheard conversations, the words and phrases came and went almost continually.

No focus, that's what the doctors said. They were sure she didn't have attention deficit disorder, despite having been medicated for that at least twice in her life; no, all the doctors and all the tests had determined that despite "somewhat elevated" levels of electrical activity, her problem wasn't physical or chemical, wasn't something in her brain—but something in her mind.

So far, none of them had been able to suggest a successful way of figuring out what that **something** was. And just about every conceivable means had been tried. The traditional couch and shrink. Hypnosis. Conscious regression, since no one had been able to hypnotize her to attempt the unconscious variety. Group therapy. Massage therapy. Various other kinds of therapy, both traditional and New Age. Including, now, painting, under the tutelage of an honest-to-God artistic genius, in yet another attempt to tap in to her inner Diana and ask what the hell was wrong with her.

One of her current doctors had suggested she try this, and Diana could only wonder if he was getting kickbacks for every referral.

Her father had spared no expense in trying to help his troubled only child, openly afraid that she might, as so many others had done, escape into alcohol or drugs or, worse, give up and commit suicide.

But Diana had never been tempted by the chemical forgetfulness that could be found in "recreational" drugs. In fact, she disliked losing control, a trait that only exacerbated her problem; the harder she tried to concentrate and focus, the more scattered her thoughts became. And the failure to control them, of course, depressed and disturbed her further, though never to the point of contemplating suicide.

Diana was no quitter. Which was why she was here, trying yet another form of therapy.

"I'll see you all back here tomorrow," Rafferty told his class, smiling, not offering a collective "Good work" because he had instead offered that individually.

Diana removed her smock and hung it on the hook at the side of the easel, and prepared to follow the others out of the conservatory.

"Diana?"

She waited, a little surprised, as Rafferty approached her.

"Take this." He held out a sketchpad and small box of watercolor pencils.

She accepted them, but with a frown. "Why? Is this some kind of exercise?"

"It's a suggestion. Keep the pad close by, and

when you start to feel upset or anxious or restless, try drawing. Don't think about it, don't try to control what you draw, just draw."

"But—"

"Just let go and draw."

"This is like the inkblots, right? You're going to look at my sketches and interpret them, go all Freudian and figure out what's wrong with me?"

"I won't even see them, unless you want to show them to me. No, Diana, the sketches are just for you. They may help . . . clarify things for you."

She wondered, not for the first time, just how much he really knew about her and her demons, but didn't ask. Instead, she merely nodded. It was something she hadn't tried, so why not? "Okay, fine. See you tomorrow."

"See you tomorrow, Diana."

She left the conservatory, going out into the gardens more because she didn't want to return to her cottage than because the gardens were an enjoyment for her. They were pretty, she supposed. Gorgeous, really, from the various themed gardens already in bloom in mid-April to the striking greenhouse that held an amazing variety of orchids.

But Diana walked through most of the charming scenery indifferently. She followed a flagstone path because it was there, crossing the arched footbridge over the man-enhanced stream holding numerous colorful koi and ending up in the supposedly serene Zen Garden, with its manicured shrubs and trees and carefully placed rocks and sand and statuary.

She sat down on a stone bench beside a weeping willow tree, telling herself she wouldn't remain long because the afternoon was waning and it got chilly this time of year as the sun dipped below the mountains. And then there was the fog, which had an unsettling tendency to creep across this valley and settle over The Lodge and its gardens so that finding one's way along the paths resembled a trip through a damp and chilly maze.

Diana definitely wasn't in the mood for that. But she nevertheless sat there longer than she had planned, finally opening the box of watercolor pencils and absently selecting one. They were already sharpened.

She opened the sketchpad and tried the pencil out just as absently, making yet another attempt to ignore the jumbled thoughts crowding her mind and concentrate on only one. Why she was having so much trouble sleeping here. It had been an issue now and then in her life, but not recently, not until she had come to The Lodge.

Nightmares had always been a problem for

her, though still not regular occurrences, but since coming to The Lodge they had gotten worse. More intense, more... terrifying. She'd wake in the dark hours before dawn, gasping in panic yet unable to remember what it was that had so frightened her.

It was less traumatic to stay awake. Just curl up in the window seat in her bedroom, an afghan protecting her against the chill of the glass, and stare out at the valley and the dark mountains that loomed above.

Looking for... something. Nothing.

Waiting.

Diana came back to herself with a little start, suddenly aware of her aching fingers. She was holding one of the pencils, and most of the others lay beside her on the bench, out of their box, their once-sharpened ends dulled now. She had the sense that time had passed, and didn't want to look at her watch to see just how much.

That was all she needed—the return of something that hadn't happened to her in months. Blackouts.

Warily, she turned her gaze to the sketchpad on her knees. And saw, to her astonishment, the face she had drawn.

Slightly shaggy hair a color between gold and brown surrounded a lean face with high cheek-

bones and vivid blue eyes. There was a jut of determination to his jaw, and humor played
around the faintly smiling mouth.

He seemed to be looking right back at Diana,
those keen eyes curiously . . . knowing.

Artistically, it was better work than she knew
herself capable of, which gave her the creeped-
out feeling that someone else had drawn this.
And lending weight to that was her certain
knowledge that she had never seen this man before in her life.

"Jesus," she murmured. "Maybe I really am
crazy, after all."

"I keep trying to tell you, Quentin, there's been
nothing new." Nate McDaniel shook his head.
"Matter of fact, since that time a few years back
when you and—what was his name? Bishop?—
helped find that missing girl out at The Lodge,
we haven't had any unsolved disappearances or
accidents anywhere in the area, let alone murders. It's been downright peaceful around here."

"Don't sound so disappointed," Quentin advised dryly. "Peaceful is a good thing." But his
long fingers drummed restlessly on the edge of
the desk, a gesture McDaniel took due note of.
Not the most patient of men, was Quentin—
which made it all the more interesting that he

kept returning here in patient pursuit of answers.

McDaniel sighed. "Look, we both know that cold cases rarely get hot just because somebody sifts through all the paperwork one more time. And God knows you've sifted through it all enough times to be sure of that. The truth is, unless some new fact or bit of information comes to light, chances are that case stays cold. And after twenty-five years, what's likely to turn up now?"

"I don't know. But something has to."

Not without sympathy, McDaniel said, "Maybe it's time to let it go, Quentin."

"No. No, I'm not ready to do that."

"But you are ready to waste another vacation sitting in the conference room with dusty files and crime-scene photographs, and drinking lousy coffee for hours on end."

Quentin frowned. "As you say, that's hardly gotten me anywhere in years of trying."

"So try something else," McDaniel suggested. "I know you always stay here in town; why not get a room or cottage out at The Lodge this time?" He watched the play of emotions across the other man's expressive face, and added quietly, "I can guess why you've avoided that, but maybe it's time you hunted those ghosts where they're more likely to be."

"I hope you don't mean ghosts literally," Quentin muttered.

McDaniel hesitated, then said, "You'd know more about that than I would."

Quentin looked at him, brows raised.

"Oh, come on, Quentin. The SCU's been gaining quite a reputation in law enforcement circles, you know that. I'm not saying I buy everything I've heard, but it's clear you guys deal with stuff that's more than a little bit out of the ordinary. Hell, I always wondered how you and Bishop found that little girl, as if you went straight to her. I've followed a few **hunches** myself over the years, but they were never as accurate as yours clearly were that day."

"We got lucky."

"You had a damned sight more than luck on your side that day, and don't try to deny it."

"Maybe," Quentin admitted finally. "But whatever we had, whatever I have, it doesn't open a window into the past. And I'm no medium."

"That's somebody who talks to the dead, right?" McDaniel strove to keep the disbelief out of his voice but, judging by the other man's wry smile, failed.

"Yeah, a medium communicates with the dead. But, like I said, I'm not a medium."

Then what are you? But McDaniel stopped

short of asking that question, uncomfortably aware of how it would sound. Instead, he said, "Maybe there aren't any ghosts at all out at The Lodge. I mean, there's been talk over the years that the place is haunted, but what old building doesn't have those sorts of stories around it? Anyway, what happened, happened out there."

"Twenty-five years ago. How many times has the place been remodeled or redecorated since then? How many people have come and gone? Christ, there aren't more than a handful of employees who were there, and I've talked to them all."

Responding to the last statement, McDaniel said thoughtfully, "Funny you should mention that. I'd forgotten, but as it turns out, there is a new employee there now who was also there twenty-five years ago. They just rehired him a few months back. Cullen Ruppe. He manages the stables, the same job he had back then."

Quentin felt his pulse quicken, even as he heard himself say, "I don't remember him. But then, there's a lot I don't remember about that summer."

"Not all that surprising. You were—what?—ten?"

"Twelve."

"Still. Maybe Ruppe can help fill in the blanks."

"Maybe." Quentin got to his feet, then

paused. "If I do want to come back and sit in that conference room again—"

"You're welcome to, you know that. But unless you do find something new out there..."

"Yeah, I know. Thanks, Nate."

"Good luck."

Quentin hadn't yet checked into his usual motel in Leisure, and when he left the police station he barely hesitated before driving his rental car the fifteen miles or so along that lonely blacktop road out to The Lodge. It was a route he knew well, yet the journey never failed to rouse in him a vaguely uneasy sense of leaving civilization behind as the winding road climbed up into the mountains and then descended into the valley that housed The Lodge and nothing else.

Though it catered to guests year-round and actually provided fair skiing for at least a couple of months in winter, the busiest time of the year for The Lodge was from early April through October.

So Quentin knew he was lucky when the front desk clerk found a room for him despite his lack of reservations. He even wondered if it was fate.

Malevolent fate.

"We have the Rhododendron Room available for the next two weeks, sir. It's in the North Wing."

In the middle of filling out the registration card, Quentin paused and looked across the desk at her. "The North Wing. Didn't that burn down, years ago?"

"Why, I believe it did, sir, but that must have been at least twenty or thirty years ago." She was new, or at least no one Quentin had talked to on his previous visits, and seemed to be not the least bit fazed by the fact that there had once been a fire here.

"I see," he said. He hadn't bargained on staying in the North Wing. Hadn't even thought about it, in fact.

"The Lodge **is** over a hundred years old, sir, as I'm sure you know, so having a fire here at least once in all those years isn't all that surprising. I was told it started accidentally, but not due to faulty wiring or anything like that. And it was rebuilt, of course, even nicer than before."

"I'm sure it was." He knew it had been. He had been in that part of the building many times. But he had never stayed there, never spent the night there, not since it had been rebuilt.

For the first time, Quentin had to ask himself if he did believe in ghosts. It was a surprisingly difficult question to answer.

The desk clerk hesitated for a moment, studying his face. "I don't believe we have another room available for the full two weeks, sir, but if you're willing to change rooms partway through your stay here, I'm sure I can—"

"No, I'd prefer to stay put, I think. The Rhododendron Room will be fine, thank you."

Ten minutes later, he was settling into what was actually a very nice, beautifully decorated suite with a small sitting room adjacent to the spacious bedroom and bathroom, when he found a card cheerfully explaining the "historic" meaning of the rhododendron flower "according to some sources."

He felt again the consciousness of malevolent fate taking a hand when he saw what the meaning was.

Beware.

"Well," he murmured aloud. "No one can say I haven't been warned."

Nate McDaniel waited until nearly the end of the day before he placed the call, not because of reluctance but simply because things got busy. So it was after five before he dug into the clutter on his desk to find the scrap of paper with the cell phone number scrawled on it.

He wasn't really surprised, though, when the call was answered immediately; few cops worked nine to five.

"Hello, Captain."

Nate knew it was Caller I.D. rather than psychic ability, but it still caught him slightly off guard, and it was that which made his tone a bit aggressive.

"Okay, you called in the favor and I paid. I suggested that Quentin might want to stay at The Lodge this time, and I'm pretty sure he went out there."

"I appreciate your help, Captain."

"Yeah, well, I'm not all that happy about it, so don't thank me. He might find something he's not looking for out there, and if it's trouble, I'm going to feel like shit. Plus, you know, I kinda like the guy."

"Just remember it was my idea."

Nate's unconscious frown deepened. "You know something. What is it?"

"All I know is that it's time Quentin settled with his past."

Nate wasn't about to call an FBI agent a liar, so all he said was, "And you get to decide stuff like that, huh?"

"No. I wish I did, but no."

"Well, I just hope you know what you're doing."

"Yes," Bishop said. "So do I."

Diana.

Opening her eyes with a start, Diana looked around her bedroom warily. It was dark, but not so dark that she couldn't see every corner. Nobody there, of course. Just her wayward mind not quite hearing voices.

She refused to hear voices.

Because that would make her delusional or psychotic, she knew that. So she wasn't hearing voices. Just her own random thoughts and fragments of thoughts, and so what if those fragments occasionally held her name?

The birds had begun to sing outside and darkness was shading into a slightly misty, gray dawn, which told her that she had indeed slept for at least an hour or two. Curled up in the window seat, wrapped in a soft chenille afghan.

She stirred and moved stiffly off the window seat, getting to her feet and beginning to unwrap herself. Stupid way for a grown woman to spend the night when there was a perfectly comfortable bed nearby; the housekeeping staff probably thought she was out of her mind—

Diana.

And maybe she was.

Diana went still, waiting. Listening.

Look.

For the first time, Diana was certain that the voice—this particular voice, at any rate—was outside herself. Like a whisper in her ear. On her left side, closest to the window.

Slowly, Diana turned her head.

The center pane of the window looked fogged or frosted, as though someone had breathed warmly on it. None of the other panes, just the center one. And on that pane, very clearly as if a firm finger had traced them, were two words.

HELP US

Diana caught her breath, staring at the words, the plea. A wave of coldness swept over her. But she found herself reaching out, very slowly, until she could touch the glass. That was when she realized that the words had been traced on the outside of the glass.

She jerked her hand away and quickly moved to the nightstand beside the bed and the lamp there. She turned it on, blinking in the light, and looked back at the window.

Gray, featureless panes of glass. No fog or frost.

No desperate plea.

"Of course," Diana murmured after a long moment. "Because I'm obviously out of my mind."

She managed to at least partially shake off the cold uneasiness she felt, telling herself it had probably been her imagination anyway. Just . . . a leftover wisp of whatever she'd been dreaming.

Probably.

She turned on a few more lamps in the cottage, checked the doors to make sure they were all locked, and then went and took a long, hot shower.

She actually wished she could believe there had been someone outside her window. Because if someone **had** been out there, then at least that would have been a flesh-and-blood thing. A real thing. Whether an attempt to frighten her, a stupid joke, or an actual plea for her help, it would have been **real**.

Not all in her head.

It was daylight, the sun rising above the mountains and rapidly burning off the mist, by the time Diana was dressed, but it was still early. It was her habit to either make coffee in her cottage's tiny kitchenette or else order room service, but on this morning she really didn't want to spend any more time alone.

She picked up the sketchpad and pencils that Beau Rafferty had given her and slipped them into an oversized tote bag and dropped her billfold and keycard in there as well, hoping she wouldn't have to have the latter rekeyed again. She'd already had to do that half a dozen times in the two weeks she'd been here, to the bafflement of the hotel staff.

She left the cottage, a bit relieved, as she moved toward the main building, to find the fog all but gone and others stirring even this early. Groundskeepers were working in the gardens, the heated outdoor pool Diana passed already boasted a couple of morning swimmers doing serious laps, and she could dimly hear the sounds of activity down at the stables.

At least three of the tables on the veranda overlooking the gardens were occupied by yawning guests with coffee and the morning newspaper. Diana had intended to find a table there and have breakfast, but instead found herself crossing the veranda and going into the main building.

The observation tower.

That was where she was headed, though she only consciously realized it when she began climbing the stairs. Part of her wanted to turn around and go back, if only to get some caffeine into her system, but she couldn't seem to make herself do that.

Which was more than a little unsettling.

"Dammit," she muttered as she neared the top. "I don't need to sightsee, I need some coffee."

"Help yourself."

Diana held on to the railing at the top of the stairs and looked at the man who had spoken, conscious of shock—but surely not as much as she should have felt—to see him there. To see **him**.

He was standing, leaning a shoulder against the casing of one of the unshuttered windows that encircled the room, a coffee cup in one hand. Despite the early hour he looked wide-awake, and was casual in jeans and a dark sweatshirt.

"The waiter brought up two cups," he continued, "so maybe he knew something I didn't. Then again, maybe it was just a screwup with room service. In any case, you're welcome to join me. There's plenty." He gestured toward a nearby small table, on which sat a silver tray with a coffeepot, cream jug and sugar bowl, the second cup and saucer, and a plate holding assorted pastries.

"I—you obviously wanted to be alone up here," she managed to say finally.

"Want didn't have much to do with it," he said. "Most of the early birds are up for a reason. Golf, swimming, the morning ritual of coffee and newspaper. I'm just up because I couldn't sleep. And up here because I might as well be looking at nice scenery if I have to be awake at the crack of dawn. How about you?"

Diana hesitated for another moment, then went to the small table and poured coffee into the second cup, vaguely surprised to find her hands steady. "I couldn't sleep either. Think maybe the place is haunted?"

She had meant it as a lame joke, but when he didn't respond right away, looked up quickly to catch a fleeting expression she instinctively identified as pain or loss. **He does think the place is haunted. And the ghosts are his.**

"I think a sleepless night could make me believe in almost anything," he said lightly, smiling. "But then the sun comes up, the world looks and feels the way it should, and I'm not quite so willing to believe. My name's Quentin Hayes, by the way."

"I'm—Diana Brisco."

"Nice to meet you, Diana Brisco."

He stepped toward her, free hand outstretched, and Diana hesitated only an instant before shaking hands with the man whose face she had sketched yesterday.

Before ever setting eyes on him.

2

Madison Sims was what her mother termed "an imaginative child," a definition Madison herself understood perfectly. It meant that her mother and other grownups didn't believe her when she told them that her so-called imaginary friends were actually real—if not flesh and blood.

Madison was a very bright eight-year-old and had caught on quickly to the fact that saying things like that made people uncomfortable. And **her** uncomfortable, since it led to conversations between her parents in hushed voices, and visits to doctors, and wary looks from other grownups.

So she had stopped talking about her friends, and when her mother oh-so-casually asked about them, had lied without a blink. Did she still see children dressed as if they had stepped out of an old movie, children who seemingly walked through walls and whose laughter and voices only she could hear?

Nope. Nuh-uh. Not Madison.

Mama wouldn't be mad at her if she told the truth, she knew that, didn't she?

She knew it. But Madison had discovered even in her young life that there was truth... and then there was **truth**. And she had learned that some truths were better kept to herself.

Besides, she didn't always see the other children. Never at home, in their almost-new house near the ocean. And seldom at the homes of other family or her "real" friends. Just, mostly, at places like The Lodge, old places.

She liked The Lodge, even though there was a sad feeling to some of the rooms and parts of the grounds. She loved the gardens, where, she had discovered the previous day, it was possible to walk for hours with her little Yorkie, Angelo, and not be scolded by the gardeners for trampling the flowers.

Where the other children liked to play.

It was still very early when she was allowed to excuse herself from the breakfast table and left her parents to finish their meal on the veranda while she and Angelo went off to explore the gardens they hadn't got to the previous day.

"Don't go outside the fence, Madison," her mother warned.

"I won't, Mama. Come on, Angelo."

The Lodge provided a little postcard map of the gardens, and Madison consulted that as she and her attentive companion paused just out of sight of the veranda. Rose Garden, she'd seen that yesterday after they'd arrived here. And the greenhouse. She'd also seen the Rock Garden the previous day. But she hadn't seen the Zen Garden, and that certainly sounded like something worth seeing.

She glanced back toward The Lodge, her gaze traveling up to the observation tower she had also seen the day before. Her eyesight was very good, and she could make out a man and woman standing up there, looking down at her.

"This way, Madison."

She looked back toward the gardens to see a smiling little girl beckoning. Feeling suddenly happy, Madison waved gaily to the couple up in the tower and then followed this new friend toward the path leading off into the Zen Garden.

"Is she yours?" Diana asked as the little girl waved up at them and then raced off with her dog toward one of the garden paths.

"No, I've never seen her before." Quentin frowned slightly, adding, "Haven't seen any other kids here, in fact, since I got here yesterday. I hope someone's keeping an eye on her. This isn't the safest place for children."

"Isn't it? Why?"

He returned his attention to Diana and smiled, neither of which was difficult. "Oh . . . streams and ponds, horses, snakes from the mountains. That sort of thing."

It was her turn to frown just a little, those very green eyes of hers direct and thoughtful. "I get the feeling that's not really what you meant, though."

Quentin was hardly in the habit of confiding in strangers, so he was surprised by his impulse to confide in this one. He was unusually drawn to her. There was something about Diana Brisco, something in those green eyes or the vulnerable curve of her mouth.

She was striking rather than pretty, with the coppery hair and very fair skin of a true redhead, paired with those unusual green eyes. Her features otherwise were ordinary, though her face held the sharpened look of someone under stress of some kind. And though the fashion magazines would have called her slender, Quentin thought she was too thin by a good ten or fifteen pounds.

She wasn't his type at all, yet from the instant he had heard her voice and turned his head to see her come into the tower, he had been conscious of the strangest feeling. It was why he had offered to shake hands with her, though that was far more a business or professional gesture than one between strangers meeting casually at a resort.

He had needed to touch her, almost as if something inside him sought reassurance that she was real, that she was here. Finally, she was here.

Peculiar, to say the least.

And now, standing no more than a couple of feet away from her, he was highly conscious of the warm scents of soap and some kind of herbal shampoo. Aware of the gold flecks in her green eyes, and even of her quiet breathing. Hell, he could almost hear her heart beating.

He told himself to turn off the spider sense, but of course that was impossible: whenever he was focused or concentrating, that "extra" sense kicked in, and all his other senses became almost painfully heightened. That was, of course, all it was. He just didn't know why he **was** so focused on her, so intent.

"I guess it's none of my business," she murmured.

The silence had definitely gone on too long.

"I don't know that it's **my** business," he told her ruefully. "But I tend to visit The Lodge once every year or so, and over time I've...become interested in its history. It's an old place, so there's plenty of history and quite a few tragedies, some of them involving children."

Diana glanced back out and down toward where the little girl had disappeared, then returned her gaze to Quentin. "I see. I didn't know that. But then, this is my first visit here. I haven't had a chance to look into the history of the place."

"I'm here on vacation," he said, not even completely sure why he wanted to steer the conversation away from The Lodge's potential danger to children when he had, after all, brought up the subject himself. "How about you?"

She took a sip of her coffee, her hesitation almost imperceptible. Almost.

"I'm attending a workshop here for the next few weeks. A rather famous artist is teaching it. Painting."

"So you're an artist?"

"Actually, no. It's more of a...therapeutic workshop." She paused again, and added in a slightly flattened, let's-get-this-over-with tone, "My doctor recommended it."

Accustomed to reading between the lines as well as weighing people, Quentin decided that the doctor was undoubtedly a psychiatrist or psychologist. But, possibly unlike other people Diana had encountered before, Quentin had absolutely no bias against or discomfort with mental or emotional issues or the people who treated them. In fact, he understood far better than most just how fragile and troubled the human mind could be.

Especially a psychic's mind.

And most especially one who might not know that's what she **was**.

He was intrigued and more than a little cautious, not quite sure how he should handle a situation he'd never before encountered. At the same time, he was conscious of something he'd felt once or twice before in his life, a certainty of being in the right place at the right time, and that compelled him to follow his instincts.

Rather than just politely accept what she said or shy away from the subject uppermost in her mind, Quentin confronted it directly.

Matter-of-factly, he said, "Our company shrink insists we take vacation time every year whether we want to or not. Plus, of course, we get the inkblots and regular appointments to sit down and talk about anything that might be bothering us."

"I guess mental and emotional health are issues a lot of companies are more aware of these days," she said after a moment.

"Especially some companies," he agreed. "In my case, it's definitely the wear and tear and just general stress of the job. I'm with the FBI."

"I never would have guessed. I mean—"

He chuckled. "I know I don't look the part, according to what's portrayed on TV and in the movies, but such is fate. The unit I belong to is a little less formal than the traditional FBI mold. Even on the clock, we seldom wear suits and ties. But we're still cops, and the cases we investigate tend to be the worst of the lot. Which is why doctors and various forms of therapy are used to help us to work more effectively."

Diana looked down at her coffee cup and, rather abruptly, said, "So it **does** help you? Therapy?"

"I hope so. None of us has had to take medical leave for emotional or psychological reasons despite several years of dealing with some pretty rough cases involving murderers, rapists, and kidnappers. So something must be working."

Her mouth twisted, and she murmured,

seemingly to herself more than to him, "And I can't even deal with everyday life."

"You seem to be dealing just fine," he told her.

"Oh, I can concentrate pretty well for twenty minutes or half an hour at a stretch. Hold a conversation that actually makes sense. Usually. But then . . ."

"Then, what? What happens, Diana?"

She wavered visibly, then shook her head with a polite, strangers-on-an-elevator smile. "Never mind. You're on vacation and I'm here for one more round of self-examination. Maybe this one will do the trick. Thanks for sharing your coffee, though. It was nice meeting you, Quentin."

He wanted to stop her as she turned to set her coffee cup back on the tray, but something told him it would be better to let her go. For now.

"Nice meeting you, Diana. See you around."

"Sure." Her tone was still polite, like the distant smile she wore as she left the observation tower.

Quentin looked after her for a long time, then turned his gaze to the morning view.

Bishop had told him once that during the early days of locating and recruiting psychics for the unit, he had found a number of psychically gifted but emotionally fragile people who could never have withstood the demands of police work. Some had barely coped with their abilities just living day to day, while others...

Others, Bishop said, had been convinced somewhere in their lives, by doctors or their own seemingly bizarre experiences, that they were mentally ill.

Because, obviously, there was no other explanation for the voices they heard in their heads, or the strangely vivid dreams they experienced, or the blackouts or headaches that plagued them. No other reason to explain why they weren't "normal" like everybody else.

Conventional medicine was fairly universal in treating such "symptoms" with medication and various other therapies, none of which involved convincing the patient that he or she was, in fact, perfectly normal, and simply possessed an extra sense or two that most other people didn't share.

So they ended up thinking they were crazy, and since their "problem" was an organic thing perfectly natural to them, the treatments and therapies attempting to fix what had never been broken failed them abysmally. And most of them went through life, if they survived at all, so emotionally and psychologically damaged that they never found peace, let alone joy.

Unless they happened to encounter a doctor able to think outside the traditional medical box. Or another psychic with the awareness and willingness to help them.

Diana Brisco, Quentin was certain, was a psychic. He wasn't sure what ability she possessed; though he could usually recognize another psychic, his own ability allowed him only to look forward—not into another's mind or emotions. He was also unsure how strong her ability or abilities were.

Strong enough that she was here undergoing "one more round of self-examination" in an attempt to heal herself. Strong enough that she had likely been medicated at various points in her life. Strong enough that now, in her late twenties or early thirties, she wore the finely honed look of someone for whom stress was a constant companion.

Yet she was also strong enough to have survived this long, sane and able to function even believing something inside her was wrong, and that said a lot about her character.

So she was strong, strong enough to handle her abilities if she only knew how to do that. And she was **here**. Fate had brought her here, now. Brought her to The Lodge, this particular place, at this particular time.

Even more, she had come up to the observation tower at the crack of dawn, her own muttered words an indication that she hadn't even been sure **why** she was climbing the stairs rather than seeking out a far more likely place to find coffee.

"Gotta be a reason," Quentin heard himself murmur. "There are no coincidences. And some things have to happen just the way they happen."

It wasn't what he'd come here to do, help a troubled psychic. But Quentin, though not a complete fatalist, had been convinced for some time that certain encounters and events in one's life **were** mapped out in advance, predetermined and virtually set in stone. Crossroads, intersections where key decisions or choices had to be made.

And he thought this might be one of them, for him. What he did or didn't do now could determine his path from this point onward, perhaps even his ultimate fate.

"The universe puts you where you need to be," he reminded himself, repeating something Bishop and his wife, Miranda, often told their team of investigators. "Take advantage of it."

The question was . . . how?

Ellie Weeks knew she was going to get fired. She **knew** it. And the reasons why she would get fired made up a long list, at the top of which was the secret, passionate affair she'd had with one of the guests a few weeks back.

Number two on the list was getting pregnant.

There had been a cold knot of terror in her belly ever since she'd used the early pregnancy test that morning—for the third time this week. Positive. All positive.

Three faulty tests in a row were hardly likely, she knew that all too well. So they hadn't been faulty. And she could no longer ignore or pretend to ignore the awful truth.

She was unmarried, going to have a baby, and the father of her child was—he had told her, by way of ending their affair—already married. Happily.

Happily married. Christ.

Men were bastards, every last one of them. Her father had been a bastard, and every man she'd been involved with in her twenty-seven years had been a bastard.

"You're just not lucky with men," her friend and fellow maid at The Lodge, Alison, had offered sympathetically when Ellie had confessed to a heartbreaking "fling" without going into details as to who the man was and where the affair had taken place. "My Charles is a fine man. He has a brother, you know."

Ellie, queasy with morning sickness and a

gnawing bitterness, had informed her friend that she never wanted to hear from another man as long as she lived, no matter how fine their brothers were.

Now, as she pushed the noisy vacuum over the carpet of the Ginger Room in the North Wing, Ellie wondered miserably what was going to happen to her. She figured she had, maybe, three or four months before her pregnancy became obvious to everyone. And then she'd be fired, out on her ass with no savings and nobody to turn to for help. With a baby on the way.

If she had the nerve, she'd contact the baby's father. But he was not only wealthy and famous, he was a politician, and Ellie had the uneasy suspicion that he'd know plenty of people who could and would take care of a little problem like a pregnant ex-lover turning up. And it wouldn't be by paying her off, either.

Ellie wasn't that lucky.

The vacuum began making an unholy racket then, and she hastily turned it off. She hadn't noticed anything in the deep pile carpet, but obviously somebody had dropped a coin or something else metallic. She knelt and turned the vacuum on its side, peering at the rotating brush head.

It turned easily under her probing touch, so she shook the vacuum a few times, until what had been rattling around inside dropped to the carpet.

It was a little silver locket, heart-shaped and engraved on the front with a name. Ellie picked it up and studied it. The sort of thing a child might wear, she thought. She used a thumbnail to try prying it open, but it stubbornly resisted her attempts, and she finally gave up.

She knew better than to merely leave it on the nightstand or dresser. Climbing to her feet, she went to her cart in the hall and got one of the envelopes provided for just this sort of thing. She wrote the date, the time, and the room name on the outside, then gave the locket a last look before dropping it into the envelope and sealing it. Then she put the envelope in one of the cart's lower compartments.

"Okay, Missy," she murmured, "your locket will be at the Lost and Found in Housekeeping. Safe and sound."

Then she went back into the Ginger Room and continued her work, the roar of the vacuum drowning the sound of her voice when she murmured aloud, "I just don't know what I'm going to do. . . ."

Diana was glad there was a workshop class scheduled later that morning. Meeting Quentin

had shaken her more than she wanted to admit;
left with nothing to do but brood over the question of how she had been able to draw a very fair
likeness of him before ever setting eyes on him,
she might well have bolted.

Instead, she found herself standing in her
usual corner of the conservatory, the easel with
her large working sketchpad open to a fresh page
before her, frowning as she half listened to the
pleasant murmur of Beau Rafferty's voice. He
was instructing his students to use their charcoal
sticks to sketch whatever was uppermost in their
minds this morning, whether it be an idea, an
emotion, a problem, or whatever else bothered
or preoccupied them.

"Don't think about what you're doing," he
told them, repeating what he had told Diana
privately the day before. "Let your thoughts
wander. Just draw."

Diana resisted the impulse to once again
sketch Quentin's face. Instead, she thought about
her predawn experience and the maybe-dream of
the plea for help traced on a windowpane.

Help us.

Us? Who was "us"? No. Never mind. It was a
dream. Only a dream.

Just another strange dream, another symp-
tom, another sign she was getting worse instead
of better.

It scared her. This illness of hers had disrupted her life from the time she was eight years old, and twenty-five years was a long time to deal with anything like that. But at least in those early years she had been able to function normally most of the time. There had been some dreams, scattered instances of thinking she had heard someone speaking to her when there had been no one nearby, even eerie glimpses of people or things, like a flicker of motion caught from the corner of her eye but gone when she tried to look straight at them.

Unsettling, to be sure, and it had worried her father when she had mentioned this or that occurrence. But it was only when Diana hit adolescence that the symptoms had begun to seriously interfere with her life.

The blackouts had been the most frightening. "Waking up" to find herself in a strange place or doing something she never would have done consciously. Dangerous things, sometimes. Once, she had opened her eyes to realize, to her terror, that she was up to her waist in the lake near her home.

Fully clothed. In the middle of the night. Just wading out toward the middle of the lake. And at the time, she hadn't been able to swim.

After that, she learned.

What had been called "disturbances" by

school officials had led to special private tutors who struggled to complete her education while doctors struggled to find the right combination of medication and therapy to enable her to function.

There were times she was so heavily medicated she'd been little more than a zombie, resulting in whole stretches of her life she could barely remember. Times when new medications caused "adverse" reactions far worse than the symptoms they were meant to treat. And many times when yet another doctor with yet another theory offered hope of a cure only to ultimately admit defeat.

Through it all, through twenty-five years of doctors and clinics and therapies and medications, Diana had, at least, learned to play their games. She had learned, through painful trial and error, which responses and answers would lead to more drugs and which signaled "improvement" to the doctors.

She had learned to fake it.

Not that she didn't sincerely try to get better. Try to listen to what they told her. Try to be as honest as she could, if only silently, to herself, in weighing what she thought and felt.

Because even with all the unsettling, frightening occurrences in her life, with all the confusion in her mind and her troubled emotional state, deep inside herself Diana truly believed she was sane.

Which, sometimes, frightened her most of all.

Beau moved among his students, offering a quiet word or smile here and there, gradually working his way back to the far corner where Diana had set up her easel on the first day. He wondered if she was even aware of what signal that sent, that she cornered herself deliberately, looking out on those around her with wary defensiveness, her back to the wall.

Probably. She didn't lack self-awareness, despite the concerted efforts of mainstream doctors to convince her that she only had to understand herself to be able to heal herself.

Which, of course, was bullshit, at least in the strictest sense. Diana didn't need to understand herself, she needed to understand her abilities and accept them as natural and normal for her.

She needed to stop believing she was crazy.

As he neared her corner, Beau was conscious of a surge of satisfaction, not unmixed with concern. Her gaze was fixed on the open workbook on her easel, but at the same time it was a distant, unfocused look. She was expressionless, yet her hand moved rapidly, the scratching of charcoal on paper not at all tentative.

Without saying a word, Beau stepped to where he could see what she was drawing. He studied it for a moment, looked at Diana long enough to note her dilated pupils, then moved away as silently as he had approached.

Within a minute or so, he began releasing the other students, one at a time. It was something he had done before, so no one was surprised. He spoke to each briefly, commenting on their work or their mood, listened if they wished to talk to him, and then sent them from the conservatory to get some fresh air or exercise or meditate in one of the gardens, whatever was appropriate for the individual.

He didn't release Diana, or even approach her again.

Instead, Beau took up a position by the open doorway, so that she wouldn't be disturbed by anyone entering the quiet building. He leaned against the casing and looked out toward the gardens, listening to the steady scratching of charcoal on paper and patiently waiting.

If Quentin had learned anything in his years with the SCU, it was that there really was no such thing as coincidence. No matter how random something appeared to be, there was always a connection. Always.

Diana Brisco was here at The Lodge in a troubled search for answers; Quentin was also here searching. The possibility that he could help her with her search told him it was also possible that she could help him with his.

He had no idea how. It seemed bizarre to suppose that she could have any connection with what had happened here twenty-five years before, especially when she had told him this was her first visit to The Lodge. But all his instincts as well as the quiet voice in his mind insisted there was a connection.

All he had to do was find it.

Another man might well have been daunted, but after too many years of sifting through the same information again and again and finding no answers at all, Quentin felt energized at the mere possibility that there was a new avenue to explore. But he had to be cautious, he knew that. Whatever else she was, Diana was emotionally vulnerable; if he pushed too hard or too fast...

So, hard as it was for him to cultivate patience, he forced himself to let a few hours go by before he sought her out. He had breakfast, and then went down to the stables hoping to talk to Cullen Ruppe, the man who had been here at The Lodge twenty-five years before.

It was Ruppe's day off.

Malevolent fate again.

Quentin was left to prowl restlessly around the stables and gardens for a while, before he finally gave in and found out—with some difficulty, given the hotel staff's famous discretion—where the painting workshop was being held.

As he approached the conservatory, he was silently debating how to handle this meeting when he was thrown off balance by a completely unexpected development.

"What the hell are you doing here?" he demanded.

Beau Rafferty smiled. "Teaching a workshop."

Quentin eyed him suspiciously. "Uh-huh. And I suppose Bishop had nothing to do with it?"

"This series of therapeutic artistic workshops," Beau replied pleasantly, "was established years ago. They've been so successful that at least two are held each year. In different parts of the country. Taught by different artists. We're all volunteers and sign up well in advance, supplying information such as the time of year or area of the country in which we'd prefer to teach. Then each of us goes through training so we're better equipped to deal with our troubled students."

"And when did you sign up?" Quentin inquired, his tone just as affable.

"About six months ago."

"Saying you thought April in Tennessee might be nice?"

"Well, it is, isn't it? I suggested The Lodge. I was told it would be the perfect setting."

Quentin sighed. "So Bishop did have something to do with it."

"With putting me here, certainly. But you know as well as I do that what happens next is always up to us. And at the end of the day, I'm just here to teach a therapeutic workshop."

"You're the one who's here to help Diana?" Quentin didn't even try to keep the disappointment out of his voice.

Beau smiled. "I'm just teaching a workshop, Quentin. I don't think either one of us believes that will provide Diana with the answers she's looking for. It may pose a few more questions for her, though."

Frowning, Quentin looked past the other man into the conservatory. He saw Diana in the far corner, standing behind an easel, her face oddly without expression as her right hand moved rapidly. From this angle, he couldn't see what she was drawing, but something about her posture and that curious absence of emotion on her face...

"Is she doing what I think she's doing?" he asked.

"Yeah, she's on autopilot. Has been for nearly half an hour now. The artistic version of automatic writing, totally from the subconscious and whatever psychic senses are tapped."

Quentin looked quickly back at the artist. "Jesus, Beau, you told me yourself that's dangerous as hell."

"It is. It's also the only way, sometimes, to unlock the door blocking us."

"Maybe it's blocking her for a reason."

"There's always a reason, Quentin. And, always, there's a moment when it's time for the door to be unlocked." He paused, adding, "Bishop said to tell you it's time."

"You mean—"

"I mean all the pieces are finally here. All the pieces you need to solve your puzzle."

Quentin stared at him. "Why do all the people around me talk in metaphors?"

"Probably to see that look on your face."

Refusing to laugh, Quentin merely said, "In plain English, did Bishop offer up any sage advice as to how I'm supposed to help Diana?"

"No."

"Free will. Dammit."

"We make our own choices and follow our own paths. Not even Bishop can control what happens once a situation begins to unfold. Obviously, this one is unfolding." Beau glanced back over his shoulder at the absorbed Diana, and added, "She'll be coming out of it any minute now. I don't have to tell you that she'll be . . . upset. Disoriented. And disinclined to put much trust in a stranger. Be careful, Quentin."

Quentin watched the other man stroll away, muttering under his breath, "Easy for you to say."

He really didn't have a clue how to handle what he strongly suspected was going to be a very difficult interlude. But that had never stopped him before, so he squared his shoulders, drew a deep breath, and went into the conservatory.

He barely glanced at sketches on other easels as he passed them, thinking only that Beau was clearly dealing with a number of emotionally disturbed persons if their drawings were any indication.

When he reached Diana, he studied her face first, noting the dilated pupils and intent but expressionless face. He wasn't sure whether he should touch her or say her name, but before either option could be put to the test, she blinked suddenly, shook her head a little, and dropped the charcoal stick she held, flexing her fingers as though they ached.

"Diana?"

She looked at him, frowning. "What're you

doing here?" She sounded not so much dazed as a little sleepy.

"I wanted to buy you lunch," he said, following his instincts.

"Oh. Well—" She glanced at her sketch, then looked back at it quickly, her face going pale and an expression of fear tightening her features.

Quentin reached out to grasp her arm, still following his instincts, and then looked for the first time at what she had drawn. And it was his turn to feel total shock.

Amazingly detailed, especially for a charcoal sketch, it was a view looking out a window from inside. A window seat with pillows framed the view, and through the panes of glass a garden scene was visible. A spring garden, judging from the smudges that were surprisingly vivid little black-and-white portraits of various flowers.

Standing in that scene, looking toward the window, was a girl. She was perhaps eight or nine years old, with long hair and sad, sad eyes. She wore a small heart-shaped locket around her neck.

"My God," Quentin said. "Missy."

3

Missy?" Diana tore her gaze from the sketch to stare at him. "You know her? You mean—she's real?" She sounded shaken now, and there was a new tension in her body, as though she were poised to run.

Quentin got a grip on himself, realizing in the same instant that his grip on her arm had tightened unconsciously. She didn't seem to notice, but he forced his fingers to relax at least a little, and summoned a smile he hoped was reassuring.

"You've captured her beautifully," he said, keeping his tone casual. "I could never forget those sad eyes."

"But . . . I don't know who she is. I don't know anybody named Missy."

"Maybe you've just forgotten," he suggested. "It was a long time ago."

"What?"

Quentin swore silently and tried again. "Look, Diana, why don't we talk about this over lunch?"

"Why don't we talk about it here?" Seemingly noticing his grip for the first time, she pulled her arm free. "Who is Missy, Quentin?"

He forced himself to look at the sketch again, consideringly this time. Asking himself if the resemblance he had first seen really existed. There was, after all, no reason to further upset Diana if he'd imagined the similarity.

Except . . . he hadn't. Because that was Missy. Not an image that merely resembled her, but **her**. The big, sad eyes. Long, dark hair. The oval face with its stubborn chin. Even the way she was standing, one foot tucked behind the other ankle, balancing easily, was characteristic.

And it was painful, how vividly alive she was in his mind.

"Quentin?"

He looked at Diana, fully aware that he wasn't much good at hiding his feelings. "Maybe it's just my imagination," he suggested.

Spacing the words for emphasis, she said, "Do you know who this girl is?"

"Was," he said finally. "Who she was. Missy Turner was murdered, Diana, at the age of eight. Here at The Lodge. Twenty-five years ago."

She stared at him, drawing a slow, deep breath, then said with what was obviously a tenuous calm, "I see. Then I must have seen a photograph somewhere."

"Do you remember seeing one?"

"No. But my memory isn't the best. Some of the medications I've been on...stole time from me."

He thought that was one of the most wrenching things he'd ever heard despite her matter-of-fact tone, and had to clear his throat before saying, "We can figure this out, Diana. But not standing here. Why don't we have lunch—out on the veranda, if you like, in the sunshine—and talk?"

Again, her wavering was visible, and Quentin spoke quickly to persuade her.

"You came here for a reason. One more round of self-examination, remember? And in the process of that self-examination, you drew an amazing picture of a little girl who died twenty-five years ago. A little girl whose murder I've been trying to solve most of my adult life. There must be an explanation for that, and I think we both need to find it. That's worth a conversation over lunch, isn't it?"

"Yes," she replied slowly. "Yes, I think it is."

"Good. Thank you."

Diana looked at the sketch a moment longer, then carefully tore that page from the pad and rolled it up. She slid it inside the oversized tote bag hanging on the side of her easel, then took off the smock she wore and hung it in place of the tote bag.

Quentin noticed that the tote bag held a smaller version of the sketchpad on the easel, but didn't comment as she put the strap over one shoulder and indicated with a nod that she was ready to leave.

It wasn't until they reached the door that she realized something, asking, "Was I here alone when you came in? Where was Beau?"

"He left when I got here." Quentin didn't elaborate and hoped she wouldn't question him further on the subject.

Diana frowned, but shrugged as though to herself. She didn't say anything else until they were settled at a table on the veranda and the attentive waitress had taken their order and left them with iced tea and a basket of rolls.

Ignoring both, Diana said, "You said you'd

been trying to solve her—her murder most of your adult life. Why? Were you related to her?"

"No."

"Then why? If it was twenty-five years ago, you had to be no more than a child yourself."

"I was twelve."

"Were you here when it happened?"

He nodded. "I grew up in Seattle, but that summer my father moved us into one of the cottages here because he was doing some work near Leisure. He's an engineer, and he was overseeing the construction of a major bridge."

"So you spent the summer here. What about Missy? Did she live here?"

"Her mother was a maid in The Lodge. In those days, some of the employees had small apartments in what eventually became the North Wing. That's where Missy lived." He shrugged. "There weren't many kids around that summer, so those of us who were here tended to do things together. Hiked, fished, rode the horses, swam. Typical summer stuff, mostly designed to keep us out of the way of the grownups."

Diana could barely remember being eight, so she was guessing when she said, "Did Missy have a crush on you?"

He smiled slightly at the word, but nodded.

"Looking back—yeah, she probably did. At the time, thinking myself so grown-up, I just saw her as a tag-along kid. She was the only girl in the group, and the youngest of us. But she was shy and sweet, she didn't mind bugs or jokes or the messes boys got into, and I . . . got used to having her around."

Still guessing, Diana said, "You're an only child."

He didn't seem surprised by the statement. "Yeah. So having other kids around all the time was a novelty for me, one I enjoyed. To me, by the end of the summer Missy had become the little sister I never had."

"By the end of the summer?"

Quentin nodded. "It was when she died. In August. It'll be twenty-five years this coming August."

"What happened?"

His face tightened, and a bleak chill entered his eyes. Slowly, he said, "There was something weird about that summer, from the very beginning. At the time, I thought it was just that The Lodge was old, and that old places had a creepy feel to them; it was something I'd noticed before then, at other places. And then, being kids, we scared each other senseless with ghost stories around campfires down near the stables, pretty much on a nightly basis. But it was more than tall tales and overly active imaginations. We—all of us—had experiences that summer that we really couldn't explain."

"Like what?"

"Bad dreams when we'd never had them before. Catching a glimpse of something out of the corner of our eyes, only to turn and find nothing there. Strange sounds we heard in the night. Places in the buildings and on the grounds that felt wrong to us. Places that felt...bad."

Quentin grimaced slightly. "When you're a kid, you're not very good at articulating something you feel, or at least I wasn't. All I knew was that there was something wrong here. And I should have told someone."

Diana, intent, frowned slightly. "You blame yourself for what happened to Missy? Because of that?"

"Not just because of that," he said. "Because Missy was afraid. Because she tried to tell me what she was afraid of—and I didn't listen. Not then, and not two days later when she tried to tell me again. That was the last time I saw her alive."

By late morning, Madison had explored most of the gardens, or at least those that interested her. Which was a good thing. She had returned obediently to the main building and inside to have an early lunch with her parents, and reluctantly promised afterward to stay inside because storms were forecast for the afternoon.

Since she was an independent child and not the sort to be destructive or get herself into trouble, her parents didn't object when she announced her intention of exploring inside as she had the gardens.

"But remember the rule, Madison," her mother said. "Stay out of other people's rooms. Why don't you go to the library or the game room?"

"I probably will, Mama. Come on, Angelo." She left her parents in their two-bedroom suite—the Orchid Room, officially—and set off with her canine companion to explore.

She did check out the game room, finding one other child in there: a boy of perhaps ten who was utterly absorbed in the video game he was playing. There were a few adults in the room as well, several grouped around a pool table and others talking quietly over games of chess or cards, also engrossed in what they were doing.

Madison shrugged and went to study stacks of board games and puzzles on shelves by several handy tables. She responded politely to one elderly lady's greeting, helpfully picking up a playing card that had fallen to the floor near her chair.

"Well! No wonder it wouldn't come out right," the lady said, staring at the half-finished game of solitaire spread out before her. "Thank you, dear."

"You're welcome." Madison's experience with elderly ladies told her that this one would talk to her as long as she stood there, so she wasted no time in moving away. It wasn't that she didn't **like** elderly ladies, it was just that she wanted to see what else the hotel had to offer.

They were supposed to stay here for a whole **week,** and Madison was determined to explore her options.

She left the game room and continued on, saying to Angelo, "I think you're the only dog here."

Angelo hesitated, whining, when she turned down the long hallway leading to the North Wing, and she said impatiently, "You didn't want to go into the Zen Garden, either, but we had fun in there, didn't we?"

The little dog whined again, but when his favorite person in the whole world continued without pausing, he hurried to catch up, ears and tail lowered in unhappiness.

"You're a baby," Madison informed him. "I told you that you don't have to be afraid of them. They've never hurt us before, have they?"

Whatever Angelo thought about that declaration he kept to himself, sticking close to Madison as she explored two sitting areas and a couple of short hallways before going up the stairs to the next floor.

"Madison!"

She smiled at the little girl beckoning from the other end of the hall, and hurried toward her. "Hey! I was beginning to think I'd never find you."

"I said I'd be here, didn't I?" her new friend replied.

"Yeah, but you didn't say where." Madison joined her at the T-junction of the hallway, looking to the left and the right to find two more shorter corridors. "What's up here? Be quiet, Angelo," she added in an aside to her whining dog.

"There's a secret place. Want to see?"

"Like a secret room or something?" Madison liked that idea. "Where?"

"Follow me." Her new friend led the way toward a dark green door at the end of the hallway.

Whining louder, Angelo followed them.

Diana pushed her plate away and said, "It's no use. I can't just eat and pretend I'm not waiting for the rest of your story."

Since he didn't have much appetite himself, Quentin didn't protest except to say, "Murder isn't the best thing to talk about over lunch."

"You should have thought of that before you suggested it."

"I did." He smiled wryly. "But I also thought you'd be more willing to sit and talk if the setting was...unthreatening. Lunch on a sunny veranda, other people near, no reason to feel crowded or cornered."

"Why would I feel that way in any case?"

"It was an impression I got this morning. That the observation tower was too small, even open as it is, that you felt uneasy there. Then again, maybe it was just me." He gazed at her steadily.

Somewhat evasively, she said, "You seem to get a lot of feelings about...places. About this place."

Quentin allowed the shift in subject, still cautiously feeling his way with her. "Some people, to varying degrees, of course, are sensitive to their surroundings," he said matter-of-factly, pushing his own mostly untouched plate away. "Our brains are apparently hardwired to pick up electrical and magnetic impulses that most people aren't aware of."

"How is that possible?" She was toying with her glass, frowning a bit.

"How could it not be? It's the way the human

brain works, Diana, by transmitting electrical impulses. Energy. And energy is all around us. It only makes sense that some people possess a stronger-than-average sensitivity to that energy. I mean, as a species we throw out an occasional genius or inexplicably gifted person, a Mozart or an Einstein or a Hawking. Their brains seem to work differently from the norm, but it doesn't make them less human." He shrugged. "I think we're just beginning to understand how the mind really works. Who knows what we'll define as 'normal' in the years and generations to come?"

Slowly, she said, "So you really do feel things about places? About people?"

"A bit, though it's not my strong suit," he replied easily. "But a place like The Lodge has such a long history it's not all that surprising that its energy would be unusually strong. Strong enough so that even I can pick up on it sometimes. A clairvoyant or a medium would probably sense a lot more."

She blinked. "You're talking about...ESP?"

"I guess some people still call it that. Or the paranormal." He shrugged again, keeping his tone casual. "The very idea of psychic ability is still denied by many in the mainstream, but as more and more research is being done, we're learning that very few things are impossible when it comes to the human mind."

"You seem to know a lot about it," she said slowly.

Quentin followed his instincts. "The unit I belong to was designed around the idea that psychic abilities could be channeled constructively and used as investigative tools. So we've done plenty of research and have several years of experiences now to study and draw on. Empirical evidence, the scientists call it. Not absolute scientific proof, but we're getting there."

"You believe you're psychic?"

He could hear the tension in her voice and answered carefully. "I have the ability to use my five senses with more control and precision than most people, given the belief that it was possible and years of practice. And, yes, I believe I possess an extra ability most others don't have or can't tap in to."

"What ability?" The tension was growing.

"Sometimes I know things before they happen."

Diana sat back abruptly and crossed her arms before her. "So you can see the future? Tell me my fortune?"

"I don't **see** anything," Quentin said. "I don't read tarot cards or gaze into a crystal ball or study the lines on someone's palm." His voice was dry now. "I just know things sometimes before they happen."

"Just," she muttered.

"It's a perfectly human ability, Diana, even if it is a rare one."

"How can you possibly know something is going to happen before it **does**? That doesn't make sense."

"It's one ability we really can't explain scientifically," he admitted. "Using today's science, that is. If time is linear, as we believe it is, then it certainly doesn't seem possible that the human mind could, as you say, perceive something that hasn't yet happened. Then again, maybe we don't understand time any better than we understand our own minds."

She drew in a deep breath and let it out slowly. "I have enough trouble with reality as it is, thank you. Even if I believed what you say is possible, I—"

"Explain your drawing," Quentin invited.

"Like I said, I must have seen a photograph."

"As far as I've been able to find out, Diana, Missy and her mother had no family. They had lived here from the time Missy was three or four. And less than a year after she was murdered, the North Wing was left nothing more than a hollow shell after a fire gutted most of it, destroying all of her and her mother's possessions. So how did you see a photograph of her? In fifteen years of searching, aside from crime-scene and autopsy photos, I've never been able to find one."

Diana was silent, clearly uneasy.

"Your sketch shows her the way she was that summer," he continued. "The heart-shaped locket around her neck? I gave her that. In late July, at her birthday party. It disappeared when she was murdered, and hasn't been seen since."

"You can't possibly know it's the same locket, not from a simple—and badly drawn—charcoal sketch. I'm not an artist, Quentin—" She broke off as their waitress appeared to take their plates and inquire about dessert and coffee, finally leaving them alone again with the latter.

"I'm not an artist," Diana repeated steadily. "And nothing in that sketch can be taken seriously. I don't even know where that—that image came from, but there has to be a perfectly rational explanation for it."

"I agree. But my idea of rational and yours might just be light-years apart."

"If you believe in the paranormal, probably so." She shook her head. "It's just... mysticism and junk science. It isn't **real**. There are valid medical explanations for why people see things that aren't there, or hear voices, or—or whatever. It's not their fault, it's just that they're sick. They have an illness."

"And what if they don't?"

She stared at him.

"What if they don't, Diana? What if all those valid medical explanations are wrong? It wasn't all that long ago that medical **science** used leeches and didn't have a clue that a chemical imbalance in the brain could cause all sorts of problems then mistaken for insanity."

"Quentin—"

"You read the newspapers, right? How often are we told that scientific or medical **facts** have been proven wrong? Technology advances, new discoveries are made, and suddenly today we know more than we knew yesterday. So we re-think. We come up with better tests, or we look at the evidence in a new light of understanding. The impossible becomes possible, even likely and predictable."

"Even so, some things are just too far-out to be believable."

"And psychic ability is too far-out for you?"

"Yes."

"Why?" He hesitated when she remained silent, then said slowly, "Why is it so much easier for you to believe that you're sick?"

"We weren't talking about me," she said, visibly tense.

"Weren't we? Diana, there's nothing **wrong** with you. That's why all the medications and the therapies haven't made a difference. You're trying to fix something that was never broken."

"You don't know anything about me."

"I know you're psychic. And knowing that, I can guess a few other things. Either you were born with the abilities, or else they were triggered when you were very young, by some sort of physical or emotional trauma. You tried to tell people—probably your parents first—about your experiences. About seeing things that didn't seem to be real. About hearing voices. About unusually vivid dreams. Maybe there were blackouts, missing time. And that's when the whole useless round of doctors and medications and therapies began."

Still tense, she said, "And where did you get your medical degree, Quentin?"

"How many doctors with medical degrees have been unable to help you?" he countered. "When is it time to consider perfectly viable alternate explanations for a so-called disease no expert has been able to treat? Next month? Next year? When you've done a roll call of the AMA? When most of your life is behind you and it's not even worth trying one more time?"

Quentin decided later that he was probably damned lucky she didn't just get up and walk away. He was pushing too hard, and he knew it; he was demanding that she suddenly question and discount what had been drummed into her for too many years and by too many doctors, and that was something that could never happen in an instant.

Diana didn't walk away. But she clearly wasn't willing to continue with the same topic. She was expressionless, but when she uncrossed her arms and reached for her coffee cup, the movements were jerky with strain.

"Look, you said you wanted to talk about this girl and her murder. I'm curious because you say my sketch looks the way she looked before she died."

"I **say**?"

"Well, if you don't have a photograph—that you can show me," she qualified hastily, remembering he'd said there were crime-scene and autopsy photos, "—you can't really prove it, can you?" She nodded when he remained silent. "For all I know, you **did** imagine a similarity. Hell, for all I know, you could be making up the whole damned thing. I met you a few hours ago; how do I know you're being honest with me?"

"You don't," he admitted.

"I don't even know you're really with the FBI."

Sighing, he said, "I left my I.D. in my room, but I'll make sure to show it to you later. I'm not lying to you, Diana. About anything."

"Are you going to tell me what happened to Missy?"

"Of course I am. As much as I know, anyway." He hesitated and then, compelled as he had been earlier in the observation tower, reached across the table and lightly touched her hand. "I'm sorry, I didn't mean to push—"

Whatever else he said, Diana didn't hear. It was as though a switch had been thrown; one instant she was sitting at a table with this man, on a warm, sunny veranda, conscious of the muted sounds of other people around them, and the next instant everything was different.

She was still on the veranda, but it was a darkened and gray space brightened intermittently as though by flashes of lightning. There was a peculiar smell she couldn't identify in the air, and it was cold. It was very cold.

Eerily, in the flashes of light she could see Quentin sitting across from her, looking at her with a slight frown, but he vanished in between them.

And when she looked down at the table, she could see in the flashes her hand gripping his strongly, as if she were holding on to a lifeline.

Between the flashes, her hand was holding . . . nothing.

She was completely alone in the grayness of almost-night.

Diana.

She didn't want to, but Diana found herself turning her head slowly to the right. There were two large potted palms flanking the steps that led down to the lower terrace, lawn, and the garden paths; at first, that's all she could see.

Then there was a flash, and between the plants stood the little girl.

Long dark hair. Big, sad, dark eyes. Pale oval face.

Missy.

In the gray twilight separating the strobelike flashes, she vanished, only to reappear in the bright white light.

Help us.

She didn't appear to speak; her lips didn't move. But with every flash she was moving closer and closer, closing the distance between them, her pallid face beginning to twist in an expression of pain, her eyes dark pools of terror.

Her hands reached out toward Diana, pleading—

"Diana!"

She jerked her head around to stare at Quentin, blinking in the abrupt return to the bright warmth of the veranda. And then in the next moment a loud rumble of thunder made her look up to see dark clouds rolling overhead, swiftly blotting out the sun and bringing a chill to the air.

"We'd better get inside," Quentin said, over the sounds of chairs scraping against the stone surface of the veranda as other guests came to the same decision. "This storm came out of nowhere."

"Did it?" she murmured, feeling very . . . peculiar. "Or was it here all along?"

"What?"

Diana realized that she was indeed holding his hand, and it required an enormous effort to force herself to let it go. "Nothing. It's . . . it doesn't matter."

"We should get inside," he repeated, frowning, as he got to his feet.

Diana rose as well, automatically. She was cold. And she was scared. Her body was tingling oddly, as if an unfamiliar energy coursed through her. And yet . . . there was something familiar about the sensation, like the distant echo of a forgotten memory.

Without meaning to say it aloud, she murmured, "Why do they call it second sight? Because you can see what's underneath the surface? Because you see what isn't there? Because you can see . . . through a glass, darkly . . ."

Quentin stepped around the table and grasped her shoulders with both hands. "Diana, listen to me. You are not crazy."

"You don't know what I just saw." Her voice was shaky now.

"Whatever it was, it was real." He glanced up impatiently as the first drops of rain began to splatter around them, then took her hand and began leading her inside.

Diana went, almost blindly. Maybe, she thought later, because she really didn't want to be alone just then. Or maybe it was because the answers Quentin offered were less terrifying than the probability of her own deepening insanity.

Madison looked up from the very old doll she had found in the trunk and frowned as thunder rumbled. "Daddy said there'd be storms."

"It storms a lot here," her new friend said.

"I like storms. Don't you?"

"Sometimes."

"I also like this room." Madison looked

around at the very pretty, very girlish bedroom, with its old-fashioned furniture and lacy curtains. "But why is it secret?"

"Because they wouldn't understand."

"They?" Madison frowned and absently patted Angelo, who was curled up next to her, trembling a bit. He hated storms, poor baby. "You mean my parents?"

"Yes."

Suddenly wary, Madison said, "It's your room, right? I mean, it doesn't belong to somebody else? Because I'm not supposed to go into other people's rooms, not without being asked."

"You can always come into this room."

Madison had the suspicion that her questions hadn't really been answered, and asked another, more pointed one. "What's your name? You haven't told me."

"Becca."

"That's pretty."

"Thank you. So is Madison."

"So this is your room, Becca?"

"It was."

"But not anymore?"

Becca smiled sweetly. "I still come here sometimes. Especially when it storms."

"Do you? I like my room at home when it storms. I feel safe there."

"You'll be safe here too. Remember that, Madison. You'll be safe here."

Madison eyed her uncertainly. "From the storm?"

"No." Becca leaned toward her and, still smiling sweetly, whispered, "It's coming."

4

Diana sipped the hot, sweet tea Quentin had ordered, looking at him over the rim of the cup. When she set it down in its saucer on the small table between their chairs, she said dryly, "The traditional remedy for shock."

He shrugged. "We didn't get to finish our coffee."

They were sitting in a fairly secluded area of the big lounge off the main lobby, where quite a few guests had also taken refuge from the storm. The space was arranged so that numerous chairs and tables in scattered groupings separated from each other by large potted plants, screens, and other decorative dividers provided for privacy and quiet conversations, yet there was still the sense of not being too isolated, too alone.

The storm continued to rumble outside, more thunder, lightning, and wind than rain. Which was usual for this valley, Quentin had said.

Diana hadn't really recovered from her experience on the veranda. In fact, she wasn't sure she ever would. And now that she'd had a few minutes to think about it, she was feeling wary, defensive, and more uncertain than she could ever remember feeling.

It was not a comfortable sensation.

"We also didn't get to finish our conversation," Quentin added. "What did you see out there, Diana?"

"Nothing." She had, at least, regained enough of her wits to know better than to describe what she thought she had seen. What she couldn't possibly have seen. No matter what he **said** he believed, in Diana's experience people found the inexplicable unsettling at the very least.

And she really didn't want to see that too-familiar look in his eyes, that don't-let-her-know-I-think-she's-nuts careful lack of shock or disbelief.

"Diana—"

"This morning, you said something about this not being a safe place for kids. Something about tragedies? I assume you meant other than Missy. So what's that all about?"

He hesitated, then shrugged. "Accidents, illnesses, unexplained deaths, kids gone missing."

"That happens everywhere, doesn't it?"

"Yeah, unfortunately. But it happens here a lot more often than can be accounted for by random chance."

"And you believe that ties into Missy's death somehow?"

"I've found that for the most part, there's no such thing as coincidence," Quentin said.

Diana felt herself frowning. "No?"

"No. There are patterns everywhere, if we only knew how to recognize them. Mostly we don't, at least until after the fact. Some of them, on the other hand, are so clear they're practically in neon. You and me, for instance."

Warily, she said, "What about us?"

"The fact that we're both here, now, isn't a coincidence. The fact that you drew a very accurate sketch of Missy, someone whose murder I'm trying to solve, and that I **happened** to be here to see it, isn't a coincidence. Even the fact that you climbed the stairs to the observation tower at the crack of dawn this morning and found me there wasn't a coincidence."

"All part of the master plan, huh?"

"All part of the pattern. It all connects, some-how, some way. And I'm guessing Missy is the connection."

Diana, thinking of the other sketch in her tote bag, the one of this man drawn before she'd ever set eyes on him, found it difficult to argue with at least some of what he was saying. But she tried.

"How could that be? I told you, I never knew anybody named Missy. I've never been here before. I've never even been in Tennessee be-fore. There was probably a newspaper article about her death or something, with a picture, and I saw it at some point years ago. Something like that."

"No." Quentin's voice was flat. "The article about her death was little more than a para-graph, and there was no picture. Plus, it never even made the big regional papers, let alone any national news media. I've studied the case for years, Diana. I've seen every scrap of informa-tion I could find—and the Bureau teaches us how to search, believe me."

Diana was silent, bothered but a long way from convinced.

"You saw her, didn't you? Out on the ve-randa."

She half shook her head, still silent.

Patiently, he said, "Whatever you saw, it was very sudden and very vivid—and it was triggered by the storm."

That surprised her. "What?"

"Remember what I said about energy? Storms are full of it; they charge the very air with electrical and magnetic currents. Currents our brains are hardwired to react to. Psychics are almost always very strongly affected by storms. Sometimes they block our abilities, but more often what we experience is far more intense than is usual for us, especially in the minutes just before a storm breaks."

More to herself than to him, she murmured, "I usually know when one is coming. But, out there..."

"Out there," he finished, "we were both concentrating on the conversation and got caught off guard by the storm. I can usually feel them coming myself." He paused, watching her. "And most of my senses tend to be heightened during storms. Just like yours are heightened right now."

Diana couldn't help thinking that he had guessed more about her and her various moods and peculiarities in a few short hours than all the doctors had in years of knowing her.

If he was guessing.

It was unsettling, and yet it had to make her wonder if there could conceivably be any truth to the other things he was telling her. The possibilities. Could there be? After all the years, all the tests and therapies and medications...could the answer to what was wrong with her really be that simple? And that incredibly complex?

"Diana, what did you see?"

"Her. I saw her. Missy." Diana hadn't realized she was going to answer until she did, and when she did, she braced herself unconsciously for his reaction.

Except that Quentin didn't react at all, at least overtly. Still watching her with focused intensity, he said, "Describe what you saw. Exactly."

Diana was suddenly reminded of one of her many doctors, expressionless, determined to be nonjudgmental no matter what she said, even while mentally cataloging her neuroses, and the memory made her grit her teeth.

Might as well get it over with.

Rapidly, her voice toneless, she said, "There were flashes like lightning or a strobe light, and she was coming toward me, closer in every flash, and I thought she said 'Help us,' but her mouth didn't move, and it was cold and I was alone except for her—" She sucked in a quick breath. "And you, in the flashes but not the gray time in between. You were there, but only because I was touching your hand, keeping you partway—there."

"We were still on the veranda?"

She searched his face for signs he was humoring her the way some of her doctors had, and didn't know whether to be relieved or alarmed that she found none. "Yes."

"No one else was there? Just the three of us?"

"Yes."

"During the flashes. Were you completely alone out there between them?"

Diana nodded. "There was—I couldn't see anybody else in the gray time. None of the guests. Not you. Not her."

Quentin frowned suddenly. "It almost sounds like you were the one slipping into her world, which I believe is far more rare than the other way around. I've always thought mediums provided a doorway, but not that they passed through it themselves. Not that I've ever heard, anyway. I wish I knew more."

"What?" Even before he could answer, Diana was shaking her head. "No. Don't tell me you believe—"

"Missy is dead, Diana. If you saw her—"

"Obviously, I didn't. It's all in my mind." She heard her own voice rise, and paused a moment to collect herself. Being too excitable or emphatic about things got her into trouble, she'd learned that well enough. "Because it isn't possible to see the dead. There's no such thing as an afterlife. When you're dead, you're gone. Period."

"You really believe that?"

"I really do," Diana said firmly.

Ransom Padgett trudged up the narrow stairs to the attic of the main building, grumbling underneath his breath. Every damned time it stormed, something went wrong with this old place. Either there was a leak, or rain washed leaves and other crap into the gutters, or else the hotel's backup water supply—designed by a thrifty original owner to be replenished by rainwater carried down from the surrounding mountains—increased pressure on the old pipes so they groaned and rattled and disturbed the guests.

This time, at least three guests on the main building's topmost occupied floor, the fifth, started complaining about noises almost as soon as the first clouds darkened the skies.

Ransom thought most of 'em had too much imagination and ought to be warned by Management when they checked in that old buildings made noises, there was just no way around that. But handling the guests directly wasn't his problem, thank God. He just fixed things.

In this case, however, he doubted there was anything to fix. He'd had trouble with squirrels nesting in the attic over the winter, and since he hadn't yet discovered how they were getting in, he figured a couple had just come back inside to take shelter from the approaching storm.

So he was mostly up here to check his humane traps—which hadn't, so far, been successful in catching any of the canny squirrels—and poke around a little so he could tell Management he'd checked it out.

He used his key to unlock the attic door and then opened it, flipping the light switch just inside. The lighting consisted of bare bulbs in metal cages scattered around the vast expanse, and there were a lot of them, but the medium-wattage bulbs didn't do much to brighten the attic. Nor did the several dormer windows or even the big ones at the north and south ends, partly due to age-darkened stained and leaded glass. And with all the old furniture, trunks, boxes, and various junk stored in the space, the clutter didn't help.

Ransom had suggested more than once that the hotel's owners have somebody go through everything and get rid of what was obviously never going to be used again. He just didn't see the sense of holding on to things like old clothing and ancient linens falling to bits, and old tools and broken furniture, but, again, he hadn't been listened to.

"I just work here," he muttered to himself as he picked his way among the refuse of time and people's lives, trying to remember exactly where he had left those traps.

He found one up under the eaves on the west side of the building, still empty—but with the dried ear of corn he had left as bait gone.

"Little bastards," he said of the squirrels, baffled as to how they'd managed to get the bait without springing the trap. This thing was **designed** to trap squirrels, after all. He tested the spring and found it in good working order.

"Now I gotta go all the way down to the garden shed and get more bait. Shit." He thought longingly of the days when a little poison did the trick, wishing he dared disobey Management and just eliminate the rodents permanently.

He set the unbaited trap back in place and began working his way toward the next one, again automatically cursing the jumble of discarded junk he had to wade through, climb over, or push aside.

He was back in the main section of the attic

and facing one of the fairly large stained-glass windows at the far north end when there was a deafening boom of thunder and all the lights abruptly went out.

Not wanting to break his neck falling over something in the darkness, Ransom waited where he was, confident that if the power didn't come back on in a minute or two, the generator would kick on. He made a mental note to either start carrying his flashlight when he came up here or else leave one by the door so he'd have it handy.

A brilliant flash of lightning abruptly illuminated the window, the grime-covered glass seeming in that instant to glow incandescent with colors.

Somebody was standing in front of it.

He'd caught only a glimpse in the flash, and Ransom frowned as darkness surrounded him once again. "Who's up here?" he demanded.

There was no answer, and as hard as he listened, Ransom could hear nothing beyond the rumbling of thunder and the scattered patter of rain on the roof above his head.

He waited, peering intently toward the window. And in the next flash he saw, as he expected, nothing.

"Trick of the light," he muttered. But he felt a

building uneasiness, and not just because the lights had failed to come back on. It was normally fairly stuffy up here, generally on the warm-to-hot side this time of year, which it had been when he'd first entered the attic.

Now it was getting cold. Uncomfortably cold.

Not at all a fanciful man, Ransom had the sudden idea that if he put his hand to the nape of his neck, he'd find all the fine hairs there standing straight out in a primitive warning that something was wrong here. Very wrong.

A nearby floorboard creaked, and he spun around, but it was very dark, and all he could make out were looming shapes.

Looming.

That was . . . strange. He'd just walked across this space, following a clear if narrow aisle down the center of the attic. Now, as far as his straining eyes could make out, there was some sort of barrier there.

"I'm imagining things," he told himself in the sort of loud, emphatic, I'm-not-afraid-at-all voice of someone walking through a graveyard after midnight. "I just moved without thinking, is all. There's nothing else up here."

It didn't occur to him until later that he should have said "nobody" else.

A loud boom of thunder made him nearly jump out of his skin, and Ransom started thinking about getting out of here, at least until the lights came back on.

Before he could move, lightning flashed again, and in the momentary brilliance, he could see what the barrier was.

As darkness surrounded him again, Ransom grappled with what he had seen. Three old storage trunks, stacked one on top of the other. Trunks he was almost positive had been, only moments ago and for donkey's years before that, shoved over underneath the eaves in the far west end of the attic.

Matter of fact, he was **sure** that's where they'd been, because they were a matched set of old steamer trunks, covered over with travel stickers the way people used to do, the sort of thing decorators were selling for a fortune these days. He'd taken special note of them there.

About thirty yards away from where they now were.

Thunder boomed, vibrating the plank floor beneath his feet, and he wished fervently that he had brought a flashlight.

A floorboard creaked again. Behind him.

He whirled around, the oath that escaped him a bit too high-pitched for his ego. Nothing looming this time, thank God, but wasn't that—?

He was facing the window again, and as he

stared a flash of lightning backlit the stained glass radiantly.

Someone was standing in front of it.

Someone without a head.

Ransom took a panicked step back, coming up hard against the trunks that had been, surely, farther away from him just a minute ago.

And the lights came on.

He blinked as his eyes adjusted, stood staring, and after a moment uttered a shaken laugh. "Jesus."

Ransom walked closer to the stained-glass window, until he could reach out and touch the old dressmaker's form. The surface he touched was cracked with age, and the dress draped around the form was old, fragile lace and silk.

"I remember you," he said to the form, comforted by the normal sound of his own voice. "You've been up here for years." He paused, adding uncertainly, "I don't think you were in front of the window, though."

One hand still resting on the form, he half turned and looked back at the trunks now stacked neatly in the center of the attic space. "And you guys definitely weren't there," he added, hearing his own uneasiness.

He walked back to the trunks, studying them. Yeah, he remembered seeing these guys. He remembered seeing these guys over at the west end of the attic, with a jumble of other stuff nobody had bothered with in years. Old furniture, and a canvas-draped thing he thought was a mirror, and—

And a dressmaker's form.

Ransom looked back over his shoulder, half expecting the form to be back where it belonged. But it stood before the window, seemingly innocuous.

Until lightning flashed outside the window again, the multicolored glass giving the sudden, brief impression of a woman with arms and a head of flowing hair standing there.

Deciding that he'd check the rest of his traps some other time, Ransom squeezed past the trunks and lost no time in leaving the attic. And he didn't want to admit even to himself that he didn't breathe easy until the attic door was closed behind him.

Closed and locked.

The lights in the lounge flickered and dimmed, but didn't go out, and though the storm was clearly building in intensity, the sounds of it were muted in there and hardly interrupted conversation.

"So you believe dead is gone," Quentin said thoughtfully. "Which means you probably aren't religious."

"So?" Diana was trying to ignore the storm, ignore the prickly, tingling-skin sensation that had remained with her even after they'd left the veranda. She looked away from him, trying to appear casually interested in the room around them, and blinked when she saw a woman at a nearby table drinking tea. The woman met Diana's gaze, smiled, and lifted her cup in a slight acknowledgment.

She was wearing Victorian dress.

"Diana?"

She started slightly and looked back at Quentin. "What?"

"We've found it's easier for some psychics to accept their abilities if they have a religious or spiritual background. For whatever reason, religion or spirituality sometimes helps the impossible seem more . . . credible for some people."

Diana sent a quick glance toward that nearby table, only to find that both the woman and the table were no longer there.

All of a sudden, she wanted something a lot stronger than sweet tea. But she took a sip of what she had, vaguely surprised to see that her hand appeared steady. "So if you can't convince

me with so-called science, you'll try mysticism?"
Her voice was steady as well, she thought.

"Different things work with different people,"
he said, smiling faintly. "We all find our reasons
for accepting what we have to accept, Diana. We
all figure out sooner or later what we believe,
what our philosophies are. Science doesn't make
religion or spirituality less valid, it's just another
option. All that matters is that we accept what
exists."

"What you say exists."

"You have firsthand proof that the paranormal
exists, we both know that."

She was tempted, but didn't look around the
room again. She was afraid of what she might
see. "All I know is that I have an illness that exists," she said, her voice flat. "I'm told insanity
runs in the family."

"Who told you?"

"My father—in a roundabout way. He never
talks much about my mother, but I gather from
the little he has said that she was certifiable."

"Was?"

"She died when I was very small."

"Then you have no real idea what she was like.
Only hearsay."

"My father wouldn't lie to me."

"I'm not saying he did. But since it obviously

never occurred to him that you might be psychic, and he undoubtedly had the same ideas about his late wife, all you can really **know** is that she also had experiences he didn't understand—and viewed as mental or emotional problems."

Diana said, "My father has done everything in his power to help me."

Aware he was treading on tricky ground, Quentin said carefully, "Of course he has. Any father would. And, like most people, I'm sure he sincerely believes in modern-day medical science. What he doesn't believe is that the paranormal exists. Which is why the possibility that you might be psychic quite likely never even occurred to him."

"Or to any of my doctors, highly educated though they were?"

"Especially them." He shook his head. "There are a few pioneers researching the paranormal—there always have been. But mainstream medical science can't prove to its satisfaction that psychic abilities are real."

"Why not?"

He lifted an eyebrow at her. "Can you prove what you experienced out on the veranda was real? Even more, could you duplicate that experience in a lab?"

"No, I can't prove it. And I sure as hell couldn't duplicate it. Because it was all in my mind." It had to be. Surely, it had to be.

Ignoring her denial, Quentin said, "Much of science is based on the belief that the results of experiments have to be duplicated, again and again, under very controlled conditions, before anything can be **proven** factual. But psychic ability doesn't work that way."

"Yeah, right."

Quentin smiled. "Unfortunate but true. My boss says that if ever a psychic is born who can completely control his or her abilities, the whole world will change. He's probably right. He usually is. But until then, until a psychic or psychics come along who **can** consistently demonstrate and control their abilities, we're left out on the fringes."

"The lunatic fringes?" she murmured.

Unoffended, he said, "You'll find plenty to say so. But we're doing what we can to build a solid reputation in order to be taken seriously. We believe we understand how most of our abilities work, if only in a general sense, and those beliefs are grounded in science. We're working very hard to train our abilities to help us better do our jobs."

Quentin paused, then added, "And don't dis-

count the fact that the FBI, not the most frivo-
lous organization in existence, was accepting
enough of the idea to allow our unit to be created in the first place some years ago."

Diana took another sip of her tea, more to be
doing something than because she wanted it.

Quentin went on, "Diana, I know this is a
possibility you've never considered. But what
will it hurt to consider it now?"

"I'd be lying to myself. I'd be looking for an
easy answer." Her reply was automatic after so
many years of being warned by doctors not to
justify, not to attempt to "explain away" her
symptoms.

"Who says the answer has to be complicated?"

"People are complicated. The human mind
and human emotions are complicated."

"Agreed. But sometimes the answers aren't
complicated at all." He smiled again, ruefully
this time. "Although, as a matter of fact, you'll
find that having psychic abilities complicates the
hell out of your life."

"Gee, that's all I need."

"I'm not handing you a magic pill. And I'm
sure as hell not telling you that your life will
suddenly be perfect, all your problems in the
past, just because there's a very simple answer
to the question of what's **wrong** with you. Nothing is wrong. Your mind just works a bit differ-

ently from what is traditionally considered the norm."

Listen to him.

Diana caught her breath, staring at the cup in her hand. It had always sounded alien, that particular whisper in her head, somehow not a part of her. It was one reason she had never been able to completely buy the doctors' various explanations—because all of them had more or less stated that what she "heard" in her mind were only aspects of her own personality.

So why did this whisper feel like someone else?

"Diana?"

She set her cup down and looked at Quentin, listening to the rumblings of the storm as it rolled around the mountains and seemed to circle the valley. Round and round and back again. She tried to listen to that and not to the whisper in her mind.

He can help you. He can help us.

To Quentin, a bit unsteadily, she said, "I've sat across from enough doctors to have heard, over the years, most of the jargon. It varied a little from one to the next, but one thing they all had in common was the absolute conviction that hearing voices made you delusional."

"If you're insane. Not if you're psychic."

A little laugh escaped her, hardly a breath of

sound. "They were all very careful not to use that word. Insane. Very careful to find nice, socially correct words and phrases to use instead. Disturbed. Ill. Confused. In need of more... advanced... therapy. I think my favorite phrase was 'in transition.' I asked that particular doctor what I was in transition from. Or to. He said with a perfectly straight face that I was in transition from a state of confusion to a state of certainty."

"Christ," Quentin muttered.

"Yeah, he wasn't the best at it. He didn't last long. Or—I didn't last long with him."

Diana...

"Diana, I know I'm asking a lot in asking you to believe that you're psychic—"

"What makes you think I am, by the way? I could have been making up everything I've told you." She was trying very hard to ignore that other voice.

"You didn't make up that sketch—so to speak. Besides, we tend to recognize each other."

"At first sight?"

"Pretty much."

"I see. So now I'm a member of a secret club?"

Quentin grinned suddenly, recalling that initial conversation with Bishop years before. "Something like that. As for recognizing others like you, you'll find it comes in handy."

"You claim to be psychic, and yet I didn't... sense... anything different about you," she said, realizing as the words emerged that she was lying. She had sensed something, had known in an instant that her life was about to change forever because of him, even if she hadn't been able to admit it to herself then.

"I'm willing to bet you did," he said, still smiling. "But you haven't been taught how to sort through the impressions of all your senses. I can help you with that."

"Sure. And then I get to recognize people as nuts as I am."

"You aren't nuts."

"No, just seriously disturbed."

"That either. Look, even if I was wrong about you being psychic and you did accept the possibility, would you be worse off than you are now?"

"I don't know."

...listen to him.

"Could you be? You've been medicated, and you've tried every form of therapy available without success. Why not take a chance and find out if I can help you? What have you got to lose?"

Instead of answering that, Diana said, "You believe I can help you solve Missy's murder, don't you?"

Quentin hesitated, then said, "There has to be a connection. You drew her picture."

"Even if I did, that doesn't mean I can help you. **If** I'm psychic, as you claim, then maybe I just...picked up her image somehow. From here, this place where she died. That would make sense—at least in your world."

He ignored that little dig. "Maybe you did. But **if** you did, it's very likely you could pick up other information as well."

"Information about Missy and her murder."

"Yeah, maybe."

"So who's helping who?"

This time, Quentin didn't hesitate. "We're helping each other, or we will be."

Listen to him. Let him help us.

Diana forced herself to stand up. "I have to think about this," she told him. "I—the storm seems to be easing up. I think I'll go to my cottage for a while." She took a step away.

On his feet as well, Quentin said, "Diana? Better stop by the front desk and have your key-card redone. We both know it won't work."

"How did you—"

"We usually have a higher than normal level of electromagnetic energy in our bodies. Tends to interfere with some electrical or magnetic things, especially those we have to carry around with us. Like watches. And keycards."

He wasn't wearing a watch.

Diana glanced down at her left arm, bare of a watch because she'd never been able to wear one. Then she stared at Quentin for a moment before turning and walking away.

Toward the front desk.

5

t was late afternoon, the storm long gone, when Quentin found Beau in the conservatory, alone, painting at an easel.

"Making progress?" the artist asked.

Quentin couldn't see what was on the canvas, and wasn't interested enough to look; he appreciated both fine art and the people who created it, but right now his mind was on something else.

"I have no idea," he replied frankly. "She hasn't called the cops or the guys with the butterfly nets—yet. But she also hasn't admitted to even the possibility that she's psychic."

"Not surprising, really. So many people have spent so many years convincing her she's sick."

"Yeah, and I hate that." Quentin scowled and began prowling among the other easels set up for Beau's students. "They've done a real number on her."

"Conventional medicine. They only know what they think they know."

"They know shit, at least when it comes to us."

"True." Beau watched the other man for a moment, then smiled slightly and returned his attention to his canvas.

"Not that you don't definitely have some sick puppies in your workshop, judging by some of these."

"Troubled people. Not sick puppies."

"No, Beau, these are some sick puppies." Quentin was staring at one canvas that bore a somewhat abstract image of a prone figure seemingly in a pool of blood. The figure was contorted in an agonized pose, and sticking out of its chest was what appeared to be a huge knife.

Unperturbed, Beau said, "Less sick when you know the background. His brother was killed in a violent mugging. Protecting him. He's still trying to come to terms with it. With the exception of Diana, all the students in this workshop are trying to come to terms with a specific traumatic event. So they aren't emotionally disturbed in the clinical sense. Ordinary people, for the most part."

"Oh." Quentin stared a moment longer, then resumed his pacing, sparing only a glance now and then for some of the other sketches and watercolors. "God knows what I'd draw," he muttered, half under his breath.

"The ghosts in your life, probably. Missy. Joey. Others lost along the way. The ones you blame yourself for losing."

"I've had my couch time this month, Beau."

"Sorry."

Quentin sighed. "No, I'm sorry. Didn't mean to snap. I'm just feeling very frustrated right now. I want to help Diana, and I'm afraid she won't let me even try."

"Be patient."

"You know something I don't?"

"No. We both know patience is something you have to work at."

Quentin sighed again. "You're here to state the obvious, is that it?"

Beau chuckled. "I'm here to teach a workshop. Come on, Quentin, you know as well as I do that there aren't any shortcuts. You and Diana both have to find your own way. Whether that's separately or together—or both—is entirely up to the two of you."

"Jesus, you sound like Bishop."

"It's something he understands. Miranda too."

"That didn't stop them from taking a hand in things last fall," Quentin said, recalling the single time in his memory that Bishop and his wife had made a deliberate attempt to change a tragic future both had foreseen.

"With great care and only because the stakes were so high. They'll always hesitate to interfere openly unless they're very, very sure that by doing so they won't make the situation worse."

"I was there."

"I know you were. And I know you understand the concept."

"That doesn't mean I always agree."

"No. It's always more difficult when you're the one . . . personally involved."

"Yeah, yeah. Look, **teaching** Diana in this workshop of yours sounds like a shortcut to me."

"No. This is a critical time for her, a turning point in her life. And what other people do at those turning points is as much a part of our journey as we are ourselves."

Quentin sorted through that, and said finally, "No offense, but you really do sound like a fortune cookie sometimes."

"So Maggie tells me."

Momentarily distracted by the mention of Beau's half sister, Quentin said, "Do she and John have that organization of theirs up and running yet? I hadn't heard."

"Just about."

"So we'll soon have a domestic organization geared toward psychic investigation and resources."

"That's the plan. If anyone can do it, John can."

"I'll say. And Maggie's doing okay?"

"She's flourishing. John's been very good for her."

"She's been great for him as well. Twenty years I tried to convince him psychic abilities were real, and she manages it in a week or two."

"Sometimes," Beau said, "falling in love removes the blinders from our eyes."

"**Very** like a fortune cookie."

Beau smiled, but kept his gaze on his canvas.

Quentin prowled a while longer, then said, "You're very plugged in to the universe, right?"

"According to Maggie."

"Okay, then. Without providing a fateful **shortcut** for me, can you at least tell me if I'm on the right track in how I'm handling things with Diana?"

"Are you following your instincts?"

"Yeah."

"Then I'd guess you're on the right track." Beau paused, then added casually, "But you might want to open up your focus a bit to include more than Diana."

Quentin stopped prowling to stare at the other man. "What do you mean?"

"I mean that right now you have a kind of tunnel vision." Beau stepped back from his canvas, set his palette down on a worktable nearby, and began cleaning his brush. "Focus on a single element, and you could miss other equally important elements. If you hadn't encountered Diana, what would you be doing right now?"

"With Cullen Ruppe unavailable today, I'd probably be... trying to get permission to go through boxes of old paperwork I know The Lodge has in storage rooms and in the basement. Because I don't have any legal authority to examine something ruled not relevant to an old crime, I've never been able to get access to stored employee records, the original blueprints of the buildings, and whatever else is down there."

"Maybe it's time to ask again."

After a moment, Quentin said, "Maybe it is."

Beau said, "I'm told the current manager of The Lodge just got the job last fall. Have you met her?"

"Not if she started last fall."

"She might be more open-minded than the

other managers were. More apt to grant a reasonable request to look through old paperwork."

"You're about as subtle as a flagpole, Beau."

"Just making a suggestion."

"But not offering a shortcut?"

"No. It's a path you would have followed on your own."

With considerable feeling, Quentin said, "Once, just once, I'd like at least one member of the unit to give me a straight answer."

Beau's eyebrows rose. "That **was** a straight answer."

"Jesus." Quentin started toward the door, then paused and frowned at the other man. "My instincts are telling me to give Diana a little time to think about things. But not a lot of time. From what she told me earlier, her abilities are strong. Strong enough to scare the hell out of her. Maybe strong enough that they'll be difficult for her to control even once she accepts their reality. And I don't know as much as I wish I knew about mediums."

"Neither do I. But like the rest of us, they're all different in most respects. Different strengths and weaknesses. No hard-and-fast rules, I gather."

Steadily, Quentin said, "I think she may have the ability not only to open a door into the spirit dimension, but to pass through it herself."

"That," Beau said, "has got to be dangerous."

"Yeah, I don't have much doubt about that. I'm afraid if I'm not careful, I could lose her. I think maybe I need some expert advice."

"I think maybe you do. Miranda raised a medium, I understand?"

"Her sister, yeah. And very successfully; Bonnie's one of the most well-adjusted psychics I've ever met."

"Say hello for me," Beau said.

Diana hid out in her cottage for most of the afternoon, but by the time the sun began to slip behind the mountains, she was too restless to stay put any longer. She picked up her tote bag, with the sketches of Quentin and Missy still inside, hesitated at the door, and then somewhat defiantly locked it behind her.

Quentin had been right earlier, and she'd had to have her keycard redone.

Diana had overheard one of the doctors talking to her father back during her teenage years when it had been so bad. He'd been talking about the "stronger than normal" electrical impulses her brain had produced during an EEG. Other tests had also shown the "abnormality."

Diana still winced when she remembered how she'd felt hearing that.

Abnormal. None of the psychiatrists or psychologists had ever used that word. But that doctor, cool and sure of himself, had used it with utter certainty.

She was abnormal. There was something wrong with her.

Unless ... there was nothing wrong with her.

Psychic? It was a possibility she had, literally, never considered. It had never crossed her mind that there could be anything so beyond her understanding at the root of her problems.

And, surely, and despite what Quentin had said, someone in all these years would have offered the suggestion if it had been possible. Wouldn't they? All the doctors and therapists, all the experts her father had taken her to see for most of her life, they couldn't all have been wrong, could they?

Could they?

Diana wandered away from The Lodge, in the direction of the Formal Garden. Though she didn't consciously think about it, the neat rows of box hedges, the symmetrical planter beds bordered by smoothly raked paths, the classical fountains, all made her feel somewhat soothed. It was all so ... orderly.

Unlike her mind. Thoughts skittered through it, half formed, just bits and pieces. She couldn't concentrate at all, couldn't focus on anything ex-

cept the haunting question of whether twenty-
five years of her life had been virtually wasted in
a futile search for a "cure" that had never existed.

Because she had never been ill.

Sitting down on an iron bench near a beautiful three-tier fountain, she considered and then
discarded the impulse to pull out the sketchpad
and draw something. Instead, she stared at the
fountain, trying and failing to put the question
out of her mind.

"Hello."

Startled, Diana saw a little boy standing only
a few feet away. He was perhaps eight years
old, an angelic child with fair hair and big
brown eyes.

"Hi," she said.

"I'm sorry you're upset."

Diana forced a smile, hoping she hadn't been
wearing the sort of expression that gave children nightmares. "I'm just having a bad day,
that's all."

He nodded, solemn, then said, "My name is
Jeremy. Jeremy Grant."

"Hi, Jeremy. I'm Diana." She hadn't been
around kids much and felt a bit awkward with
this one. "Where are your parents?"

He gestured vaguely toward the main building of The Lodge. "Back there. Can I show you
something?"

"Show me what?"

"A place." He tilted his head slightly to one side, still solemn. "Sort of a secret."

She wanted to ask him why he'd want to show his secret place to a stranger, but instead said, "It'll be getting dark soon, you know."

"I know. We have time. It isn't far."

"Okay, sure." Anything beat sitting there while her mind chased itself in useless circles, she thought. "Lead the way." She got up and followed as Jeremy turned and began walking along the gravel path toward the far end of the Formal Garden.

Diana thought idly that if this child wanted to go beyond the gardens, she'd protest. The sun had set behind the mountains now, and there was a growing chill in the air. It would be dark in less than an hour. And she had no intention of being responsible for someone's child, not even on a good day.

Even as she thought that, she realized that Jeremy had paused beside one of the raised planting beds to allow her to catch up, and when she did, reached confidingly for her hand.

"It's just over here," he told her.

Diana allowed herself to be guided down another path to where the Formal Garden intersected the English Garden. This area was filled with riotous blooms on shrubs and plants, the paths wound leisurely among them, and it possessed a more natural, less manicured feeling than the other gardens.

"Jeremy—"

"This way." He led her toward one corner where the landscapers had apparently decided to allow an existing granite rock formation to become part of the garden. Several large boulders jutted up from a bed of smaller rocks and gravel, softened only by moss and a very few tenacious flowers growing in the stony area.

"They were going to put in a waterfall," Jeremy said. "Changed their minds, I guess. The gardeners never dig here."

"No wonder, with so much rock," Diana said. "Is this what you wanted me to see?"

"Around to the side," Jeremy said. "See that rock with all the moss near the bottom? Look behind that."

Suddenly suspicious, Diana said, "Nothing's going to jump out at me, is it, Jeremy? A frog, or some kind of bug? Because I don't like those."

He smiled sweetly. "No, I promise. No frog or bug. Something you need to see." He released her hand. "Just look behind the rock."

Diana looked at him for a moment longer and then, still wary, picked her way carefully among the rocks until she could see behind the one the child had indicated. At first, she had no idea what it was she was supposed to see. More rocks, looked like, more grayish granite, most of them jagged except for a piece that was paler and smoother, worn by a river somewhere, she supposed.

"Jeremy, what—" She looked back over her shoulder, surprised not to see him there. She turned completely around, gazing all around the area, but saw no sign of him. "Fast little kid," she muttered, trying to figure out how he had moved so quickly and so silently.

She looked back down at the rocky ground at her feet, more warily sure now that some nasty surprise lay in store for her if she poked around here. Even so, she found her gaze fixed on the rounder, smoother stone, and hesitated only an instant before crouching to touch it.

It didn't really feel like a rock, she thought. When she tried to move it, the gravelly soil imprisoning the lower part of it gave it up easily. And it wasn't until she turned it slightly that she realized in horror what it was.

It fell from her nerveless fingers, clattering against the stone, and came to rest so that the empty eye sockets stared up at her and small white teeth seemed to grin.

The skull of a child.

"Are you sure?" Bishop asked.

"As sure as I can be," Quentin replied. "She only told me as much as she did because it freaked her out and her guard was down. God knows if she'll talk to me about it again. All I know is what it sounded like to me."

"And she was touching your hand? When she said she was alone on the veranda except for you and Missy?"

"Yeah. Said there were flashes, like a strobe, and that's when she saw us. Said something about me being there only because she was touching me, keeping me partway there. In the—what did she call it?—the gray time in between, I think she said, she was completely alone out there. Didn't see anybody else, including me. Or Missy."

"You weren't aware of anything paranormal?"

"Nothing I saw or sensed." Quentin leaned back against the headboard of his bed, the cell phone to his ear. "But I could tell something was going on with her. She was pale, her eyes were fixed and dilated, and her hand was like ice. But the storm was about to break, and we both know storms scramble all my senses as often as not. I'm either blocked or really distracted."

"Obviously they don't block Diana."

"No. If anything, I'd say they affect her

strongly the other way. Isn't Hollis like that too?" he asked, naming the unit's only medium.

"Yes. Much more apt to sense spiritual energy, and her spider sense is intensified as well. She says it's like all her nerve endings are raw and exposed."

"That can't be fun," Quentin noted.

"She's still learning to cope with all her abilities, so, no, not fun. And it must have been terrifying for Diana."

"I'll say. She's clearly a medium, and a strong one. Probably how she was able to draw that sketch of Missy. She doesn't know the first thing about sorting through psychic impressions, so to her it's all a jumble. What she feels, what she thinks, what she senses. Hell, probably what she dreams as well. Pretty much a state of constant confusion. And all the doctors and meds and therapy over the years have only made things worse for her."

Bishop was silent for a moment, then said slowly, "Quentin, you do realize that virtually all psychics with a background and condition similar to Diana's never learn to incorporate their abilities into their lives and function normally?"

"Those we know about so far, yeah. But she's strong, Bishop. Really strong. If I can just get through to her, I know I can help her."

"I just don't want you to be...disappointed...if you aren't successful. Talented as they may be, some psychics really are beyond our ability to help."

"Not Diana."

Accepting the other man's determination, Bishop said, "All right. Then, judging by what you've told us, probably the most important thing is for you to keep her grounded. Literally."

"What do you mean?"

"She told you that she was able to see you and Missy at the same time out on the veranda because she was touching you, keeping you **partway** there. Right?"

"Yeah. But she can't possibly understand how her abilities work, not when all the doctors have spent a lifetime convincing her she's simply crazy."

"I'm sure that's true—consciously. But we know our abilities come with instincts, and it's likely that some part of her, however deeply buried, does understand how they work. If she really was shaken off her guard when she told you about this, then it's very possible that she told you the absolute truth. She was able to see you when that psychic door was open because she was touching you. You were, in a very real sense, anchoring her on our side of the doorway. That could also explain the strobelike flashes;

because you were anchoring her, she wasn't able to get a complete fix on the other side."

Quentin digested that, then asked slowly, "So she needs an anchor? A lifeline?"

Miranda, also on the speaker phone in Bishop's office, spoke up then to say, "Most mediums we've encountered don't; they're able to exert enough control to . . . stand back, in a sense, when they open that door. To look through, but not travel through. To keep themselves safely on their own side. But a medium like Diana, untrained and at the mercy of her own powerful abilities, may well be unable to do that. Without an anchor."

"So . . . what would happen? Worst-case scenario, if she were to cross over psychically, pass through that doorway she opened, without an anchor on this side, what would happen?"

"What mediums do," Bishop said, "leaves them wide open to spiritual energy, and we know a great deal of that energy is negative. Anger, grief, loss, regret, hate. Even a strong medium with good control is vulnerable to those destructive energies; a medium with strong abilities but lacking control could easily find themselves yanked into that other dimension we've theorized but can't prove exists."

"It's a miracle that hasn't already happened to Diana," Quentin said.

"How do you know it hasn't?"

That surprised Quentin. "Could it have?"

"Easily. If she has a history of blackouts, especially. Judging by what she said to you, she recognized that **gray time** between the flashes well enough to have given it a name. Which means she's been there before, probably many times over the years."

Quentin gave himself a mental kick for having missed that. "Without an anchor?"

"Her instincts could be good enough to have pulled her back to our side eventually. Find out whether she's experienced blackouts. If she has, and if they've increased in intensity or duration over the years, then Diana may be reaching a point in her psychic development when an anchor will become necessary for her own safety. At least unless or until she learns how to exert more control."

Quentin stared across his pleasant room, not seeing any of it. "And without an anchor, one of these visits to that gray time would be . . . permanent? She wouldn't be able to come back?"

"It's possible, Quentin. We don't know for sure. We've encountered psychics so damaged they were catatonic, beyond anyone's reach. Those we could read at all were . . . a blank slate. Empty. Were they the physical shells of mediums psychically trapped on the other side? We don't know. Could Diana suffer that fate? We don't know."

Quentin drew a breath and released it slowly. "You're a comforting bastard today."

"Sorry."

He sighed. "You two knew Diana would be here now. But you didn't set it up so she would be?"

"No," Bishop replied. "Her doctor had already signed her up for the artistic workshop to be held this spring. All we did was place Beau as the instructor."

"And have him suggest The Lodge as a setting?"

"Yes."

"To help her?"

"To help both of you."

"Wait a minute," Quentin said, realizing. "How did you even know about Diana? To know that her doctor had signed her up for the workshop, you had to be—what?—watching her?"

There was a brief silence, and then Bishop said, "It's taken years to build the unit, Quentin, you know that. And you know that I spent a great deal of time in the early days checking out various reports of psychics and paranormal events."

"Which was it, with Diana?"

"I had a source in a major psychiatric research hospital in the Northeast. He told me about Diana. Years ago."

"I gather you never tried to recruit her."

"No."

"Why not?"

"Because she was so heavily medicated at the time it would have been useless and potentially harmful."

"But you kept her on your watch list."

"Yes."

"Okay." Quentin was grappling with yet another puzzle. "But why were you so sure she needed to be here? Is she connected to The Lodge? To what happened here twenty-five years ago?"

"You tell me."

"Bishop."

"I'm not trying to be deliberately obscure, Quentin. We don't know what the connection is, only that one exists. You and Diana are both meant to be there, now. Beyond that, there isn't much we can tell you."

"Has it ever occurred to you," Quentin said politely, "that one day one of us might just get really pissed off about your chess playing?"

"I don't play chess."

"The hell you don't."

Sounding a little rueful now, Bishop said, "If

it ever becomes a game to me, Quentin, I sincerely hope you kick my ass."

"You're a black belt," Quentin pointed out. "I'm only going to kick your ass if you let me. Or if I'm armed."

"Good thing you're usually armed."

"I could get Galen to help me," Quentin said thoughtfully, referring to one of the more mysterious members of the unit. "I'm sure he'd welcome the opportunity. I've got a hunch he's always wondered who's tougher."

"He knows," Bishop said.

"Yeah? I wish I'd been there for that."

"Nothing to see." Without elaborating on that tantalizing statement, Bishop got the conversation back on track. "About Diana. I don't have to warn you to be careful."

"She really is strong, Bishop."

"In a place like The Lodge, a place with a long and troubled history, a medium is likely to find it all too easy to be drawn, even unconsciously, to the doorway between our world and the world of the dead. No matter how strong she is, it's a dangerous situation."

Miranda said, "There's one more thing to keep in mind, Quentin. Since Diana can't yet reliably distinguish between the usual senses and her extra ones, it's entirely possible that she's opened that door numerous times since she arrived, without even being aware of it. Mediums are hardwired to do just that, to provide a doorway. And she could have left it open long enough to allow some of that spiritual energy to cross through."

"You're saying this place is probably haunted."

"For want of a better term."

Bishop said, "Energy always has a purpose, remember that. Whatever may have come through the doorway Diana opened will be acting in very specific ways. The aim is almost always to find peace, closure, to settle with the past. To resolve whatever it is that's keeping them trapped just on the other side of that door and preventing them from moving on. A medium provides them with the opportunity. And some of them may have been waiting a long time."

"Missy," Quentin said.

"Missy, almost certainly, given what Diana's experienced so far. Which means you've got your best chance to solve Missy's murder. If you can help Diana."

"By keeping her grounded."

Miranda said, "Follow your instincts, Quentin. You've got good ones. And she needs your help."

"How do I persuade her to trust me? I'm telling her that everything she's believed all these years is a lie, that expert after expert in her life has been wrong, even if not maliciously. That her own father may have made her situation worse because he didn't consider this one possibility. In her place...hell, I wouldn't believe me."

Miranda replied immediately, her voice certain. "Build a connection with her. You understand her and what she's been going through. You believe her. You know she's not crazy. She needs your certainty, Quentin, because they've left her with none of her own."

A soft knocking at his door caught Quentin's attention, and he said, "I'll do my best. And I'll check in again later."

"We'll be here," Bishop said.

Quentin closed his cell phone and got off the bed to go out into the sitting room and answer the door. He was normally cautious enough to check the security peephole out of habit, but this time as soon as his hand touched the door handle, he knew who was on the other side.

Diana stood there, visibly stiff, both hands working the strap of the tote bag she carried over one shoulder. Her face was pale, and her eyes seemed huge, darkened.

Before Quentin could speak, she did, her voice almost toneless. "Can you come? There's...something I need to show you."

6

Nate McDaniel scowled as he watched two of his people working cautiously in the heat and glare of the big outdoor lights. "I don't have to be an expert to know that this body has been in the ground a long time," he said. "Years, at least."

"According to the head gardener," Quentin said, "there used to be a lot more topsoil in this area, with only a foot or so of the largest boulder sticking out. That would have been at least ten years ago. By the time the garden extended to include it just a couple of years ago, they decided to use the boulders as part of the scheme and just plant a few hardy flowers."

"Which I suppose at least partly explains why no one knew there was a grave here."

Quentin shrugged. "I honestly don't remember spending any time here over the years. It's too far from the main building and stables to have interested me as a kid. And five years ago, when Bishop and I helped in the search for that little girl, the gardens had already been covered by the staff and your people."

"Yeah. Christ, I wonder what else we've missed."

Quentin shook his head. "How many acres of gardens are there? Twenty? Thirty? Plus the rest of the valley and all the mountain bridle trails. Worse than a needle in a haystack. Maybe if the search dog had been able to work, he'd have found it."

"Maybe."

"In any case, at least it's inside the fence. Protected from predators and scavengers in the mountains. So the bones may tell a forensics expert a lot."

"You mean, other than the two facts we can be pretty damned sure of, that this was a child, and that the cause of death was probably decapitation? I don't have to be an expert to see that, either."

"DNA for identification," Quentin said. "Dental records are often unreliable when it comes to kids. Once the age of the remains is determined, we'll have to get a sample from a family member of every child reported missing in the area within the right time frame."

"Shit." Nate followed that weary curse by adding, "And **how** did she say she found it?"

Quentin glanced to one side, where Diana sat on a bench made of slabs of granite and watched the work going on a few yards away. She hadn't been willing to return to her cottage except briefly to grab a jacket when he had insisted, and she was still clearly upset, but she had said very little.

"You heard her," he said to the cop. "She was walking out here, leaned against that boulder— and happened to look down. Maybe the storm earlier today or the ones last week washed away enough of the topsoil and gravel to expose what had been buried here. The top of the skull looked different enough from all the rocks to catch her attention. It sure as hell caught mine."

"And then she went to you."

"She knew I was an FBI agent."

Nate shook his head, but more another weary gesture than negation. "This is a hell of a thing. I know you always suspected that at least some of the missing kids on that list of yours had been murdered, but this is the first time we've found anything to support that."

"According to that list of mine, there are three unsolved disappearances of children from this general area in the last twenty years, four if you count a supposed runaway."

"Okay, so maybe you were right to believe something was going on here."

"Maybe?"

"Quentin, we have an undoubted murder twenty-five years ago, the killer never caught. No question about that. And we have this skeleton, which may or may not be identified as one of the missing kids. But—"

"There are other missing kids. Missing adults as well."

"You say. And I'm not saying I don't believe you—it's just that in most of those old cases you've dug up, official reports were never filed. Or if they were, there was every reason to believe the disappearances could be explained in ordinary ways. Estranged parents taking their kids. Runaways. And then there's the mountains; you know as well as I do it's damned easy to get lost up there—and virtually impossible to find somebody who has."

"Yes, I know that. I know there have been wanted fugitives—federal fugitives—who disappeared into these mountains for years despite exhaustive efforts to find them. And some of them were never seen or heard from again. But there's something more, something going on here, at The Lodge."

Nate shook his head again, but said, "Well, after this you may have a better argument to use in persuading the hotel's management that taking a look at their records is in order. But I don't think a judge is going to force them if they say no, especially if we can't connect this child to The Lodge."

"He—or she—was buried here. That's enough of a connection for me."

"Yeah. I had a feeling you were going to say that." Nate sighed as he watched his people work. He zipped his jacket, adding a muttered, "When did it get so cold?"

Quentin could have answered, "**Twenty-five years ago.**" But he didn't, of course. He just waited silently while Nate's people worked to uncover bones buried years in the ground.

Madison knew she wasn't supposed to be in the garden. In any of the gardens, now that the police were here. Her mama sure wouldn't like it, she knew that. But she was too curious to stay away.

And small enough to slip unseen through the gardens until she was within sight of what was happening.

"They found Jeremy," Becca said.

Madison held Angelo close to make sure he didn't start whimpering, and said to her friend, "They're digging up bones."

"Uh-huh. That's Jeremy."

Madison frowned at her. "If he's just bones, how come you know him?"

"He isn't **just** bones. That's all they see, though. All of them except her." Becca nodded toward the pretty lady sitting on a rock bench off to the side.

"She saw Jeremy when he wasn't just bones?"

"Uh-huh. He wanted them to find him, so he showed her where he was." She nodded as though to herself, adding thoughtfully, "I expect he was ready to leave."

"Leave The Lodge?"

"He's been here a long time."

Madison asked, "Have you been here a long time, Becca?"

"Yeah, I guess." Becca gazed off toward the police officers working in the very bright light, and added wistfully, "It used to be okay, really. Still is, sometimes. But mostly now it's just scary."

"Because of...what you told me? What's coming?"

Becca nodded. "It's been here before. And it keeps coming back."

"Why?"

"Because they don't know how to stop it. They can't stop something they can't see. Something they don't believe in."

"But you believe in it."

"I have to, don't I?"

Madison thought about that, absently hugging her small dog close as she watched the grownups working. Then, slowly, she said, "The lady who saw Jeremy could probably see it. Probably believe it. Don't you think?"

"Maybe. Maybe she could." Becca turned her head and looked back at Madison. "Maybe that's why she's here. But she'll have to hurry."

"Tracing the movements of a kid after years... How lucky would we have to be to find out anything at all about whatever led up to his death?" Nate swore under his breath. "And we're starting cold, with shit for leads."

"Pretty much." Quentin couldn't help glancing toward Diana even as he spoke.

Nate was paying attention. "Or do we maybe have a little more than that? What's her story, Quentin? Did she really just stumble over the skull?"

"She didn't tell me any more than she told you about that."

"About that? What else did she tell you?" Nate lowered his voice. "Is she gifted too? Psychic?"

Quentin was a little surprised that the cop asked the question openly, but he barely hesitated before replying. "In her case, it's more of a curse than a gift. And not one she's happy with or knows how to use effectively. She might be able to help us, but she's just as likely to join the dozen or so guests already packing up and leaving."

Momentarily distracted, Nate said, "I heard one of them tell the manager that he couldn't afford **this sort** of publicity, and he sounded real nervous about it. I guess the others are leaving for the same reason, because they're afraid to find themselves in the middle of a media nightmare. Especially if they have secrets or . . . indiscretions . . . of their own to hide."

"Probably. The Lodge's reputation for discretion is a strong lure for plenty of people looking for a private, stress-free vacation. This—especially if we find more—is just the sort of thing to really screw that up. When word gets out that two children were murdered here, even if years apart, the media's not going to ignore it. Then again, this place is so remote, and the locals are so accustomed to minding their own business, I'm not all that sure it **will** get out. Anytime soon, at least. Plus—"

"Plus, The Lodge is one of the largest employers in the area," Nate finished for him. "People around here have a vested interest in minding their own business. You've always thought that, haven't you?" He was matter-of-fact rather than offended, largely because he believed the same thing and understood the mind-set, having grown up in Leisure.

"It's been obvious. Even after I found brief mentions in the Leisure newspaper morgue of various **accidents** and disappearances over the years, I could never follow up. Nobody seemed to know anything. Nobody seemed to remember or to want to talk about it. Whatever the excuse, the meaning was clear. Whatever happened at or near The Lodge was not my business. And I've never had the legal authority to force the issue."

"Hey, Captain?"

Nate and Quentin both stepped forward at the summons, joining the two officers who made up the Leisure Police Department's Crime Scene Unit.

"Found something," Sally Chavez told them.

"Other than bones?" Nate wanted to know.

"Yep. See for yourself." Kneeling, she leaned back so that both Nate and Quentin could do that.

The skeleton, now half uncovered and with

the skull repositioned where it belonged, lay stretched out on its back, legs straight and arms at its sides.

As if it had been laid out carefully for burial. Quentin made a mental note of that, bothered by it even though it wasn't particularly uncommon. Some killers took special care with the disposal of their victims, and some did not.

Both men saw immediately what Chavez had invited them to see.

"A watch?" Quentin bent closer.

"Yeah," Chavez said. "Right wrist, so he may have been a southpaw."

"He?" Nate asked.

"Guess. Mostly from the watch, which looks like a guy type to me. From the size of the skeleton, this was a kid, and gender is a lot more difficult to determine from skeletal remains if death occurred before puberty. I don't see any obvious signs denoting gender. What I can tell you is that the watch undoubtedly had a band made of some kind of material that must have rotted away. Clearly not metal. Probably not plastic; that stuff lasts forever."

"That isn't really a child-size watch," Quentin said. "More of an adult watch he was meant to grow into—maybe given for some sort of accomplishment."

Nate grunted. "I got one when I made Eagle Scout."

"Can we get a closer look?" Quentin asked Chavez.

"Just a sec. Ryan, will you get a few shots of the watch, please?"

Her partner, a silent young man, stopped brushing dirt away from the foot end of the skeleton long enough to pick up a nearby camera and take several pictures.

Chavez carefully worked the half-buried watch loose with gloved hands, looked at it briefly, then slid it into a clear plastic bag and handed it up to her captain.

"Looks like we got lucky," she said.

Quentin and Nate both straightened, and the latter said, "Looks like. The back is engraved. He was named MVP of his Little League team. Ten years ago."

"Jeremy Grant."

Quentin and Nate both turned, startled, as Diana spoke. She was standing several feet back, certainly not close enough to have been able to see the watch. Her face was tense, her voice a little shaky.

"That's what it says, isn't it? What's on the back of the watch? His name is—was—Jeremy Grant."

Quentin stepped toward her. "Diana—"

"Just tell me."

"How the hell did you know?" Nate demanded.

Her gaze remained fixed on Quentin. "Tell me."

He had been advised to keep her grounded, and Quentin had the certain sense that right now it was a literal thing, that if he didn't provide an actual physical anchor for Diana, she would be gone.

Maybe in more ways than one.

He crossed the space between them and took one of her cold hands in his. "That's the name on the watch." He kept his voice low so no one else heard them, but also matter-of-fact. "You saw him?"

A little sound escaped her, not a laugh and not quite a sigh. "Saw him? Oh, hell, I talked to him."

Stephanie Boyd, manager of The Lodge, had her hands full. Not only had a dozen of her guests checked out without hesitation as soon as a skeleton had been found in one of the gardens, but those who were left had been vocally unhappy about the situation. They wanted her to reassure them that this was a one-time unfortunate event, that the police would soon be gone, and that no media would get wind of it.

So far, there had been no media that she knew of. She was crossing her fingers that continued. But, who knew?

And now she had a new worry.

"Captain, you can't be serious," she said to Nate McDaniel, trying hard to keep the dismay out of her voice.

"I'm sorry, Miss Boyd, but I am serious." He sounded serious. He also sounded frustrated. "It may be a cold trail, but I have to treat this as an active murder investigation. We expect dental records and DNA will positively identify the remains as those of Jeremy Grant, age eight when he disappeared from here at The Lodge ten years ago. His father worked here as a gardener at the time, but died himself of cancer a few years later. The mother relocated; we're trying to trace her now."

"You can't know that child was murdered on the grounds of The Lodge," she heard herself objecting. "Or by anyone connected to this place."

"He was buried in the English Garden, Miss Boyd."

"That wasn't part of the formal gardens then, Captain."

"No, but it was inside the fence. On the grounds of The Lodge."

She leaned back in her chair and stared at him across the desk. Her office felt more than usually small with his rather large presence occupying it. "Correct me if I'm wrong, but you have no evidence aside from the location of the remains that this is in any way connected to The Lodge."

"Miss Boyd—"

"Make it Stephanie." Dryly, she added, "From the sound of things, we're going to be seeing quite a lot of each other, at least for a while."

"I'm afraid so—Stephanie. I'd like to be able to offer Jeremy Grant's mother more closure than just the information that her son was murdered." He paused, then added, "And I'm Nate."

She nodded rather absently. "Just how do you mean to conduct an investigation into a ten-year-old crime? There are certainly a few long-time employees here who probably remember when the boy disappeared, but evidence? How can you possibly find anything after all this time?"

Nate didn't want to admit that the two aces he was counting on were one obsessive FBI agent with an even older murder to solve and one fragile guest and maybe-psychic who, if Nate was any judge, was about a whisper away from some kind of breakdown.

So all he said was, "We have to try, Miss—Stephanie. Now, obviously, it'll be better if we can conduct our investigation and interviews as quietly as possible. Which means keeping things inside The Lodge as much as we can. We don't want to be transporting employees back and forth from here to the police department, do we?"

"That has the nasty ring of a threat, Nate."

He lifted both eyebrows. "Not at all. Granted, without more evidence than I have that a crime was committed here, I don't have the legal authority to force you to turn over a room or cottage or other adequate space to me so that I can set up and conduct interviews here at The Lodge."

"No, you don't. And after ten years, I doubt a judge would grant you the right to do that."

Nate kept his tone pleasant. "But I doubt any judge in the county would forbid me to investigate this crime, especially given that it's the murder of a child. So you can have it one of two ways, Stephanie. Either I ferry employees back and forth—in police cars—from here to the station to be interviewed, for however long that takes, or else you do set aside a space for us to do what we have to do quietly and discreetly here on the grounds of The Lodge."

She didn't like either of the alternatives, but she knew damned well she was stuck with them.

Discarding her manager's hat for a moment, she said, "You really believe that child was murdered here?"

Nate hesitated, then said, "It gets worse. Another child was murdered here twenty-five years ago, and there could be more."

"What? Jesus."

"I guess they didn't tell you about any of that when they hired you." It wasn't a question.

"We didn't really discuss the history of The Lodge. That history, anyway. Twenty-five years ago? And you think that is related to this? Two murders that occurred fifteen years apart?"

Nate sighed. "It's reaching, I admit. But it's not unheard-of for a serial killer to operate over that span of time."

Even more startled and dismayed, she said again, "**Jesus.** Serial killer?"

"Just a possibility. But one I have to investigate, surely you see that?"

"All I see is a hotel on the front page and empty of guests," she said. Then she grimaced. "Sorry. I know that sounds callous, especially with children dead. But . . . if this boy was killed ten years ago, and nothing like that has happened since, then—"

Nate hated to do this to her, but interrupted to say, "In the last twenty-five years, we have here at The Lodge or in the area three children dead of illnesses, one reported runaway, two so-called accidental deaths, two undoubted murders—counting what we found today—and two unsolved disappearances of children. We also have at least two adults who disappeared without a trace while they were staying here."

It took a full minute before Stephanie could say, "How much of that happened since the little boy?"

Nate ran through the facts in his head—the ones Quentin had provided—and said slowly, "One kid disappeared nine years ago; two of the ones who died of illnesses died six and eight years ago; and the runaway was seven years ago. So, since Jeremy Grant disappeared, we have four kids dead or missing."

"You said some of them died of illnesses. Can't we discount those? I mean . . . You know what I mean."

"I know. And, no, we can't discount them. I'm told in all three cases the attending doctor ascribed the deaths to some kind of fever, which is why the police weren't involved at the time."

"Wouldn't that fall under the definition of natural causes?"

"Not necessarily. I'm also told some poisons would present that way." He was hoping she wouldn't ask who'd told him all this.

Stephanie propped her elbows on her blotter, rubbed her face with both hands, and muttered, "Oh, shit."

Nate felt more than a twinge of sympathy for her, helped along by the fact that she really was a very attractive woman. He'd always had a soft spot for brown-eyed blondes, especially when they were nicely woman-shaped rather than absurdly thin, as fashion so often pushed them to be. And she wasn't wearing a wedding or engagement ring. As soon as those thoughts occurred, he reminded himself that his first marriage had ended badly and that he liked living alone and being unattached.

He did.

He was almost positive he did.

But when she uncovered her face, he couldn't help but notice that her brown eyes were both intelligent and humorous, even now.

"So, Nate, you seriously believe that we might have a serial child-killer who's been operating here at The Lodge or at least in the area for the past twenty-five years?"

He yanked his mind back to work, hesitated, and said, "I believe it's possible. And, to complicate your life even more, you have a guest staying here who also believes it, and he's had experience with just this sort of thing."

She frowned. "The FBI agent?"

"You knew he was staying here?"

"Well, yeah. He has his weapon, and when he checked in he was good enough to inform us of that as well as furnish his badge number so we could verify his identity."

"Which you did?"

"Standard procedure. Somebody walks in here carrying a gun, I sure as hell want to know they're legit. So, yes, I personally called to verify Agent Hayes's identity." She frowned again. "Is this why he's here? Was he expecting to find skeletal remains in one of our gardens? Because I was told he was here on vacation, nothing more."

"Call it a busman's holiday." Nate sighed. "Quentin was a kid staying here twenty-five years ago when that first little girl was murdered. He never forgot it. And it never sat right with him that the case went unsolved. The last ten or twelve years, he's been coming to Leisure pretty regularly, looking for whatever information he could find on that and the other deaths and disappearances possibly connected to The Lodge."

Shrugging, Nate added, "And so he's pretty much the expert on all this. Carries the facts and details in his head."

"Sounds like a man obsessed."

"You could say that. I have."

Stephanie nodded slightly. "He'll be helping you investigate this child's death? All the deaths and disappearances?"

"Unofficially. Although he's going to tap Bureau resources to help us out with DNA and that sort of thing. The Leisure Police Department isn't really equipped to handle the kind of forensics work we're likely to need in investigating old crimes."

"I see. Well, I understand the point you made earlier about keeping this investigation as quiet as possible. Needless to say, I agree with that. So I'll allocate a room for your interviews, and I'll make available to you those employees who were here during the times you're investigating. I assume you'll provide a list with the relevant dates?"

"Of course," Nate responded, thinking of the busy night ahead of him.

"All I ask in return," Stephanie continued, "is that you **do** keep your activities as low-key as possible and don't disturb my guests any more than you absolutely have to."

"Agreed."

"I assume you mean to start first thing in the morning?"

Nate nodded. "Jeremy Grant was in the

ground out there for ten years, so one more night isn't likely to change anything. The remains are on their way to the state medical examiner. So, yeah, we'll get started on the interviews in the morning. Plainclothes, no uniforms. We will do our best not to disrupt your routines any more than necessary."

"I appreciate that. And Agent Hayes?"

"Agent Hayes will be approaching you for permission to go through old employee records and other paperwork stored here at The Lodge. I'm asking that you grant that permission."

She sighed. "I'll check with the owners, but under the circumstances, I'm sure they'll okay it."

"Thank you." He got to his feet and was on the point of leaving her small office when he found himself hesitating. "Stephanie, I know this is not what you signed on for, and I'm sorry it's happening on your watch."

She smiled slightly. "Don't worry about me, Nate. I'm an army brat. We learn early to cope with the unexpected."

Nate was tempted, but in the end decided not to ask her if the unexpected included the paranormal.

He'd find out the answer to that soon enough. They both would.

"You don't understand." Diana's voice was rock-steady in a way that only those holding on to control with teeth and fingernails could manage. "I talked to him. I took his hand and—and it was warm and solid. Flesh and blood. He wasn't cold, or wispy, or any of the things a ghost is supposed to be."

Quentin stirred an extra spoonful of sugar into the tea and then put the cup into her hands. "Drink this."

She stared at the cup for a moment, then looked around her, frowning. The sitting room was surprisingly large and comfortable, occupying part of an open space that also included the kitchenette and a small dining table.

Both the big sofa and the oversized chair in which she sat were plushly comfortable, and were grouped along with a large, square coffee table around a gas fireplace with a plasma TV placed above the mantel.

"We're in my cottage."

"Yes. It was closest. Drink the tea, Diana."

"How long have we been here? Oh, Christ, I didn't black out, did I?"

Which, Quentin thought, answered at least one of Bishop's questions.

"Not as far as I could see," he said matter-of-factly. "But you're in shock, and no wonder. I'm told it takes quite a while for a medium to adjust."

"I'm not a medium." But for the first time, her protest was more defiant than certain.

Again keeping his tone prosaic even though what he was saying certainly wasn't, Quentin said, "You met and talked to Jeremy Grant, and he's been dead for ten years. Either you're a medium, or else you imagined the whole thing. I know damned well you didn't imagine it, at least partly because there's no way you could have known whose grave you had found."

"A hallucination—"

"Probably wouldn't have given you his name, don't you think? Not the correct name, at any rate."

She stared at him.

"Drink the tea, Diana."

After a moment, she took a sip of the steaming liquid and grimaced, either because it was so hot or because it was so sweet. "I...don't remember coming here," she said finally.

"Shock, like I said. After you told me you'd talked to Jeremy, you didn't say anything else. It seemed to me the best idea would be to get you inside and give you a little time to come to terms with all this."

"I'm sure that cop had questions."

"Oh, he has plenty."

"Then—?"

"He'll talk to you tomorrow. He and his people will be talking to everybody tomorrow. Or at least everybody who was here or might know something about what happened to Jeremy Grant ten years ago."

"I don't know anything about that."

"He didn't happen to mention how he died, huh?"

She stared at him wonderingly. "No."

"Yeah, they never do. My boss says it's the universe reminding us that nothing is ever easy." He took a sip of the coffee he had ordered for himself, and added, "I think it sucks, though, frankly. I mean, you have this cool—and scary—ability to communicate with the dead, and they seldom tell you anything you couldn't figure out for yourself."

Diana cleared her throat. "It doesn't seem . . . quite fair," she agreed.

"No. It's like most psychic abilities. They come along with limitations, just as the other five senses do. Mine, for instance, never work when I need them to. I can't look into the future and see who's going to win the World Series this year, or if it's going to rain tomorrow, or even whether I'll be able to solve whatever case I'm working on at any given time. Hell, I can't even reliably predict the turn of a card. In fact, using tests developed years ago to measure psychic ability, I score below average."

Intent now, she said, "And yet you're psychic."

"And yet," he agreed. "Sometimes I just know things. They don't appear in my mind in neon, and I don't get visions. Sometimes I hear a faint whisper, as though someone is telling me something. Other times I just...know."

"And you really believe that?"

Quentin smiled at her. "Of course. I've seen and experienced too much in the last twenty-five years not to."

"Twenty-five years. Since Missy died?"

He nodded.

"You weren't psychic before then?"

"I wasn't born an active psychic, no." He shrugged, keeping it as matter-of-fact as he could. "One theory is that most if not all humans have latent psychic abilities, unawakened senses, maybe left over from more primitive times when we needed that edge just to survive. It could be something we're evolving away from, since our survival as a species doesn't seem to depend on it."

"Is that what you think?"

"Not really. I think it's more likely that we're evolving toward the ability to more effectively use our brains. Maybe because of the increased levels of electromagnetic energy in the modern world. That's a viable theory."

Diana nodded slowly. "Sounds like it."

"Sure, it makes sense. Anyway, for most people, whatever extra latent senses they possess remain dormant, inactive. But for some of us, there's a trigger, usually early in life. An event of some kind that creates just the right electromagnetic spark in our brains to activate what lies dormant."

"What sort of event?" she asked.

"Traumatic, usually. Physically, a severe injury or blow to the head. An actual electrical jolt. Or some kind of emotional or psychological shock."

"Which was it for you?"

"The latter."

"Missy's murder?"

"Only partly." He drew a breath, still finding it difficult to talk about even after all these years. "The real shock came when I was the one to find her body."

7

Diana leaned forward and carefully set her cup on the coffee table. "You...never told me just how she died."

"She was strangled." Quentin paused, then forced himself to go on, holding his voice steady. "I found her in what's now the Zen Garden, ironically. The little stream there was natural to the area, and we played there quite a bit."

"Were you looking for her?"

"Yeah. It was past suppertime, and she hadn't met the rest of us on the veranda as usual so we could eat together. It wasn't like her to just not show up, and it worried me. I kept thinking about how afraid she'd seemed earlier that day, for at least a couple of days, about how she'd tried to tell me what scared her."

"What had she said?"

"Nothing that made any sense to me. She said that she heard things, especially at night. And that . . . there was something else inside her sometimes."

"Something else?"

"That's the way she put it, something else. There was something inside her sometimes, and it made a sound like her own heartbeat."

Diana frowned slightly. "Does that make sense to you now?"

"Have you ever heard in your mind something that sounded like your own heart beating, Diana?"

Instead of answering that directly, she said, "You think Missy might have been psychic? A medium?"

"Have you?"

She shook her head. "No. I've . . . heard a lot of things inside my own mind, but never anything that sounded like a heartbeat. At least, not that I remember."

It was Quentin's turn to frown. "Still, that doesn't mean she wasn't psychic. It would explain why she was hearing things that frightened her."

Diana hesitated, then said, "Somebody killed

her, Quentin. Somebody real. It's pretty obvious she had good reason to be afraid."

"You don't have to remind me of that."

"What I mean is... if you've been looking for a paranormal explanation all this time—"

"That's why I was never able to solve her murder?" He shook his head. "I'm a cop, Diana. Psychic or not, the first thing we're taught to look for is the reasonable, rational, likely explanation. Because, more often than not, that's what we're going to find."

"It wasn't there, in this case?"

"The cops who investigated the case twenty-five years ago never even had a decent suspect. I've gone over all the reports on their investigation, and conducted my own investigation for years, however unofficially. Even interviewed dozens of people who were here or in the area at the time. And I have nothing new to show for it."

He drew a breath and let it out slowly. "Missy was strangled with a piece of twine from a bale of hay that had come from a field just yards away from where her body was found. A field filled with freshly baled hay. All that tells me as a cop, all it would tell any cop, is that the murder weapon was near to hand and convenient, which most likely means the murder itself was impulsive or opportunistic rather than planned.

Something triggered his rage or his need, and he used the first weapon he could reach to kill her."

"He?"

"Odds are, the killer was—is—male. Women virtually never kill children unrelated to them, and Missy's only relation here, her mother, was helping in the kitchen for hours that day, reportedly under observation by a dozen other people the whole time. Beyond that, nothing at the scene offered any indication of who killed Missy or why."

Diana frowned and, not even sure where the question came from, asked, "Why did he even need the twine? I mean...she was just a little girl. Wouldn't it have made more sense if he had used his hands?"

Quentin nodded slightly. "An educated guess is that she was probably strangled from behind with that twine because he didn't want her to see him, or else didn't want to look into her face as she died."

"Why?"

"Maybe because watching her die would have meant he'd have to admit to himself that he was a killer."

"How could he delude himself that he wasn't?"

"Easily. People do it all the time, you know that. Delude ourselves. Mostly in minor things.

We delude ourselves into believing that we won't be one of the ones let go when our company starts layoffs. That our favorite sports team has a shot at a championship. That we really can afford that shiny new car calling out to us from the lot."

"All of which is a long way from denying you're a killer when you're choking the life out of someone," Diana pointed out.

"Yeah, it's a leap. But I believe by the time he picked up that twine and wrapped it around her neck, this killer had gradually reached that point. It may have taken him years to get there, but he had. Possibly for the first time. By then, by that day, he could kill, but didn't view himself as a killer."

Quentin had seemingly been cool and clinical up to that point, but the detachment left when he continued, his voice going quiet and a little rough. "Whatever happened out there, whatever triggered it, he killed Missy. She was left in that stream, her body wedged in among the rocks, the twine still wrapped around her neck."

He paused, then added softly, "Her eyes were open. When I first saw her, she seemed to be looking right at me. Pleading with me. As if I could help her. As if I should have."

"Quentin—"

"By then, she'd become the little sister I'd

never had. Someone I couldn't imagine my life without. And I stood there, frozen, staring into her eyes, knowing that I had failed her. As a brother. As a friend. I hadn't listened to her. I hadn't protected her. I hadn't helped her. I hadn't saved her. It was . . . it felt like I'd been kicked in the stomach. Everything around me faded, grew dark, until all I could see was her. Her eyes. That pale, pale face. And the twine wrapped around her neck, cutting into her skin. Such a strangely small, ordinary thing to have snuffed out a life. To have stopped a smile and silenced a laugh forever. Just twine. Just twine from a bale of hay."

Diana wasn't entirely sure she wanted to hear any of this, yet at the same time she couldn't remember ever feeling so focused, so clear-minded. There were no scattered thoughts, no random flashes of information, no whispers in her head. There wasn't even the earlier shock and fear at the certain knowledge that she had on this day spoken casually with a ghost.

There was only this man and his low, hurting voice, painting for her a horrific, tragic image she could see so clearly it was as though she had stood there herself and seen that murdered little girl.

Her long, dark hair moving in the water as though it and she were still alive, big dark eyes open, staring up . . .

"It wasn't a... sexual crime," Quentin continued, obviously with difficulty. "At least, that was the official conclusion, and I haven't found any evidence to believe otherwise. She was fully dressed, and no bodily fluids were found on or near her, though being submerged in water means we can't be certain there wasn't something on her clothing or body that was washed away. There were no bruises, no signs of trauma other than what had killed her. No defensive injuries. They scraped under her fingernails, took clippings. But there was nothing, no evidence to help identify her killer.

"She probably died there in the stream or nearby; there was nothing to indicate it might have happened somewhere else. Nothing to indicate that she fought her attacker, or even that she struggled at all. The last person to see her alive, as far as they could determine, was me."

That surprised Diana. "You?"

"Yeah. Late that afternoon. I was coming back up from the stables, and met her near what's now the entrance to the Zen Garden. That's when she tried one more time to tell me that she was afraid, that there was something...wrong here. But I was hot and tired and just wanted to go to our cottage and take a shower. I thought she'd had a nightmare, or maybe was just making up a story, for whatever reason."

"Could there have been a reason?"

He shrugged. "Because the other kids and I had been spending more time riding the horses, and she never went along since she was afraid of them. Because the summer was winding down and we were all getting a little bored, a little tired of one another's company. Whatever. So I brushed her off." He paused, then added steadily, "They fixed the time of death as just under two hours later."

"And nobody saw her in all that time?"

"Nobody admitted to it. In all fairness, they probably wouldn't have noticed her. She was— she had the knack of slipping past people without really being seen."

"Like a ghost?"

"Like a ghost."

In the privacy of her office, Stephanie Boyd grimaced as she held the phone to her ear. She was pretty good at keeping her thoughts and feelings to herself, but it was a relief now to relax physically as she couldn't allow herself to verbally. With this man, at any rate.

Her boss had, not surprisingly, reacted badly to the news of the remains of a child being found on the grounds of The Lodge. His reaction was even worse once he grasped the probable ramifications of the police investigation already under way.

"You couldn't stop them, Stephanie?"

"How?" she asked, repressing the urge toward sarcasm. "The police are bound by law to investigate something like this, and I have no authority to stop them. Offhand, I can't imagine any local judge or politician trying it, either, not when it concerns the death of a child."

She drew a breath. "Setting aside, of course, the fact that it could only further damage the reputation of The Lodge if we seemed in any way reluctant to find the truth of this tragedy, we are morally compelled to do whatever we can."

"Of course. Oh, of course." Doug Wallace tried hard to sound as if he cared about the long-ago murder of a little boy. And he almost pulled it off. Almost.

Stephanie kept her own tone brisk and businesslike. "Under the circumstances, I believe our best course is to cooperate fully with the authorities. The police captain in charge of the investigation has assured me that he will do his utmost to conduct all relevant inquiries as discreetly as possible." She decided not to mention the FBI agent who was, after all, here very much unofficially.

Wallace sighed. "Yeah, I've heard that before."

Pressing, Stephanie said, "And I have your permission to extend our cooperation to the police, to make our records available to them?"

"Christ. Is that really necessary?"

Unconsciously, Stephanie tilted her head to one side. "Is there any reason why it would be a problem, Mr. Wallace?"

He was silent for a beat or two, then said, "Stephanie, you're aware that most if not all our clients—our guests—value their privacy."

"Yes, sir." She stopped it there, waiting. In her experience, silence quite often produced answers where insistent questions wouldn't.

"We have had some Very Important Clients."

"Yes, sir."

He sighed again, impatient. "One of the services we offer is discretion, Stephanie. The very reputation of The Lodge was founded on that. Our specialty, as it were, the lure to get people to such an isolated spot. So if a Very Important Client checks in with a companion not his wife, we respect his privacy. If an actress recovering from cosmetic surgery or the unfortunate repercussions of an ill-judged affair wishes her presence to remain...well...secret, we oblige. If a group of businesspeople requires a secure and discreet setting in which to discuss the future of their company, we provide that."

"Yes, sir."

"Dammit, Stephanie, we mind our own business. And our paperwork reflects that."

Evenly, she said, "Sir, I very much doubt that the records of any of the situations you describe could possibly be relevant to this police investigation and would, therefore, be of no interest to them."

Wallace swore, not under his breath. "Stephanie, what I'm trying to tell you is that there have been occasions in the past during which **no** records were kept. Officially or unofficially."

"Sir, I was never told that anything of that nature would be part of my duties," she said stiffly.

"No, of course not. We don't do that sort of thing these days," Wallace was quick to say. "We keep a private ledger—which I'm sure you **were** told about since I told you myself—for those more discreet occasions. But there were regrettable instances in the past in which Lodge employees accepted...um...additional gratuities...to keep a guest's name or the situation entirely off the books."

Somewhat grimly, Stephanie wondered what she'd gotten herself into. It had seemed like such a nice little job. "I see, sir."

Wallace's tone was strained but steady. "I don't know how thoroughly these police officers mean to examine our books and other records, or what they expect to find, but someone familiar with hotel accounting would certainly notice some...discrepancies."

Stephanie knew. "Such as food and beverages charged to supposedly unoccupied rooms. Such as spa services booked and not charged."

"Yes, yes, exactly those sorts of things." Wallace drew a breath. "I can assure you that all monies were reported and accounted in accordance with the law. We merely protected the anonymity of our clients."

And Stephanie believed in the Easter Bunny. She wondered how many secrets this place really held. And which of them would blow up in her face the instant they were exposed.

"Yes, sir." There really wasn't much else she could say, at least as long as she kept this job.

He cleared his throat. "My point being, of course, that if the police should look closely at our books, they could conceivably find things that could send them off on quite useless and needless tangents in their investigation of this child's tragic death."

Baldly, she demanded, "What do you expect me to do, sir?"

"You're on the scene," Wallace said, his tone persuasive. "You can...guide...the local police. Keep them focused on details relevant to their investigation."

"Guide them, sir?"

"Don't be deliberately dense, Stephanie. You can make certain that the police aren't allowed to paw indiscriminately through our accounts and records. Boundaries. Boundaries must be set."

"I've already been asked to allow access to employment records and historical documents stored in the basement."

"I don't see how those could be relevant."

"I've been assured it's simple procedure. The police need to know who was here at the time this child was murdered, and since ten years have passed, they'll need whatever paperwork they can find."

"You need to see those records first, Stephanie."

"Sir, are you asking me to interfere with that investigation?"

"Absolutely not." He sounded offended now, though also harassed. "I'm not suggesting you keep anything of value from the police, merely that you take a look before they do. Weed out what your common sense tells you cannot possibly be relevant. And notify me should you find anything . . . unusual."

"Unusual, sir?"

"Just anything that might strike you as odd, that's all. Nothing to do with this murder, obviously."

Stephanie had pretty good instincts, and right

now they were practically doing handstands to get her attention. Trying to "guide" the police away from discrepancies in the bookkeeping was one thing; actively searching through documents herself in order to report back to Wallace was something else entirely. And suspicious as hell.

What did he expect her to find?

"Stephanie, I'm making a perfectly reasonable request that you keep in mind the best interests of your employers, that's all."

Stephanie was tempted, but decided not to try and pin him down to more fully explain his meaning. He was adept at sidestepping, for one thing. For another, she really didn't want him worried enough about what she might do to hop on a plane out in California and come here himself. Not before she figured out what this was all about, anyway.

If there was anything army brats learned young, it was that the more information you had in hand, the better your likelihood of making the best decision possible. Nobody could sneak up on you if you knew where they stood.

In other words, protect your goddamned flank. And your ass, while you were at it.

Keeping her own tone calm but just faintly impatient, she said, "Very well, sir. I'll take a look downstairs and report to you anything that seems to me unusual. And I'll work as closely as possible with the police, to keep fully abreast of the investigation."

"Good." Wallace sounded a bit wary rather than satisfied, as if he realized that Stephanie had not quite sung the team fight song. "Good. I'll expect regular updates, Stephanie. No matter how this plays out."

"Yes, sir." She crossed her fingers. "With the weekend looming, I doubt much will get done until Monday, at least. I'll call then with an update."

"Very well."

She cradled the receiver, then leaned back in her chair, propped her feet on the desk, and thought about this.

Item: there were discrepancies in The Lodge's accounts, and possibly other paperwork as well. Item: Douglas Wallace, properties manager for the very wealthy group of investors who owned The Lodge, was worried about the wrong person finding the wrong thing while sifting through that paperwork. Item: whatever Wallace was worried about might or might not have something to do with the murder of an eight-year-old boy ten years ago. But either way, Wallace was just this side of scared and not hiding it well.

Which meant bad news any way you cut it.

Final item: Stephanie Boyd was sitting in the hot seat.

"Shit," she muttered. "I knew this job was too good to be true."

"You can't blame yourself," Diana said.

"Rationally, I know that." Quentin shrugged. "I've told myself to let it go and move on with my life. God knows other people have told me the same thing. But whether psychic abilities, a guilty conscience, or simple instincts, something inside me has insisted all these years that I had to find Missy's killer. And let her rest in peace. It's something I have to do. Something I'm meant to do."

Recalling the thin face and sad eyes she had seen and drawn, Diana said slowly, "I wish I could tell you she was already at peace. But . . ."

"But you can't. You saw her, which means she's still in—for want of a better term—limbo. Even after all these years, she hasn't been able to move on."

"On to where?"

He smiled slightly. "Do you want me to say 'heaven'?"

"I don't know. Would it be true?"

"Not a question I can answer. Whatever I

know of the future tells me nothing of the spirit realm. Or anything beyond this life. So far, anyway."

Diana frowned. She sipped her cooling tea, then said, "My sketch of Missy. I drew that before I saw her."

Quentin knew what she was asking. "It's a form of automatic writing. Your subconscious and psychic abilities were on autopilot, more or less."

"Why?"

"We have a few theories. Automatic writing or drawing is almost always triggered by stress. I know of only a couple of psychics who are able to deliberately tap in to the ability; for the rest of you, it tends to manifest itself because something is being suppressed."

She stared at him.

"Your abilities have been trying to surface for most of your life. Trying to. Between the meds and therapies and denial, they've been pushed down again and again. Beaten back, imprisoned. But something that powerful finds a way, sooner or later, to escape whatever's restraining it. You said something about blackouts earlier."

Diana frowned uneasily. "I did?"

"Yeah. I'm guessing the blackouts began sometime during your early teen years, during the physical and emotional chaos of adolescence. And that either they've grown stronger with time or else tend to occur when you're under unusual levels of stress."

Grudgingly, she said, "The latter."

Quentin didn't let her see how relieved he was by that information. If the blackouts were erratic and stress-related, then it was less likely that Diana's abilities were becoming a danger to her.

Less likely. Not impossible.

"Which means?" Diana prompted.

"Which means—or probably means—that you black out only when your abilities can find no other way of breaking free."

She set her cup down on the coffee table and leaned back, crossing her arms over her breasts. "Okay, now you're really creeping me out. You make these so-called abilities of mine sound as if they have a mind of their own."

"Energy, Diana. Your brain is naturally designed to tap in to energy, and it has to also be able to release it. Think of steam building up inside a pot holding boiling water. If the lid's on tight, the pressure can intensify until it's a destructive force, until the container itself is endangered. Some of the steam has to be allowed to escape."

"Okay, but—"

"The energy you tap in to has to have an outlet, something your instincts have always known. If you can't provide that release valve consciously, by allowing yourself to undergo the sort of visions you experienced earlier today, then your subconscious will find a way to do it for your own safety. The blackouts."

"I don't remember what happens then." She hesitated, then added, "But I...I've awakened in strange places. Doing strange things sometimes."

"I'm not surprised. Psychic blackouts are an extreme response, which means the energy level just before they occur has to be tremendous."

"Then what happens? Once a blackout is... triggered?" Diana wasn't sure which was strongest in her, curiosity or fear.

Quentin shook his head. "I have no way of knowing, not for certain. Psychic abilities are as unique as the individuals who possess them; the unconscious release of stored energy could take just about any form. What sort of strange things have you awakened in the middle of?"

"I was in a lake once. Up to my waist." She shivered. "I couldn't swim at the time. Now I can."

He frowned. "What else?"

"Driving my father's Jag. Very fast. I was fourteen."

"Jesus."

"Yeah. Scared the hell out of me."

"When you came out of the blackout, you didn't have any sense of where you were going or why?"

"No, just—" It was Diana's turn to frown. "Just...a pull."

"Pull?"

"Yeah. As if something—or someone, I suppose—had been calling me, drawing me toward them."

"Where were you headed?"

"I was so shaken up by it I hardly noticed where I was."

"Think. Try to remember."

"It's important?"

"Maybe."

Concentrating, Diana tried to push past the remembered terror and panic and recall more than emotions. What had she done? Slowed the car, looking for a sign, her hands cold and sweaty on the steering wheel and her heart pounding. In the darkness before dawn, everything had looked alien, and she had felt so alone there weren't even words for it.

"I was on an interstate highway," she remembered as a sign flashed through her memories. "Heading south. Took me more than an hour to find a phone and call my father. He was...not happy. As scared as I was, or so it seemed to me."

She paused, then added, "There was a new clinic the next week. A new doctor. A new treatment."

"I'm sorry, Diana."

She looked at him. "That was one time I was more than willing to try whatever treatment the doctors offered. I was fourteen years old, Quentin, and I woke up on an interstate highway at five o'clock in the morning driving my father's Jaguar at nearly eighty miles an hour. I was afraid I'd been trying to kill myself. I think my father was afraid of the same thing."

"And the doctors?"

"Did they believe I was suicidal?" Her shoulders lifted and fell. "Over the years, some did, I'm sure. But I never did any of the things suicidal patients were supposed to do. Never tried to slit my wrists or hurt myself in any other way. If you discount the blackout experiences, of course. I never tried to hoard medications. Never talked about killing myself, never drew pictures to indicate suicide was on—or under— my mind."

"What about the blackouts? Frequent?"

"There haven't been that many, really. Maybe two a year, and mostly I come out of them in my bed or just sitting in a chair. Like I've been asleep. Dreaming dreams I can never remember."

"The subconscious tends to be a good

guardian, and protects us from what we can't or don't need to endure," Quentin said. "I wouldn't be surprised if realizing you're psychic now doesn't open a few doors for you, though. You may begin to remember those dreams. And those experiences."

That was a scary possibility, Diana thought. Maybe even more scary than not remembering anything. She said, "One of my doctors became convinced that the blackouts were caused by an adverse reaction to one or more of the drugs prescribed for me. That was almost a year ago."

"He took you off everything?"

She nodded. "The first couple of months were . . . hell. It was a supervised withdrawal, so I had to be hospitalized. Watched. So many of the medications had been prescribed to quiet my mind and keep me calm."

"Sedatives," Quentin said. "Antianxiety meds. Antidepressants."

"Yeah. When all those were taken away from me, even gradually, it was like I went into hyperdrive. I lost twenty pounds because I couldn't be still. I talked so fast no one could understand what I was saying. I couldn't sleep, and nothing could hold my attention more than a few minutes at a time. My father wanted them to put me back on the meds because of the state I was in. But the doctor, bless him, held firm. And after the first weeks, my mind was finally clear enough so I could be firm too."

After a moment, Quentin asked, "How long had it been since you'd been completely off medications?"

Diana didn't really want to tell him, but finally said, "The first medications were prescribed when I was eleven. From that point on, there was always something, usually more than one drug at a time. But always something. I'm thirty-three now. You do the math."

"More than twenty years. You've spent two-thirds of your life drugged."

"Just about into oblivion," she agreed.

8

Madison said, "I don't think this is such a good idea."

"Why not?" Becca wanted to know. "We have to do something, and we don't have much time. Trust me, you don't want to be here when it comes back."

"Are you sure it **will** come back?"

"Of course I'm sure. It always comes back."

"Maybe this time—"

Becca shook her head. "It's going to keep coming until they stop it. And they won't be able to stop it until they know. Until they **understand**."

Madison hesitated, then said unhappily, "But

she looked so scared. When he left her alone a little while ago, and she locked the door behind him. Even if she is a grownup. She looked so scared."

"I know. But she can change things here, or at least she might be able to try. She's the one we've been waiting for, I'm sure of it. She saw Jeremy, and that's what matters most, what we have to remember. I think she's seen Missy too, so—"

"Who's Missy?"

"You haven't met her yet," Becca said. "She's been here even longer than Jeremy was. She usually stays in the gray time, though, and doesn't come out much, even when somebody opens the door."

"Why not? Isn't she lonely there?"

"I expect so. But she's more afraid of what happens out here. I expect that's because she knew what it would do to her even before it did."

"Really?"

"Uh-huh. She was special, like you are. I expect she's trying really hard to find a way to stop it this time."

"So she can leave The Lodge?"

"I expect so."

Suddenly irritated, Madison said, "Well, I **expect** it won't be easy, or she could have done it by now."

Becca chuckled. "Does it get on your nerves, me saying 'expect' so much? My mama always said it. Used to get on my nerves too. But now I like to say it, I s'pose because it reminds me of her."

Her ready sympathy stirred, Madison said, "Your mama isn't here?"

"Not here at The Lodge. She's on this side of the door, but I can't see her, of course. Can't talk to her. We were just supposed to stay here a little while, her and my brother and me. They stayed a long time, looking for me. They stayed longer than they meant to, looking for me. But they couldn't find me, of course. They had to go home, sooner or later. So they did."

"And left you here?"

"Well, they couldn't take me with them. They couldn't see me. And even if they had, I didn't have any bones to show them, not like Jeremy."

Madison eyed her new friend uneasily. "I'm glad you don't have any bones, Becca, 'cause I'd just as soon not see them."

"Fraidy cat."

Staunchly, Madison said, "Yes, I am. I don't like bugs, either, or snakes, or anything gross." She bent down and picked up Angelo, who had begun to whine a bit, telling herself the action was to comfort him rather than her.

"Well," Becca said, "all I can say is that you'd

better help us try to stop it when it comes back this time. Because if we can't..."

Madison waited, watching as Becca turned frowning eyes toward the cottage several yards away.

"If we can't," Becca continued softly, "there'll be more than bones for them to find. For them to see. A lot more."

Quentin paced the sitting room of his suite, restless and more than a little uneasy. Diana had closed down immediately after telling him about spending most of her life medicated, her face without expression and eyes going shuttered, and after the day she'd had he hadn't dared push her to continue talking.

Not yet, at least.

He was, truthfully, grateful for the time to try to sort through what she had told him so far. He wanted to help her, needed to, and he had nothing to go on except the instincts that urged him to probe carefully, to ask questions when she seemed ready to talk and to offer bits of information about the paranormal as she seemed able to accept it. It was all he had to guide him, that and what she told him about her life and experiences.

A horror story if he'd ever heard one.

Two-thirds of her life spent medicated.

Jesus.

Quentin found it hard not to blame her doctors, and especially her father, for not being open-minded enough to at least consider the possibility that there had been nothing **wrong** with Diana from the beginning. But they hadn't. Faced with the inexplicable, with experiences and behaviors they didn't understand and were frightened by, they had acted swiftly, with all the supposed knowledge of modern-day medicine, to "fix" her "problems."

Even before she hit puberty, for Christ's sake.

And they had left her only half alive. A pale, colorless, vague, and passionless copy of the Diana she was meant to be.

Christ, no wonder she looked out on the world with wary, suspicious eyes. Finally off all the mind-numbing medications, Diana was clearheaded for the first time since childhood. Truly aware for the first time of the world around her. And not just aware, but painfully alert, with the raw-nerved sensitivity of most psychics.

She knew, now. No matter what she was willing to admit aloud or even consciously, she knew now that she had been kept half alive, less than that. Knew that those she had trusted most had betrayed that trust, even if they had done it in the name of love and concern and with all good intentions. They hadn't kept her safe, they had kept her doped up and compliant. They had sought to hammer away all the sharp, unique edges that made her Diana.

So she could be **healthy**. Like everybody else.

It had been in her voice when she'd told him, a haunted awareness of all she'd lost.

"I'm thirty-three now. You do the math."

He thought it must have been like waking from a coma or a hazy dream to find that everything that had gone before had not been real. The world had turned, time had moved on... and Diana had lost years.

Years.

Quentin paced a while longer, more rather than less restless as time passed. He found himself, finally, in his dark bedroom, standing at the window, looking out on the night. And it was only then that he realized he could see Diana's cottage from here, his third-floor suite high enough to overlook the shrubbery and ornamental trees between The Lodge and her cottage.

Watch.

He went still, holding his breath as he tried to concentrate, to hear the faint whisper in his mind.

You have to watch tonight.

Long moments passed, and he allowed himself to breathe again as he realized there would be no more. Just the realization, the understanding. That he had to stand watch tonight, for Diana's sake.

Perhaps for her safety.

He could see both the front door and the private little patio door from here, clearly visible because the doors of all the cottages were well lit, just as the paths linking them to The Lodge were well lit. For convenience as well as security.

Without even making the conscious decision to do so, Quentin focused, concentrated. Everything went fuzzy for an instant, and then the cottage stood out in sharp relief from the landscaping around it. The door seemed so close it was as if he could have reached out and turned the handle.

Since he needed to enhance only his vision, his other senses more or less went dormant. He heard only silence. Smelled nothing. When he leaned a shoulder against the window frame, he wasn't aware of the contact. His mind was quiet and still.

Bishop had warned him not to do this. Enhancing only one sense at the expense of all the others would exact a price, a painful one. Quentin knew. He knew if he kept this up for hours he'd have a pounding headache tomorrow, that his senses of smell and taste and touch and hearing would be muffled, maybe for the entire day. He knew his eyes would ache and be sensitive to the light, strained by being forced to work harder right now.

There was also a danger, Bishop believed, of losing the capability entirely. Pouring extra energy into one's senses to enhance them was one thing; totally shutting down one or more of those senses for an extended period of time was something else again. Balance. It was all about balance.

Quentin knew. He also didn't care.

He needed to watch Diana, so that's what he did. Leaning against the window frame, no longer even conscious of the room he was in, he watched.

And waited.

"If he didn't think so before, the man certainly thinks you're nuts by now," Diana muttered to herself as she got out of the shower and dried off. "Way to go, telling him all the gory details. Everybody knows they don't keep you drugged to the gills for a couple of decades if you don't have a **lot** of problems."

The worst thing was, Diana wasn't at all sure what Quentin's gut-level reaction had been. Oh, he'd been all compassion and understanding on the surface, saying all the right things, insisting that being medicated for most of her life didn't mean she was sick. Just that the doctors hadn't understood.

Oh, yeah, she believed that. Probably about as much as he really believed it. But she couldn't tell what he thought, not for certain. She didn't think she was very good at reading people's expressions, due mostly to a lack of practice; drifting through life on her medicated cloud, what other people thought or felt hadn't seemed, very often, to matter.

It mattered now. She didn't know why, or at least didn't want to admit it to herself, but it mattered to her what Quentin thought of her. And he undoubtedly thought she was hopelessly damaged goods. It shouldn't have hurt, that, because she'd always known it.

Now he knew it too.

Angry at herself and so tired that her thoughts were going in even more circles than usual, Diana pulled on a pair of silky pajama bottoms and a matching camisole. It was still fairly early, but she needed sleep and she needed it badly.

She went into her lamplit bedroom and turned down the bed, then sat on the edge and hesitated for only an instant before opening the nightstand drawer. The prescription bottle rolled a bit with the movement of the drawer, then stilled. She picked it up reluctantly.

This medication remained in her system only a few hours, only long enough to allow her to sleep. Her doctor had promised that, had sworn it, and since he was the one who had taken her off all the other medications, she believed him.

Still . . . the bottle was full.

Diana resisted taking as much as an aspirin now. Even with the scattered, restless thoughts and inability to focus on anything for very long, the raw emotions and almost painfully sharp senses, she preferred this state to what had gone before.

She had, mostly, drifted through more than twenty years of her life. She didn't want to drift anymore.

But she needed desperately to sleep, and she was afraid of what might happen if she didn't. So she shook a couple of pills into her hand and took them, washing them down with a sip of water from the bottle on her nightstand.

She got into bed and turned off the lamp, then lay back on the pillow. She felt an impulse to go to the window as she had so many nights before, but with an effort ignored it.

Sleep. She needed sleep. All this would make sense to her if she could only sleep.

Her mind continued to chase itself in circles

for some time—she refused to look at the night-stand clock to see just how long it went on—but eventually quieted.

And, finally, she slept.

Diana opened her eyes and sat up in bed, oddly unsurprised to find herself in the gray time.

She knew it was still night, even though her bedroom was lit with that oddly flat, colorless twilight she recognized. It was always the same, in the gray time. Never darkness or light, just . . . gray.

She thought she had slept for hours, but didn't bother looking at the clock on the nightstand. It wouldn't show her anything. One of the truly spooky traits of the gray time was that there was **no** time there. Here. Clocks, whether digital or not, were faceless, featureless.

Wherever this place existed, it lay somewhere outside time; Diana had figured out that much. Yet she also had the sense that it was a place of movement, a place between the living world she knew and whatever came after it.

Not the spirit realm Quentin had spoken of, not exactly. More like the doorway, the corridor, connecting the two worlds.

She threw back the covers and got out of bed, aware of the chill of the room, a chill that even seeped upward through the plush carpet so that her feet felt like ice. She knew she should find her slippers or shoes, find a jacket or at least a robe, but didn't bother. It wouldn't make a difference, she knew that. It was always cold in the gray time. Cold to the bone.

Diana left her bedroom, vaguely interested to see how featureless the cottage seemed without color or shadows, but not interested enough to stop. There was somewhere else she had to be.

She left the cottage, stopping on the path that led from her door. Waiting. The lights out here looked strange and dull, not bright but merely a paler shade of gray. The shrubbery and flowers planted in pots and beds all around the cottage were eerily still and held that same one-dimensional appearance, like a grayish copy of a picture that had once held vivid color.

Not a breath of air stirred the cold twilight, though a faint, slightly unpleasant smell lingered. It wasn't something Diana had ever been able to identify, though it was somehow familiar. There were no night sounds, no pulse of life. There never was.

"Diana."

She turned slightly and looked at the little girl standing several feet away. A pretty child, with what seemed, in the colorless grayness, to be very fair hair surrounding a heart-shaped face.

"Hello." Diana noted the hollow sound of her own voice, the almost-echo. Different from the child's voice, which was perfectly clear. That, also, was normal for the gray time.

"You have to come with me," the little girl said.

Diana shook her head slightly, not negation but impatience. "The last time I followed one of you, it was to a grave."

The little girl frowned. "But Jeremy was on the other side. Your side. You know the difference. And you know the rules."

Diana did know, and quite clearly. In the gray time, her memory was perfect, her understanding absolute. For all its eerie strangeness, the gray time was a place in which she felt in control. But she also knew the dangers involved.

"I know this is not a safe place for me to be, in between two times. Two worlds."

"You can't stay long," the little girl agreed. "Keeping the door open is dangerous, that's one of the rules. And if you close it while you're still inside, you'll be trapped here. I don't expect you'd like that."

"No. I don't expect I would."

The little girl smiled. "Then we'd better hurry."

"What's your name?" Diana asked, because she always did.

"Becca."

Diana nodded. "Okay, Becca. You're the one who called me?"

"Yes."

"Why?"

"There's something you need to see." Another frown drew her brows together. "And we really do have to hurry."

"I've spent hours here before," Diana protested, but followed nevertheless as Becca turned and led the way toward the distant stables.

"I know. But being on our side here—here at The Lodge—is much more dangerous for you. Besides, he'll be here soon, and he won't let you stay."

"He? Becca—"

"This way. Hurry, Diana."

Knowing from long experience that protest was useless, Diana followed her guide. They were always like this, taking her places, insisting that she see what they wanted to show her, do what they asked of her. Or just listen to them.

She had listened to a lot of them, over the years.

"Why is it more dangerous for me to be here while I'm at The Lodge?" she asked, hoping for at least one answer.

"Because it started here."

"What started here?"

"Everything."

Diana wondered if she'd expected the "answer" to make sense. Tough luck, if she had.

"Becca, I don't understand."

"I know. But you will."

Diana picked up her pace, since Becca definitely had, and followed the little girl into the first of three barns making up The Lodge's stables. They walked down the long, silent hall, past stalls with their half-open Dutch doors. Diana didn't have to look to know that each stall appeared empty.

She also knew there were a dozen horses stabled here. **Here** in this barn at The Lodge. Not **here** in the gray time.

It had taken her a while to get accustomed to that.

There were no animals here, not because they lacked whatever energy or spiritual essence survived death, Diana believed, but because non-human creatures seldom lingered in the gray time, caught between two worlds due to guilt or anger or unfinished business. Only people did that.

"Not much farther," Becca said over her shoulder.

"Becca, is this about you?"

"I called you, didn't I?"

"We both know that doesn't mean anything. I had one guide who called me a dozen times, and it was never about him."

Becca stopped about halfway down the hall and turned to look steadily at Diana. "This time, it's about you."

"Me?"

"Yes."

"What do you mean?" Diana crossed her forearms over her breasts and rubbed her upper arms with her hands, trying to fight off the chill. Not that it helped. It never did.

"You were always meant to come here, Diana. To The Lodge. You've been tied to this place your whole life."

"How could that be? I've never been here before."

"Connections."

"Is that supposed to make sense? Because it doesn't."

Becca shook her head slightly, but said, "Things have to happen the way they happen. When they happen. Do you think it was an accident that the doctor took you off all the medicines when he did? That there's been just enough time to get your mind clear and all those chemicals out of your body?"

"Just enough time?"

"Enough time for you to be ready when you came here."

Diana was conscious of a new chill, a deeper one. There was something wrong here, something different. She had talked to guides for more than twenty years, and this...this wasn't the way those conversations had gone.

Like Jeremy and his bones, most of them had needed her to act on their behalf. To find something for them. To pass on some sort of information. To finish their unfinished business. It wasn't about her. It was never about her.

Becca nodded, as though she had heard those unspoken thoughts. "It feels different, doesn't it? That's because you're here, really here, in the flesh. You could do it sometimes before, when you blacked out, but never when you were asleep. When you were asleep, it was just...like a dream. Only a part of you was here, on this side. The medicines mostly kept the rest of you from crossing over."

"I'm not dead," Diana said slowly.

"No, of course not. That's not what this is about. It's time, Diana. Time for you to start remembering the places you go to when you sleep or black out. Time for you to realize what you can do. What you've been doing most of your life. Time to come here, and meet him, and begin to find the answers you need. It's all part of your journey."

Confused, Diana said, "But I won't remember. When I'm awake. I never remember."

"You never remembered before because of the medicines. They couldn't keep you from doing what you had to do, but they could keep you from remembering. Think about it. You haven't blacked out since they took the medicines away."

"The drawing. The painting."

"He explained to you. That was different from the blackouts. That was just like a kind of day-dreaming."

Diana was silent.

"If you let yourself remember now, let yourself understand and believe, there won't be any more blackouts, Diana. There won't need to be. It'll still be easier to open the door and come here when you're asleep, but you'll be able to do it when you're awake. Whenever you want to. If you believe."

"It's not that simple."

"Isn't it? You're halfway there. You've been remembering your dreams," Becca said.

"Nightmares," Diana said involuntarily. "And I don't remember, I just . . . They scare me."

"They're supposed to."

That young, grave, sweet voice sent another of those deeper chills darting through Diana, and she fought an urge to take a step back. Instead, she said, "You called me. Brought me down here. Why?"

"To show you something. So you'll really start to believe."

"Show me what?"

"A secret place."

"Becca—"

"There are secrets everywhere, Diana. Remember that." She pointed off to the side, where the door to this barn's tack room stood closed. "One of them is in there. Tell him to look for it. Tell him it's hidden there."

"What's hidden there? Becca—"

The little girl tilted her head to one side, her expression solemn. "In the attic too. There's something you need to see up there. It's important, Diana. It's very important."

"Why?" The question had barely emerged when a sudden flash made Diana blink. For an instant, just a split second, she thought she smelled hay, thought the grayness all around her changed. "Becca, why?" she repeated quickly.

"Because it's the truth. And you need to know the truth. Until you know that, you won't understand what's happening here."

Another flash brought Diana the smell of hay and horses and the sight of fluorescent lights stretching down the barn's hallway. She felt a sudden warmth grip her upper arms and realized instantly what was happening right now, this moment.

She was being pulled back.

"Becca, what is it? What is the truth?"

Another flash. Then another. She could see Quentin now, in the flashes, standing before her.

"I can't tell you, Diana. You have to find it out for yourself. You and him. You need him. Because—"

"—it's coming," Diana said as she opened her eyes.

"What's coming?" Quentin demanded, his hands tightening on her bare and chilled upper arms.

A horse snorted nearby, making her jump, and the strong if pleasant scents of hay and horses were suddenly thick in her nostrils. The strips of fluorescent lights down the barn's hall seemed so bright they hurt her eyes. She wondered vaguely if they remained on all night, then decided that Quentin had probably turned them on when he had followed her into the barn minutes—or maybe hours—before.

Her feet felt like ice. She felt like ice.

"Diana, what are you doing down here? It's five o'clock in the morning."

She blinked up at him, for a moment totally baffled, her mind a blank. But then she remembered.

She remembered all of it.

"I was . . . following," she murmured.

"Following what?"

"Not what. Who."

Quentin's frown deepened, but before he said anything else, he took off his zip-up sweatshirt jacket. "Here, put this on. Your skin's like ice."

Diana looked down at herself, abruptly aware of her very skimpy attire. The silky camisole was clinging to her chilled flesh like a second skin, leaving nothing to the imagination. Feeling heat rise in her cheeks, she hastily shrugged into the jacket, wrapping herself in the warmth and scent of his body.

"Christ, your feet are nearly blue," Quentin said. "The stable manager used to keep extra boots and sometimes shoes in the tack room, but it'll be locked. I need to get you back to the cottage."

Realizing more by intuition than any movement of his that he meant to pick her up and carry her, Diana took a step toward the tack room and said, "The door isn't locked. And we...we can't leave yet."

"Why not?"

Without answering, Diana went to the door, only dimly aware that her feet really were numb; she could barely feel the rough pavers beneath them. She turned the door handle and stepped up into the wooden-floored tack room.

It was Quentin who flipped on the light switch as he entered close behind her, saying, "Good, they still keep the extra stuff here." He went to the other side of the large space, where a low shelf held riding boots and several pairs of shoes.

Diana stood looking around her. Secret place? Was there a secret place here? All she saw was a tack room, a roughly eighteen-by-twenty-foot space crowded with saddles on stands, and bridles and halters and lead ropes on pegs, and numerous utility trays on shelves holding brushes and combs and hoof picks and other grooming equipment and supplies.

"Sit down, Diana." He took her arm and led her to one of the two long benches placed back-to-back down the center of the space. Diana sat on the nearest end of the bench, but reached for the shoes he held in one hand before he could sit down beside her.

"I'll do that. You take a look around in here."

He frowned down at her. "What am I looking for?"

Diana hesitated only an instant before replying, "A secret." She bent over to pull on the fairly new-looking but definitely too-large running shoes he had found for her.

"Everything's pretty much out in the open here," Quentin noted, looking around. "Except for the first-aid cabinet over there, I don't see any closed storage at all. What kind of secret could be hidden here?"

Diana didn't hear in his voice any sign of humoring her, and she saw only intent interest in his face when she straightened and looked up at him, but she was still wary of saying any more than she had to, at least for now.

Not because she feared he'd think she was crazy, but because she was afraid she'd convince herself of that fact if she started talking.

"Diana?"

"What're **you** doing down here, anyway?" she asked abruptly.

Quentin replied matter-of-factly, "I looked out my window last night and realized I could see your cottage. And something told me to watch. That little voice I hear sometimes. So I did. Saw you come out and head toward the stables a little while ago. It seemed like a good idea to follow you." He paused, then added, "It wasn't a blackout, was it? Your eyes were closed. You were walking in your sleep."

"Something like that."

"Something **like** that? Diana—"

"Could you just please look around in here?"

Quentin didn't move. "Does this have something to do with the murders? The disappearances?"

She drew a breath. "You tell me. A... guide... brought me down here. A little girl, maybe twelve years old. Said her name was Becca."

Barely hesitating, Quentin said, "Rebecca Morse disappeared from The Lodge nine years ago. No trace of her has ever been found."

"Then I guess this does have something to do with the—the murders. Because she led me here. In the gray time."

"And told you what?"

"That this place held a secret." Diana looked around the neat, silent tack room. "Becca told me that there were secrets everywhere. She told me to tell you to look for the one hidden in here."

"Me? By name?"

"No. She said 'him.' But she was talking about you." Diana shivered and drew the jacket even tighter around her. She should have felt lost in all the material, except that it was warm and smelled very pleasantly of him, and that gave her an odd and very unfamiliar feeling of security. She wished she could luxuriate in it. "There's something hidden here, Quentin, and we need to find it."

Still without moving, he said, "In that case, we need to call Nate and then talk to the manager of The Lodge. Before we do anything else. This is private property, Diana, and we're in here after hours and without permission."

"You sure as hell are," a grim voice agreed from the doorway.

9

Cullen Ruppe was a dark man in his fifties, powerfully built through the shoulders and arms, and with a longtime rider's slim hips and strong legs. He was also, Nate had informed Quentin under his breath, apt to view himself as a badass, possibly why he was apparently hell-bent on giving everybody a hard time.

Nobody was searching his tack room, not without permission from Management or, failing that, a warrant.

"I can't get a warrant," Nate told Quentin in a low voice as he joined the other man near the entrance end of the long barn, leaving Ruppe scowling just outside the tack room door. "Not on the word of a maybe-psychic who could have been walking in her sleep for all we know."

Quentin kept his voice low as well when he said, "I believe her, Nate. I believe we need to search that tack room."

"Yeah, I know you believe her. The question is, what do I tell Steph—Ms. Boyd—to convince **her**?"

"You said she was agreeable when you talked to her last night."

"Yeah, but she wasn't happy about the situation. Now I'm supposed to get her up at dawn to okay this? Look, what do you really expect to find in there?"

"I don't know. Something. Something to help us figure out who murdered Missy and Jeremy Grant—and who knows how many of the others."

"You're expecting a lot of a lousy tack room, Quentin. People in and out all day, every day. What could be hidden in there?"

"I don't know," Quentin repeated. "But I think we need to find out."

Nate pursed his lips and blew out a slightly impatient breath. He looked tired, which wasn't surprising; he might have gotten five or six hours' sleep before Quentin's call pulled him out of his own bed, but it was more likely he'd been working in his office until well after midnight.

"You're asking me to go out on a pretty god-damned long limb here," he said finally. "We both know a thorough search of that room is going to mean checking under floorboards and behind walls. If we don't find anything after all that, the owners of this place are going to raise hell."

"I know. I wouldn't ask it, Nate, if I wasn't convinced we'll find something worthwhile in there."

The cop studied him for a long, silent moment, then sighed again. "Ah, shit. Okay, I'll go roust Ms. Boyd, see if I can think of a reasonable explanation to give her. You got any suggestions?"

Quentin was more or less accustomed to coming up with reasonable explanations for psychic "hunches" or leads, since the SCU members often found themselves in that position, but this time he was stumped. Absolutely nothing he knew of in the information he had on the missing and dead kids connected them in any unusual way with these stables. Nothing.

No connection, no warrant.

"I wish I did, but . . . sorry."

"And I don't suppose Ms. Brisco is ready to go public with this psychic stuff?"

"I doubt it. She's only beginning to believe it herself."

"She believes enough to insist there's something hidden in that tack room. Because another ghost told her so?"

Diana had already returned to her cottage to get dressed—at Quentin's insistence—by the time Nate had arrived, so the cop hadn't yet spoken to her. About any of her...encounters, including the one the previous afternoon. Which was probably why he sounded frustrated.

Probably.

"The ghost of another one of the missing kids told her so, Nate. Rebecca Morse. That's one missing kid you should definitely remember; you worked on her case."

Nate was frowning now. "Yeah. Yeah, I worked on it. She went out to play in the gardens one morning, and nobody admitted to seeing her once she stepped off the back veranda. We never found a trace of her. My boss at the time decided her father had snatched her; there'd been an ugly divorce. But we couldn't trace him."

"Trust me, the father didn't snatch her. Or, at any rate, she never left The Lodge." Quentin glanced toward Ruppe, and added, "I'll wait here while you talk to Ms. Boyd, if you don't mind."

"You suspect Ruppe?"

"He was here twenty-five years ago. He's here

now. That's all I know." Quentin was also wary of the fact that Ruppe had turned up here when, if Quentin hadn't followed her, Diana would have been alone and vulnerable. Maybe the stable manager would have posed no threat to her even so, but Quentin wasn't prepared to accept that as a given.

There had to be a reason, after all, why his own abilities had sent him down here after her. Maybe he had just needed to wake her, to pull her from the gray time before she remained there too long. Or maybe the threat to Diana had been of the flesh-and-blood sort.

Quentin didn't know. Yet.

"Considering the precious little we've got," Nate said with another sigh, "I can't say as I blame you for what's probably grasping at straws."

"I know he was questioned after Missy was murdered. I read the file." He had memorized it.

"Then you know the cops at the time couldn't find a whiff of anything suspicious about Ruppe."

"I know. But like I said, he was here then. He's here now. If nothing else, maybe he knows something he doesn't know he knows."

Nate considered that and nodded. "Yeah, maybe. People do, often enough. But don't question him, Quentin, not yet. He woke at what he states is his usual time and came down from his apartment to find two guests poking around in his tack room, so he's got a right to be rattled and pissed. Let's not make things worse until we've got reason to, okay?"

Quentin nodded. "Understood."

"Are you okay? You look a little..."

Thinking he probably looked a lot, Quentin grimaced and said, "Headache. A real bitch of a headache." Plus his ears felt as if they were stuffed with cotton, like his sinuses, and his eyes burned and ached. He was definitely paying the price for his all-night vigil.

"You should take something for that," Nate said.

"Yeah. Yeah, I will." Quentin didn't bother to explain that painkillers couldn't touch this sort of thing. Nothing ever had, except time and rest.

Nate headed off toward The Lodge's main building, leaving Quentin and Ruppe eyeing one another across nearly half the distance of the barn's long hall. Quentin knew Ruppe undoubtedly had work to do; managing a stable comprising three separate barns and more than thirty horses was a full-time job even if others did most of the grunt work. The horses were already restless in anticipation of their morning feed, stamping their hooves and snorting softly; the maintenance crew would be showing up any moment to feed them and begin mucking out the stalls.

The clipboard hanging by the tack room listed three trail rides scheduled for today, as well as half a dozen classes for those beginning riders who wanted to do more than just hang on for dear life during future trail rides.

Ruppe clearly didn't have time to stand around all morning, much less engage in a pissing contest with the cops or Quentin. But it was just as obvious that he was jealous of his authority, and not about to give ground unless forced by Management to do so.

Quentin knew the type. He'd come up against them often enough in his years as a federal cop. He also knew that Nate was right in saying this wasn't the time to question the stable manager, badly as Quentin wanted to do that.

Nate would probably point out, however gently, that there was really no hurry, after all; Missy had been gone twenty-five years, and a few more hours or days or even weeks wasn't going to change that.

Probably.

But the restlessness Quentin had been conscious of last night had shifted abruptly into a deep, cold sense of foreboding this morning when Diana had opened her eyes so suddenly to make an eerily familiar statement.

"It's coming."

And it had required all his willpower to allow her to leave his sight. To walk away from him, back up the well-lit paths to her cottage in order to change. Because that was exactly what Missy had said to him twenty-five years before.

The last time he had seen her alive.

Ellie Weeks ate a piece of plain toast and sipped hot tea, longing for the black coffee that was her usual morning pick-me-up. But pregnancy and black coffee didn't appear to go together, at least where she was concerned; drinking the tea was infinitely preferable to puking her guts out. Besides which, The Lodge's head housekeeper, Mrs. Kincaid, had been watching her very closely the last few days, and Ellie couldn't afford to do anything even remotely suspicious.

Not again, at any rate.

Hitching her chair closer to Ellie's in the staff dining room, Alison Macon whispered, "Did you hear? About last night?"

Ellie looked at her fellow maid blankly for a moment, then nodded. "Yeah. They found some old bones in one of the gardens."

Alison was clearly disappointed that she couldn't be the bearer of dramatic news, but nevertheless managed to make her whisper theatrical.

"It was a kid. A little boy, I heard. They found his watch buried with him."

Wrapped up in her own worries and problems, Ellie said, "Bad luck for him."

"But, Ellie, they're saying he was **murdered**."

"They're also saying it was years ago," Ellie pointed out.

"But aren't you afraid?"

"Why should I be?"

Alison appeared at a loss, but only for a moment. "There could be a **murderer** here at The Lodge."

"Yeah, and he could be long gone. Probably is. Why stick around and let himself get caught?"

With a visible shiver, Alison said, "Well, I'm scared."

"Be careful, then. Stay inside The Lodge. If you have to go out alone, don't wander off the paths."

"You're really not afraid, are you?"

"I'm really not." Not about that, at any rate. Some faceless killer that was maybe still hanging around years after his crime couldn't hold a candle to the very real worries gnawing at Ellie.

A baby.

I can't raise a baby. Not all by myself. I can't have an abortion. What else is there?

"You're so brave," Alison said admiringly.

"If you say so." Ellie drained her cup, hoping it would settle her jumpy stomach, and pushed back her chair. "Fifteen minutes before we're supposed to start work. I'm going out to get some air first. I'll meet you in the supply room."

Alison nodded, but absently, her gaze already directed across the room to another maid who might not have heard about last night's discovery.

Ellie got up, making a show of looking at her watch for the benefit of Mrs. Kincaid. A show of pausing, considering, deciding she had time. Then she left the dining room, moving briskly, someone with a specific place to go.

The staff dining room was in the lower levels of the South Wing, along with the kitchens and other maintenance areas. Also in that wing were the very few small suites reserved for those comparatively few employees on the housekeeping staff who lived as well as worked in The Lodge.

Ellie occupied one of those, at least for now. But not once everybody knew about the baby. When that happened, she'd be out on her ass. Mrs. Kincaid was hard-nosed about that sort of thing. An unmarried maid turning up pregnant? No, she wouldn't have it. Not at The Lodge. So Ellie would be lucky to get a week's pay and half an hour to pack her stuff and get out. No job, no home. And no one who gave a shit what happened to her.

She didn't go to her suite. Instead, she stepped out one of the service entrances to stand on the small concrete porch. A metal pail half filled with cigarette-littered sand stood more or less behind the door, mute testimony to the usual reason employees lingered in the area.

But there was no one here now, and when Ellie glanced around warily, she didn't see a sign of anyone in the area. She reached into the skirt pocket of her uniform and pulled out her cell phone. And a slip of paper with a phone number printed in shaky handwriting.

It hadn't been easy to get, this number. Contact information on the guests—the **special** guests—was kept in a locked file drawer in the manager's desk. Everybody knew that. Well, everybody as curious as Ellie and who had reason to wonder about those secretive VIPs. Good reason.

Ever since that first pregnancy test had been positive, Ellie had spent way too much free time lurking outside the manager's office. It was one reason Mrs. Kincaid was watching her so closely now, because there was no good reason for her to have been in the administrative section of the hotel except in passing.

She had passed through a lot. Luckily, she'd gotten her chance before Mrs. Kincaid became too suspicious. And her luck had held when Ms. Boyd had left her office door closed but not locked.

The file drawer had been locked, but desperation and panic had apparently lent Ellie magic fingers, because the metal nail file she tried had actually unlocked the thing.

And without telltale damage. She hoped.

Ellie wasted another precious minute wondering if that miracle heralded a change in her luck, then drew a deep breath and carefully placed the call.

She got his voice mail, which she'd been counting on, and left the careful message she had rehearsed half the night.

"Hey, it's Ellie. From The Lodge? I'm sorry to call you like this—I know I promised not to get in touch. But something's happened and I really need to talk to you. I don't want to make trouble, honest. But this is something you should know. So if you could call me back? Please?"

She didn't bother to recite her cell number, since she knew his would record it automatically along with her message. Instead, she merely added, "It's important. Thanks." And ended the call.

There. The ball was in his court.

All she could do now was wait.

"I don't blame them for not believing me," Diana said as she and Quentin stood watching Nate McDaniel, Cullen Ruppe, and Stephanie Boyd form a clearly tense huddle in front of the tack room. Ruppe was arguing angrily against the invasion of his domain, Nate was arguing for a search he couldn't legally justify **or** present any rational reasoning behind, and the manager of The Lodge was clearly annoyed and frustrated by the entire situation.

With a sigh, Diana added, "In the sane light of day, I don't really believe it myself."

Quentin was hardly surprised by that. As dramatic as her ghostly encounters had been thus far, he knew very well that she was struggling to overcome a lifetime of conditioning. Such radical shifts in thinking were seldom quick or easy turns.

"There's a difference, though," he said to her. "This time, you remember what happened. Right?"

"If it happened. It all seems like a dream now.

And maybe it was. Maybe I was just walking in my sleep."

Instead of arguing with her, Quentin asked, "Did it feel like that? Like a dream? Or did it feel like you were someplace you'd visited before?"

She was silent.

"Diana?"

"Dreams feel that way sometimes, we both know that. Familiar even when they seem . . . different from most dreams."

"Were there shadows?"

That surprised Diana, and she looked up at him. "What?"

"Were there shadows?" His tone was steady, his gaze holding hers. "If there's any light at all in this world, there are also shadows. Even in the darkness, there are shadows, areas of deeper black. There's depth, dimension. It's one of the qualities we associate with our world. With its substance, its reality. Did you feel and see that last night? Were there shadows?"

Diana dug her hands deeper into the pockets of her light windbreaker, wondering if she would ever feel warm again. The sun was up now, the air warming. That should have made a difference, she thought. She wondered why it didn't.

And she wondered how he could possibly know about the lack of shadows in the gray time. Had she told him? She didn't remember that.

He was waiting patiently, and finally she heard herself answer him. "No. No shadows. No dimension. No darkness, no light. Just gray."

"Where you were alone with Rebecca."

"It could have been a dream."

"It was real, Diana. A real place, apart from this one. Even if you don't want to admit it, somewhere deep inside yourself you have to know that." Without waiting for her to respond, he added thoughtfully, "You've obviously been there many times before. I wonder why you've remembered this time?"

"Because the drugs aren't in my system anymore." She grimaced slightly, wishing she hadn't answered that.

But Quentin was nodding. "That makes sense."

"None of this makes sense."

"Of course it does, given one simple fact. That you possess a mediumistic ability."

"And that there's an existence beyond death. Don't forget that part." She wanted her tone to be mocking, but to her ears it only sounded strained.

"Oh, that's a given." Quentin sounded utterly calm. "I've seen way too much to believe anything else."

"I wish I believed it," she murmured.

Quentin wished she did too. It would, he thought, make all this at least a bit easier. He wasn't aware that he was rubbing the back of his neck until he felt Diana's gaze on him.

"Headache?" she asked.

He merely nodded, unwilling to explain that he was coping with the painful results of a night spent watching her cottage.

She frowned, then said, "Give me your right hand."

Quentin did, wishing all his senses weren't so muffled; he could barely feel the cool touch of her hands as she held his between them, palm up. Her thumb moved near the center of his palm, massaging slowly in a small circle.

"One of the doctors I saw over the years," she said, "was very good at this. He said it was a form of acupressure, his own personal variation. I used to wake up with headaches sometimes, until he taught me to do this."

Quentin was about to tell her that neither acupuncture nor acupressure had ever had the slightest effect on his headaches when suddenly the pounding in his head lessened, his eyes stopped burning, and he actually felt his ears pop as his hearing cleared.

He was abruptly so conscious of her touch it

was as if all his focus was there, held in her hands.

"It's supposed to open up blocked energy channels," she added, her tone a bit rueful. "New Agey stuff, I suppose, but—"

"Wow," he said.

"Better?"

"Much. In fact, the pain is gone."

"Good." For an instant, she seemed unsure, then let go of his hand and put both her own back into the pockets of her jacket. "I'm glad."

Even no longer touching her, his awareness of her remained so heightened that it was almost a tangible thing, as though she had channeled some of her own energy to heal his pain, leaving behind a faint impression of the energy's path between them. He felt it so strongly that he could almost see it.

Was she a healer as well? It wouldn't be un-precedented among psychics; Miranda's sister Bonnie was both a powerful medium and an amazing healer. And it made sense given the theories and experiences of the SCU. A brain hard-wired to tune in to the specific energy signature of death and whatever lay beyond might be reasonably expected to also possess an affinity for the energy signature of life—and possibly be able to channel that energy to heal.

"You're staring at me," Diana said.

Quentin debated silently, but decided in the end that telling Diana she might be a healer wasn't important at the moment, and could even compromise her dawning acceptance of her mediumistic abilities. So all he said was, "Next time I get a wall-banging headache, I'll know who to come to for the cure. Thanks."

"You're welcome."

He wondered what she was thinking, and in wondering half-consciously narrowed his focus even more, blocking out everything else around him to concentrate on her. It was surprisingly easy.

Even more strongly than the previous morning in the observation tower, he was aware of her scent, the sheen of her hair, and flecks of gold in her eyes. Aware of her breathing. Aware of—

"You're cold," he said.

Diana sent him a quick glance, hesitated, then said, "That's another thing about the gray time. It's cold."

"You're remembering more, aren't you?"

She nodded slowly. "It's—I'm different in the gray time. Comfortable, even confident. When I'm there, I understand. When I'm there, I have no doubts."

"You're the same person in both worlds, Diana. It's just that in this world you weren't allowed to explore and understand who you were meant to be. The medications prevented that."

"But they're gone now," she murmured.

Quentin wanted to continue the discussion, but it was cut off when Cullen Ruppe stalked angrily toward the opposite end of the barn hall and Nate and Stephanie Boyd turned and came to meet them.

The cop was triumphant but didn't let it show. Much.

The manager of The Lodge was merely resigned. "Well, he's not happy," she told them. "What do you want to bet he hits me up for a raise before the day is out?"

Diana shook her head. "I'm really sorry about all this."

"He'll get over it," Stephanie replied with a shrug and a sudden smile. "Anyway, I'd much rather there were no doubts in anybody's mind that The Lodge cooperated fully with the investigation into the discovery of that child's remains."

Uncomfortably, Diana said, "This might not be connected. I mean—I think it is. It's not something I can prove, though. And I'm not sure what we'll find. Or even if we'll find anything in there. It's just...I just believe..." She sent Quentin a frustrated glance. "Say something, dammit."

"Welcome to my world," he said.

Stephanie looked between the two of them curiously. "I gather from what Nate told me that this hunch of yours is of the psychic variety?"

Quentin lifted a brow at the cop, who responded by saying dryly, "Well, I couldn't think of anything else to tell her. It was the truth or no search of the tack room."

"I much prefer the truth," Quentin said. "Bizarre as it often sounds to those hearing it."

"I found it bizarre," Stephanie admitted. "But then, I found the discovery of a child's skeleton in one of our gardens bizarre. And in my experience, bizarre things are often connected in one way or another."

"In my experience as well," Quentin agreed.

"So let's see if there's a connection here. As manager of The Lodge, I'm hereby granting permission for Captain McDaniel to search the tack room—assisted by whomever he deems necessary and appropriate. I ask that you please not destroy property, but I do grant permission to open up the walls or remove floorboards, as long as it's done carefully."

"Which," Quentin said appreciatively, "is much more than we had any right to expect. Thank you, Ms. Boyd."

"Stephanie. And don't mention it. You'll find

a toolbox in there somewhere you may use. You also have my permission, Agent Hayes, to go through whatever records and other paperwork are stored in the basement of The Lodge."

Quentin was about to ask that she drop the formality when Diana spoke.

"And the attic?" she asked.

Stephanie appeared mildly surprised, but shrugged. "I doubt there's anything useful up there; as far as I can determine, it's a dump for old furniture, outdated decorations, and decades of lost-and-found items. But feel free. Search to your heart's content. All I ask is that absolutely nothing be removed from the tack room, the basement, or the attic without my express permission."

"Agreed," Quentin said.

"Fine. Then you guys have at it. I've got to go up to the main building for a while, but I'll be back. Always assuming, of course, that you don't find very quickly that there's nothing in the tack room to interest you."

Nate checked his watch, and said, "We've got a couple of hours before anyone's expected to need the use of the tack and equipment in that room, right?"

Stephanie nodded. "And Cullen has been asked to go on with his daily routine rather than hover in there watching you. I'd take advantage of the time, if I were you." She half lifted a hand in a casual salute and left them.

"I say we listen to the lady," Nate said. "Quentin, I'm assuming you'd prefer we conduct the search ourselves?"

"Yeah. Time enough to bring in more of your people when we find something."

"You're very confident we **will** find something," Diana murmured.

"I know we will." And, suddenly, it was true. Quentin knew without a doubt that they would find something in this old barn, something important. But this time it wasn't a whisper in his mind that told him. It was an echo of that chill foreboding he had felt earlier.

It's coming.

He didn't know what it was, not yet. All he knew was that it was what he had sensed here during a childhood summer twenty-five years ago. What Bishop had sensed here five years ago. And what Diana had in some way touched only hours ago.

Something old, and dark, and cold. Something evil.

It was near. And for the first time, he could feel it.

Nate McDaniel had argued for the search because Quentin had asked it of him. But he never
expected to find anything, not really.

Which made it all the more ironic that he was
the one who found it.

The preliminary search of the fairly large,
open room had been quick and simple. And
revealed, as expected, nothing. So then it was
time to begin tapping the plaster-over-lath walls
in search of a hollow spot, with Nate and
Quentin beginning at the same point and moving in opposite directions around the room.
They used the handles of a couple of screwdrivers to more effectively sound out the
walls.

"Think they could have a few more saddles in
here?" Nate demanded in exasperation, stretching to reach around and above one hanging on a
wall-mounted rack nearly as tall as he was.

"It **is** a tack room," Quentin reminded him
dryly.

"There are maybe a dozen horses in this barn,
and I've never seen one wear more than one
saddle at a time; there must be thirty saddles
in here."

Diana said, "It's easy to accumulate tack over
the years. Different-sized saddles for different
horses, changing styles, the preferences of different riders. Plus tack that gets worn or damaged

and never repaired. Every tack room I've ever seen looks a lot like this one."

Surprised, Quentin paused to say, "For some reason, I didn't expect you to be a rider."

"Oh, yeah." She didn't elaborate.

He frowned slightly as he looked at her. She was standing in the center of the room, her gaze almost idly wandering from saddle to saddle, from bridle to halter to utility tray. Anyone watching her might suppose she was slightly bored, paying little attention to the search going on around her, even daydreaming.

But Quentin recognized the expression. He'd seen many psychics wear it in moments of quiet, that inward-turned, almost meditative waiting. The half-conscious stilling of the usual five senses so that the other ones could be heard.

Since she'd had no training, he didn't know whether someone else could help her focus or would merely be a distraction. He flipped a mental coin.

"Diana?"

"Hmm?"

"What do you hear?"

"Water. Dripping."

"Where?"

"Underneath us."

Before Quentin could question her further,

Nate broke the quiet with a decidedly surprised exclamation.

"Holy **shit**."

Quentin turned to see that the cop had somehow managed to shift one of the heavy floor-standing racks nearly a foot to one side, presumably to better get at the wall behind it. But he wasn't staring at the wall. He was staring at the floor.

"What?" Quentin went to join him.

"Either I'm out of my mind, or else I'm looking at one side of a trap door."

"You're kidding."

"Take a look." Nate went down on one knee, tracing with one finger the clear break in the seemingly solid floorboards. "Here. The edge was hidden by the base of this saddle rack. And I'm betting that if we move the rack on the other side of this one, we'll find the hinges."

The two saddle racks were back in an awkward corner, each piled with several old saddles and musty-smelling saddle blankets, and that plus a number of cobwebs made it obvious that they were well out of the usual traffic pattern of the room. They might well have sat undisturbed for years.

Diana came over to join the men, watching silently as Quentin and Nate carefully pushed the two heavy saddle racks out of the way.

It was a trap door, the hinges that had been hidden by the second rack old, heavy iron. There was no handle, but when Quentin wedged one of the screwdrivers into the edge opposite the hinges, it lifted easily.

They all saw the rough round opening in the ground beneath the door, large enough for a big man to pass through. They all saw the heavy iron ladder bolted seemingly to the granite bedrock and disappearing into the darkness. And they all felt and smelled the wave of damp, chilly air that wafted up as soon as the door was opened.

"Water," Diana murmured. "Dripping."

10

I don't know what's going on," Mrs. Kincaid said to Stephanie, "but I'm telling you that girl is up to something, Ms. Boyd."

Stephanie took another sip of her strong black coffee, wishing she'd been granted another hour or so of sleep this morning. She hated mornings as a rule, and this one was turning out even worse than usual.

"What do you expect me to do, Mrs. Kincaid?" she asked, keeping her tone brisk but pleasant. "Ellie Weeks hasn't done anything wrong. So far, anyway. Certainly nothing to merit any kind of warning from me."

"I realize that, Ms. Boyd," the housekeeper

responded, her tone stiff. "And as head of the housekeeping staff, it is of course my responsibility to issue any such warnings. I simply thought it best to keep you informed."

Informed of what? Stephanie wanted to ask. But she didn't. Instead, she said, "I appreciate that, Mrs. Kincaid. And I trust you'll continue to do so."

"Naturally I will."

Stephanie nodded. "Great. And I wanted to inform you that the police have asked to review old paperwork and historical documents stored in the basement, as well as go through whatever's in the attic, so don't be alarmed to find any of them or Agent Hayes in the areas of the hotel normally out of bounds to guests."

The housekeeper frowned. "The attic?"

"Is there a problem?"

"I don't know what they expect to find in the attic."

"Neither do I, but since they're investigating the death of a child here at The Lodge, I certainly don't want to declare any area at all off-limits to their investigation."

"No, of course not." But the housekeeper's frown lingered. "I do hope you remind them, Ms. Boyd, that both the attic and basement are merely storage areas and, as such, are not cleaned or aired on a regular basis."

It was, Stephanie thought, rather amazing how some people became so protective of their domains. First Cullen Ruppe down at the stables, resisting a search of his tack room, and now Mrs. Kincaid worrying about her reputation due to dust in the basement and attic.

Trying not to sound patronizing rather than soothing, Stephanie said, "I'm sure they'll understand that, Mrs. Kincaid."

"I hope so, Ms. Boyd." The housekeeper rose to her feet and turned to the door, then paused and looked back at Stephanie behind her big desk. In a rare moment of loquaciousness, she said, "I've been here a long time, you know. Longer than anyone else on the staff. And my mother worked here before me, as housekeeper."

Surprised, Stephanie said, "I didn't know that."

Mrs. Kincaid nodded. "That Agent Hayes—he was here as a child, with his parents. Twenty-five years ago. I remember him."

Since the housekeeper rarely had any direct contact with guests, Stephanie was even more surprised. "After so many years?"

With another nod, Mrs. Kincaid said, "That was a bad summer, and not one I'm likely to ever forget. One of our maids then had a little girl who was murdered. The police never found out who killed her." She paused, then added, "He was a friend of hers. Agent Hayes. They said he was the last one to see poor little Missy alive. Other than the murderer, of course."

Stephanie didn't know what to say.

Returning to the subject that had brought her to the office, the housekeeper said, "I'll keep an eye on Ellie, Ms. Boyd. You don't have to worry about that."

"Fine." Stephanie wasn't about to remind Mrs. Kincaid that watching the girl was her own idea.

Apparently satisfied, the housekeeper left the office, closing the door softly behind her.

Stephanie sighed, then drained her coffee and got to her feet, deciding to return to the stables and see if the search of the tack room had turned up anything.

She had a feeling it had.

A very bad feeling.

Nate flatly refused to allow anyone to go down that ladder until the backup he called for arrived.

"There's no way in hell," he told Quentin, "that you're going down there without me. Which means neither of us is going down there until I get someone here to watch our backs."

Diana was reasonably sure that Quentin

wasn't happy about the delay, even though he agreed readily. She was very sure of her own emotions on the subject.

She did not want to go down there.

Not that either of the two cops had said or implied that she would, but she knew. She knew that she was meant to see whatever was down there, just as Quentin was. That she had to go down that ladder and into the darkness.

Shivering, she dug her hands deeper into the pockets of her jacket. Why was she still cold?

Nate checked his watch, then said, "Look, it'll take a good half hour or more to get some of my people out here and get set up. You two go get some breakfast. I'll wait here."

"You haven't eaten either," Quentin said.

"Yeah, well. Send somebody down with a gallon of coffee and an egg sandwich, and I'll be fine."

From the tack room door, Stephanie Boyd said, "I can take care of that." Her gaze was on the uncovered and open trap door, and she added incredulously, "You found something?"

Quentin took Diana's arm and guided her past the other woman as Stephanie stepped into the tack room. "We found something, all right. Nate, if you even **think** of going down that ladder without me—"

"I won't, I won't. Go eat breakfast."

"There's a ladder?" Stephanie was even more incredulous.

Diana couldn't help smiling wryly as she and Quentin moved out of the tack room and out of earshot. "Why do I think she's going to want to go down that ladder too?"

Quentin must have heard something in her voice, because his question was immediate. "Don't you?"

"Not really."

"Why not? Something you sense?"

Diana took a breath and let it out slowly, shifting just a bit as they walked to remove her arm from his light grasp. "It's a black hole in the ground, Quentin. Doesn't seem very inviting. My usual five senses are telling me that much."

He didn't bother to remind her that she was responsible for the fact that they even knew about that black hole. Instead, he said, "You don't have to tell me you'd have been far happier if we hadn't found anything at all in there."

That surprised her, and she shot him a quick look.

"So you could tell yourself once again that you were just imagining things," he explained.

Diana couldn't think of anything to say in defense of her defensiveness, so she changed the subject. "What can an old hole in the ground possibly have to do with murdered children?"

"I have no idea," he admitted.

"If you've been investigating this place for years, how did you miss it?"

"I haven't been investigating this place—unfortunately," Quentin said. "At least, not on site, and not farther back than the last twenty-five years. I have a feeling what we found is a hell of a lot older than that."

"The trap door? Or the hole itself?"

"Both, I'd say. That barn's been there a hundred years, or close to it; it was one of the original structures here. I know that much from the postcards they sell in the gift shop, the ones showing this place around 1902, just after it was first built."

"You think the hole must have been . . . excavated . . . before the barn was built?"

"Probably. It would have been hell to dig the thing from inside that tack room. You saw the ground; unless that was a natural opening, somebody had to bore or blast through solid granite at least partway down. It could have been an old well at one time; the size is about right. Maybe it went dry, or the water was bad and it couldn't be used anymore."

"What about the ladder?"

"I've never seen one in a well, even an old one. Looks to me like that hole's been used in some other way."

"Which means we'll find more than water at the bottom."

"More than possible."

Diana shook her head. "The hinges didn't squeak. Did you notice that?"

"Yeah. Old iron hinges with no rust and no squeaks. Which means that somebody's taken care of that trap door."

"It was hidden."

"But in such a way that the saddle racks could be moved aside with very little effort."

"Why?" Diana demanded, hearing the strain increasing in her voice.

"We can't even guess about that, not until we see what's down there."

"And none of you—as kids—found the trap?" She glanced at him in time to see a quick frown.

"Not that I remember," he said.

Diana was silent for a few moments as they continued up the path from the stables to the main building of The Lodge. It was still very early, but the usual dawn risers were up and stirring: gardeners and maintenance people, somebody splashing in the pool, someone practicing their serve on the tennis courts. A morning jogger passed them with an absent nod, his eyes already fixed on the looming mountains whose winding trails challenged hikers and joggers.

For most of the guests, it was just another

morning, punctuated as usual with habit and ritual.

Diana wondered what it felt like, that normalcy.

When they stepped up onto the veranda, they pretty much had their pick of tables for breakfast. Only two were occupied, one by a young couple and the other by the little girl Diana recognized from—was it only yesterday morning?

It felt like weeks since she had stood with Quentin in the observation tower and looked down on the little girl and her dog on the lawn below.

Now, the dog was lying across the little girl's lap, and she sent Diana a shy, fleeting smile before continuing to gently stroke her sleeping pet.

"She's up early," Diana murmured.

"Again," Quentin agreed. He indicated a table near the one they had occupied the day before, and as they sat down added, "So far, I've only seen her and one other kid, a little boy. A few teenagers coming and going. As I said, this place doesn't really cater to families."

A waitress approached them with a bright "Good morning" and the coffeepot, effectively ending the discussion for the time being. They accepted coffee and ordered breakfast, neither needing to see a menu.

Diana wrapped her hands around the hot cup,

again conscious of a chill she found difficult to understand. The sun was warm on the veranda, on their table. The air was warm and smelled fragrantly of flowers mixed with the sharper scent of bacon cooking.

It had been more than two hours since she'd come out of the gray time. So why was she still cold?

"Diana?"

She met his gaze reluctantly.

"What's bothering you?"

She heard a little laugh escape her.

Quentin smiled. "Okay, dumb question."

Before he could ask a more reasonable variation of it, Diana changed the subject. "You said that you didn't remember if any of you found the trap door that summer."

"That's right."

"I guess...I assumed your memories of the summer would be vivid. That you would have remembered everything because of how traumatic Missy's murder was."

Quentin looked down at his coffee, that slight frown returning. "An understandable assumption. And I don't know why it isn't so. Some things stand out, of course, as clear as snapshots in my mind. Other things..." He shook his head. "There are gaps I can't really explain. A fuzziness to some of my memories."

"Maybe because of the shock of finding Missy," Diana suggested.

"Maybe."

"You were awfully young, Quentin. And it has been twenty-five years."

"Yeah. Still. I should remember more, and what I do remember should be clearer." He shrugged. "Maybe if I could be hypnotized, I could get at the memories. But since that isn't possible..."

"You can't be hypnotized?"

"No. And neither can you." He sipped his coffee, adding, "Psychics are always in that percentage of people who can't be hypnotized. No one knows why."

With some feeling, Diana said, "Just once, I'd love to be able to say you were wrong about something like that. About me."

"Sorry."

"No, you're not."

"Okay, I'm not. Diana, I know all this is hard for you. I get that, I really do. But you have to admit that continuing to deny the paranormal when you're experiencing it on a regular basis is just a little bit stubborn."

"You think so?"

"Just a little bit."

"Well, pardon me for needing more than twenty-four hours to get used to the idea."

Quentin chuckled. "Point taken. I can be impatient sometimes."

"No, really?"

"Sorry. I'll try to do better. And try to remember this is all very new to you."

"I suppose it was something easy for you to accept?"

He hesitated, then grimaced. "It was fairly easy for me to accept the existence of my abilities. But it didn't make my life any easier when it first dawned on me that I was different. Especially since my father, being an engineer, didn't have a whole lot of tolerance for anything that couldn't be scientifically weighed, measured, and analyzed. Still doesn't, really."

"How does he feel about the work you're doing now?"

"He wasn't very happy that I chose to use my law degree in police work, but we're still on speaking terms. Which is something, I suppose."

"And your mother?"

"My mother thinks I walk on water." He grinned. "Being her only offspring, I can do no wrong. But... I think it used to spook her when I'd tell her the phone was about to ring, or that my father would be getting an unexpected bonus, stuff like that. We don't really talk about it now."

"That must be lonely."

He thought about it. "In some ways, I guess. Or at least it used to be. But finding a home with the SCU, where the paranormal is the rule rather than the exception, changed everything. For most of the team, it's the only time in our lives we haven't felt isolated and alone."

Diana could well believe that. "Do your parents know you're with the Special Crimes Unit?"

"Yeah. But they don't know what's really special about the unit."

"So . . . they've never really come to terms with what's a very large part of your life."

"No. And your father may not either, if that's what you're thinking."

Diana wanted to again express her irritation that he was so adept at picking up on her insecurities, but it seemed a wasted effort. She contented herself with a sigh he'd have no trouble interpreting and looked away from him, allowing her gaze to wander around the veranda.

To her surprise, several of the tables were now occupied.

Or . . . were they?

The woman in Victorian dress she had seen the day before sat alone at one table, again raising her teacup slightly as her eyes met Diana's. Nearby, a man sat at another table, his rough work clothing and heavily bearded face making him obviously different from the usual hotel guests or staff; he, also, was staring at Diana, and nodded somewhat brusquely when she looked at him.

Diana tore her gaze away from him only to see two small children sitting at another table. Both little boys, both wearing clothing of a style she vaguely recognized as belonging to another time. Both solemnly returned her stare.

Dimly aware that Quentin was speaking with their waitress, Diana looked at the table nearest theirs, watching as a tall woman dressed in a very old-fashioned nurse's uniform rose to her feet and took a step toward her.

"Help us," she said.

"Help us," the little boys echoed.

"It's time," the working man grunted.

"Diana?"

She started and looked at Quentin. "What?"

He was frowning, and indicated the table between them, now holding their breakfast.

"Oh. Right." She sneaked a glance at the nearby tables that had been occupied by other-worldly people, finding them now empty. "Right." Part of her wanted to tell Quentin what she had seen, but another part of her was already doubting, questioning.

Had she really seen them? Had they really

been ghosts? And if she had, if they were, then what did they want of her? How was she supposed to help them? What did they expect her to do?

"Diana, are you okay?"

She took a sip of her coffee, trying to think. To decide. "Just . . . cold. I'm just cold, that's all."

"Maybe a hot meal will help."

"Yeah. Yeah, maybe." She'd have to tell him, she knew that. Sooner or later. And maybe he could explain it all rationally, maybe he would offer a logical reason why, after two weeks of relative peace here at The Lodge, she had suddenly begun encountering ghosts.

Nate was wary enough of rousing media attention that he called in only two of his detectives for backup, explaining to Stephanie that they were the two who were already scheduled, in any case, to help him in interviewing staff members later. So Zeke Pruitt and Kerri Shehan arrived quietly in an unmarked police car and made their way without fanfare down to the stables, as ordered.

Both, however, registered considerable surprise when they saw the trap door and what lay beneath it.

"That's a hell of a thing," Pruitt noted, almost admiring, presumably of the effort undoubtedly involved in its construction.

Shehan, more to the point, said to Nate, "Are we thinking this may help explain some of the mysteries on Agent Hayes's list?"

"You've been looking into that?" Nate asked, not really surprised. Kerri Shehan was the sharpest detective he had, and he'd more than once been conscious of the guilty knowledge that her abilities were going to waste in his small, usually peaceful town.

Now he was very glad he hadn't encouraged her to move on to bigger and better things elsewhere. He had a feeling he was going to need all the brainpower he could get.

Zeke Pruitt, approaching middle age and perfectly happy with the usual mundane work the few Leisure detectives dealt with, groaned before his partner could answer their captain's question. "She was up at the crack and at her desk, poring over stuff in the historical database and linking to newspaper morgues all over the state. Stuff about The Lodge and its history, even local legends. Wouldn't even let me finish my coffee before she was reading to me out loud."

He eyed the trap door, adding, "Have to admit, though, this does make all the old stories about people going missing around here a bit more interesting."

"We don't know yet whether there's any connection," Nate told them.

"How was it even found?" Shehan asked, studying the way the saddle racks had obviously been pulled aside.

"Luck," Nate replied firmly as Quentin and Diana came into the tack room.

Neither one of them disputed the statement. Neither did Stephanie, who came in behind them just in time to hear it.

To Nate, she said, "Okay, Cullen's been informed that this tack room is off-limits until he's told otherwise. He's not happy, but he's got his orders. Any of the horses needed from this barn will be taken to one of the others to be groomed and saddled." She frowned toward the trap door. "Always assuming that thing isn't just an abandoned well or something equally innocuous."

"Let's see. No need to move all this junk—I mean tack—out of the way if we don't have to." Nate got one of the powerful police flashlights his detectives had brought, and went to shine the light down through the trap door.

Since there was so little room there, nobody came along to peer over his shoulder, but it was safe to say everyone in the room was holding their breath to hear the verdict.

He didn't make them wait, straightening after only a moment to say, "It's not a well. Zeke, help me clear a little more space around here, okay?"

"What did you see?" Quentin asked as the burly detective began helping Nate move the heavy floor-standing saddle racks back away from the trap door.

"The shaft goes straight down about fifteen or twenty feet, then it looks like it turns almost horizontal. West, toward the mountains."

"A tunnel?" Stephanie asked in disbelief.

"Maybe. But something just occurred to me. There was a lot of mining in these mountains in the years before The Lodge was built, at least according to one of my high school history teachers. I wouldn't expect to find much of anything underneath us here in the valley, but we're close enough that this could, originally, have been an air shaft."

"And nobody noticed it when they built this barn?"

"You're assuming the trap door was cut in later," Nate said. "And maybe it was. Or maybe it was here all along. Are there any original blueprints for this barn?"

She grimaced. "God knows. Did they even **do** blueprints for barns? I mean—weren't they just . . . raised?"

Nate lifted an eyebrow at her. "A barn like this one? I'm betting there were blueprints."

With a sigh, Stephanie said, "Well then, maybe Agent Hayes can find them in the basement."

He said, "I'll certainly look. And it's Quentin." He waited for her nod, then said to Nate, "I don't know enough about mining—modern or historic—to disagree with you; my father is the engineer in the family. But don't air shafts usually angle upward to the surface from major tunnels?"

"Yeah, if it's a planned shaft. But miners also made use of natural shafts and crevices, old wells—whatever was handy. At least according to that teacher I mentioned. It was a hobby of his, exploring old mines and caves, and he went on and on about it, boring most of us senseless."

Stephanie said, "Some of it sunk in, obviously."

"Yeah. Who knew it might come in handy one day?" Nate eyed the cleared space around the trap door, and added, "Zeke, you and Kerri stay topside for now; make sure nobody else comes in here. Quentin, if you're ready, grab a flashlight."

"I'm coming too," Diana heard herself say. She kept her hands jammed in the pockets of her jacket, still so chilled that it required an effort not to shiver visibly.

Nate said, "Shit," but with more resignation than anything else. He looked at Quentin, brows raised.

Quentin was looking at Diana, but even though she refused to meet his eyes, he nodded to the cop. "I think she needs to go down there. Even more, I think we need her to."

Stephanie said to Diana, "You're a better man than I am, Gunga Din. I'm curious as hell, but you couldn't get me down there at the point of a gun." She sat down on the long bench with an air of making herself comfortable. "I'll wait here until you guys get back. And I'm sure I don't have to remind any of you that you go down there at your own risk."

"Noted," Quentin said, accepting another flashlight from Pruitt and preparing to follow Nate down the ladder. He paused only long enough to direct a steady question to Diana. "Are you sure about this?"

"Yes." She was sure, but that didn't make her any less frightened. And it didn't do a thing to warm her as she put her cold hands on that cold iron ladder and followed the two men down into the cold ground.

———

With Angelo at her heels, Madison walked down through the gardens in the general direction of the stables, but turned off that path and made her way to the English Garden.

"They wouldn't let us in the first barn anyway," she told her little dog. "Becca says it'll be closed to guests all day. Maybe even longer. So you won't have to pretend you're not afraid of the horses."

Angelo looked up at her intently as they walked, his ears alert and tail waving. But he looked less happy just a minute or two later, when Madison chose the path that would lead to the little gazebo in the distance.

He whined uneasily.

"Angelo, you're beginning to get on my nerves," she told him. "Becca said to meet her in the gazebo, so that's where we're going. I told you that."

The little dog hesitated, actually pausing for a moment as his mistress continued on, then hurried to catch up with her, ears and tail lowered now.

"I like Becca," she informed him, compelled to defend her preferences. "She's fun. And she knows all about this place. Besides, you know as well as I do that we could get into real trouble if we didn't have Becca to warn us about the bad stuff."

Angelo stuck close, silent but still obviously anxious.

Madison turned her attention ahead of them, and quickened her step when she saw Becca waiting for them in the center of the white-painted gazebo.

"Hey," she called.

Becca waited until Madison and Angelo joined her before responding. "Hey yourself. Did you have breakfast?"

"Sure. Pancakes. They were good."

Becca nodded slowly. She seemed to hesitate, then said, "They've found the door."

"You said they would."

"Yeah. The thing is... I maybe took Diana down there too soon."

11

When they reached the bottom of the vertical shaft, they discovered that there was indeed a rough tunnel, angling slightly downward for several yards before leveling off and running more or less straight and level toward the west. There was just barely enough headroom for Quentin, the tallest of the three, to stand upright, but the tunnel was narrow, and they had to go single file. Their flashlights lit the space quite well, but threw odd flickers and shadows as they picked up the irregular surfaces of the passageway.

The stone floor underfoot was slippery in some places and virtually dry in others, so that they had to be careful walking. The air was damp and just chilly enough to be uncomfortable. It also held a disquieting scent of old earth and stale water, and the mustiness of a place too long closed up and left dark.

"But the air is reasonably fresh, especially for this far down," Quentin commented, keeping his voice low since the hard surfaces of the passageway, they had quickly discovered, threw sounds back at them.

"Which means that, somewhere, there's another opening to the surface," Nate said.

"Bound to be," Quentin agreed. His fingers tightened around Diana's. He had taken her hand as soon as she'd reached the bottom of the ladder, and though he hadn't said anything, he was worried about how cold it was.

He was worried about her.

"I'm fine," she murmured just then.

She was a half step behind him, but he was able to see her face when he looked quickly back over his shoulder. In the backwash of illumination from the flashlights, her face seemed almost ghostly pale.

And he sensed more than saw that inward-turned attention, the quiet waiting for whatever would come. Consciously or not, she was tuning in to her abilities. Probably, he thought, how she had picked up on his concern for her.

Probably.

"Are you sure?" he asked.

"I'm fine," she repeated, then added, "Listen."

It took another moment, but then he heard it, the dripping and faint gurgle and splash of water ahead.

"I think it widens—" Nate began, then broke off as the passageway did indeed widen very abruptly. In fact, it opened into a cavern of some kind.

There was immediately a feeling of vast space all around them, and when Nate swept his flashlight in an arc, they were able to see that they stood at the mouth of a cavern that had to be sixty or eighty feet across and a good twenty feet high. They could see the narrow mouths of what appeared to be at least three other passageways leading off from this central chamber.

They could also see the water they'd only heard before, a stream running fairly rapidly in a narrow channel that appeared off to their right, wound among and around several rock formations in the cavern, then vanished somewhere on the other side.

The cavern had the look of something utterly natural rather than man-made, perhaps formed eons ago when the narrow stream had been a powerful underground river.

Nate was the first to speak, asking Quentin,

"How far do you think we've come from the barn?"

"Fifty yards, more or less."

"Just into the mountains. Jesus, I knew Kentucky had Mammoth Cave National Park, with a shitload of natural caverns and underground passageways, but I had no idea we could have something like this in Leisure."

"You really did pay attention to that teacher," Quentin said absently, shining his own light in a slower probe around the vast cavern.

"I guess I did. But, Quentin, if this is natural rather than a mine, why keep it quiet? Tourists pay to visit places like this one."

"Maybe not if the only access is made up of vertical shafts like the one we came down. It's one thing to invite tourists to walk into a nice big cave, but quite another to ask them to use twenty feet of ladder and walk half the length of a football field in a very narrow tunnel to **get** to that nice big cave. None of us is claustrophobic; I'm betting the passageway we just walked would give most people fits of panic."

"It's a point," Nate admitted. "Still, you'd think at least the locals would know about this, and I'll swear I never heard a word about it."

"They didn't want you to hear," Diana murmured.

Both the men looked at her, with Quentin

aiming his flashlight carefully to illuminate her face at least somewhat without blinding her. In the eerie, indirect wash of light, her face was shadowed, the planes and angles of it distinct and yet curiously unfamiliar.

For just an instant, Quentin thought he was looking at someone else.

"Diana?"

"They had to keep it quiet," she said, her voice low, almost dreamy, and distinctly different from her normal tones. "They'd already built The Lodge, put so much money and time into it. They couldn't let it all be for nothing. When the first murders happened, when they realized what lived here, what fed here, they had to... protect their investment. And in those days, men took the law into their own hands."

"What did they do?" Quentin asked quietly.

"They hunted him down. And when they caught him, they put him here. Shut him underground. Left him to die here. Alone."

"Him?" Nate's voice was so wary it was just a bit unsteady. "Diana, who're you talking about?"

Her head tilted slightly, as though she were listening to a soft, distant voice. "He was evil. He walked like a man and talked like a man, but he was something else. Something that fed on terror. Something without a soul."

Quentin tightened his grip on her hand, fear-ing that if he let go of her, he'd somehow lose her for good, because he had the apprehensive sense that some part of her was already elsewhere, tied to the here and now only by the flesh-to-flesh connection of their linked hands.

He wanted to stop this, to pull Diana back from wherever that absent part of her was, but every instinct told him not to. Not yet. This, whatever it was, was important. This was something she had to tell them. Something he had to listen to.

"It's coming."

He hadn't listened to Missy.

He intended to listen to Diana.

"They thought he was an animal, so they trapped him like one," she murmured. "They had no idea . . . what he was really capable of. No idea how rage could give him the strength to keep going. They had no idea death wouldn't stop him. They destroyed the flesh, but that only set the evil free."

Quentin kept his voice low when he asked, "Who are they, Diana?"

She looked at him, seemed to see him for the first time, even though her eyes held a peculiar flat shine. "They created The Lodge. Just a handful of men, wealthy men. They didn't intend it to be a place of secrets, but that's what it became. After that night, after they buried a killer alive and swore they'd never tell.

"But people around here...some of them knew. There were stories. There always are. A whisper here, a question there. Then years passed, decades, and it was just legends. Superstitions. And most everybody forgot what had roamed these mountains—and been buried alive inside them."

Abruptly, she stepped out into the cavern, moving with the certainty of someone who knew where they were going.

"What the hell?" Nate muttered.

"Let's find out," Quentin told him, holding on to Diana's hand and shining his flashlight to illuminate her way.

Still muttering, Nate said, "I don't mind telling you the hair on the back of my neck is standing straight up." He had his free hand on his weapon.

Quentin knew how he felt. There was something almost unbearably creepy about being in this dark, dank underground place and listening to Diana's soft, serene voice speaking of a horrible past event that had the power to send chills up the spine. It wasn't so much what she said as how she said it, her voice almost sweet, almost...childlike.

Quentin felt a stronger chill when he realized that, when he suddenly understood that it wasn't Diana they had been listening to.

When the voice coming out of her struck a chord of familiarity so deep inside him it was like a splinter of ice in his heart.

Before he could react to that, before he could even try to somehow break the trance she was in, she led them into one of the passageways on the other side of the cavern. But this passageway was short, only a few feet, opening into another, smaller cavern.

Even before their flashlights showed them what was there, Quentin could smell it. The old, old stench of decay, of blood spilled and flesh rotted and moldering bones.

Death.

"Jesus Christ," Nate breathed.

"This is where it brings some of them," Diana said in that sweet, childlike voice that was, now, sad and contemplative. "They die where he died."

Quentin dropped his flashlight in order to catch her as she abruptly collapsed, and when the light rolled across the stone floor and came to rest against a rock, the beam starkly illuminated a grinning human skull lying on its side at the base of a tangled mound of bones.

From their position not far from the gazebo, Madison watched worriedly as the tall blond man carried Diana from the barn and up the path toward The Lodge.

"Is she all right?"

Becca shook her head slowly. "I don't know. I thought she was ready, but... maybe not."

"Did—did it get her?"

"No. No, it needs her. Just like we need her. But it doesn't know what she is yet. We have to make her understand, so she can help us. Before it figures out what we're doing and tries to stop us. That's why Missy thought this was the best way."

"What was the best way?"

"To speak through Diana."

Madison frowned. "How could she do that?"

"Diana can see us, you know that. Open doors for us to come to this side. She can visit the gray time too. She can be the voice for one of us if we need to speak to someone on this side. But what makes her really special is that she can cross over all the way."

"You mean..."

"I mean she can walk with the dead."

"Even though she's alive?"

Becca nodded. "It's really, really dangerous for her. Especially now, when she doesn't understand what she can do. She could lose her way, get trapped in our world or in the gray time between."

"What would happen then?"

"She'd be one of us. She'd be dead too. Or as good as."

Madison shivered again, wishing she'd worn a jacket but knowing it wouldn't have mattered. "Then she shouldn't do that, Becca. She shouldn't cross over. Somebody should warn her not to even try that."

"Yeah. I expect you're right. The thing is... once she finds out about Missy, once she **understands** that part of it, she'll probably try anyway. And maybe she's supposed to."

"Maybe?"

"Well, I don't know for sure." Becca frowned. "Maybe that's what's needed. So she can fight it. Face it the way nobody else has ever been able to do. So it can be destroyed once and for all."

"That's where it is? On the other side? You didn't tell me it was dead, Becca."

"Part of it died. Part of it is still alive. And that's the part they can't see, the part we have to fight. We've waited a long time, until we were strong enough. And until we had the one thing we needed most. Somebody to help us fight it. Somebody strong enough to open the right door."

"Diana?"

"Diana. If she can. If he can help her."

"I've sent for a forensic anthropological team," Nate told Stephanie, sounding as tired as he felt. "God knows how long some of those bones have been down there, but we have to find out as much as we can about them."

She pushed his coffee cup across the desk to him and poured one for herself, surprised that her hands were steady. "And you have no idea how extensive the caves and tunnels might be?"

"Not a clue. When Diana collapsed, the priority was to get her out of there, so we didn't keep exploring. I did point my flashlight through a couple of other openings, and it looked like they led to longer passageways, but there's no way to know for sure without going back down there." He shook his head. "Frankly, I'd rather not."

"I don't blame you," Stephanie murmured.

With a sigh, he said, "I don't know that it's a place for cops anyway. When I called Quentin's cell a few minutes ago, he said there was an FBI unit that specialized in exploring and mapping underground passageways. Said he'd get in touch with them." Nate paused, adding wryly,

"I decided not to ask him why such a unit even existed."

Stephanie thought about that, then said, "It does seem odd, doesn't it?"

"Yeah."

"Umm. How's Diana?"

"Asleep, he said. Closer to unconscious, I gather. But apparently normal after an experience like that. **Normal**. Jesus."

"What happened to her down there?"

"Beats the hell out of me. All I can tell you is that I had the creepy feeling somebody else was using Diana to talk to us."

"Somebody else? Who?"

"I have no idea. But it sounded an awful lot like a kid."

Stephanie picked up her coffee cup and took a quick sip. "Okay, now you're creeping me out."

"I'm not surprised." He sighed. "Quentin was shaken by it, I can tell you that. And I'm pretty sure not much shakes that guy. I think he's seen things that would give you and me nightmares for years."

They drank their coffee in silence for several minutes, both thoughtful, and then Stephanie spoke slowly.

"Part of my job is to worry about the reputation of The Lodge. But in all honesty, I think whatever is down in those caves needs to see the light of day—no matter what happens afterward."

Nate was both relieved and somewhat impressed. "You could lose your job," he pointed out. "I mean, your bosses aren't apt to be at all happy to find cops and feds crawling all through those caves, especially once they start bringing up the bones we found down there. We don't have a hope in hell of keeping this quiet then."

Stephanie grimaced. "You know, I don't much care. After what I've learned about this place in the last few days, I'm beginning to think I'd rather work somewhere else anyway."

"Don't go too far," Nate heard himself say. And felt his ears get warm when she smiled at him.

"We'll see," she said, adding briskly, "In the meantime, you might as well take advantage of my authority here while I still have it. I'll okay, in writing, the forensics team and Quentin's FBI spelunker people to do whatever they deem necessary in those caves. I'll also put in writing my permission, speaking as manager of The Lodge, for a thorough search of all historical documents and records stored here."

"Thanks." He was trying not to wonder whether his not-so-veiled interest in her was returned. "I've already got some of my people back at the station looking into whatever public historical documents we can find on The Lodge and this general area. Plus they're pulling every scrap of paper we have on all the unsolved disappearances and questionable deaths here. Copies of everything will go to Quentin as well as to me."

"You really believe all this is connected? That there's some mysterious...something... at work here?"

"Christ, I don't know what to think. We know at least two murders were committed here. We've got what may be a network of passages and caves, one of which contains human skeletal remains. I don't know if Quentin was right to be obsessed all these years. I don't know if he's psychic, if Diana is."

He scowled. "For all I know, there's a bear or pack of wolves responsible for all those bones down in that cave, and the murderer of those two kids is long gone."

"Except you don't really believe that."

He met her steady gaze and sighed. "No. No, I don't really believe that. I've never been a fanciful man, but I can tell you that what I felt down there was something unnatural. Even the smell was both strange and oddly familiar, like something I've only been aware of in dreams. Nightmares. As if my conscious mind couldn't identify it, but some much deeper part of me could."

"Your instincts, maybe."

"Maybe. I had the feeling I knew what was down there, but didn't want to know—if that makes any sense."

"I don't know if any of this makes sense, but, yeah, I think I know what you mean." She sighed. "So far, everything we've found or think we've found suggests a killer of some kind operating in the past."

"Yeah."

"So is there any reason I should warn my guests? Any reason to believe there's a danger in the present?"

Nate hesitated. "Honestly, I don't know. My training and experience say no."

"But?"

"But...a lot of old crimes seem to be coming to light, and my experience also tells me that means something has changed. Maybe it's a simple matter of Quentin being here again, pushing for answers, just when Diana shows up with the ability to somehow uncover what's been hidden all these years. Maybe it's just...perfect timing."

"But?" Stephanie repeated.

Nate remembered the bone-deep cold he had

felt down in the caves, and shook his head. "It's nothing I can put my finger on. Certainly nothing concrete enough to make me offer a warning to your guests, or even to suggest that you warn them."

Stephanie worried her bottom lip with her teeth, frowning a little. "And I don't want to cause a panic—**or** an exodus. But I think I'll increase our security on the grounds. Can't hurt."

"No," Nate agreed. "It can't hurt."

Quentin stood in the doorway to Diana's bedroom and watched her a moment, reassuring himself that she was still sleeping deeply. He had removed only her shoes and covered her with a light afghan, and she lay on her bed just as he had left her more than two hours before.

He reminded himself that it wasn't unusual, after an extreme or prolonged use of any psychic ability, for the psychic to need sleep and lots of it, and common sense told him that channeling the spirit of a little girl murdered twenty-five years before certainly qualified.

Still, it was difficult for Quentin to make himself move away from the door. He didn't want to leave her, even to step into the next room. She was certainly getting a baptism by fire when it came to her abilities, and he wanted to make it easier for her; knowing he couldn't was frustrating and curiously painful.

Finally, he returned to the living room area of her cottage, where he had set up his laptop. The Lodge being a highly service-oriented place, it provided high-speed Internet access—and an obliging staff more than willing to fetch his computer from his own suite and deliver it to him here.

Nate had also been obliging enough to grant him the authority he needed to search various databases, and for the first time Quentin was going back much farther than twenty-five years.

"They created The Lodge."

What Diana had said down in the caves gave him a starting point he'd never had before, and Quentin intended to take advantage of the information. He needed to find all the information available on the men who built The Lodge, and the murderer they may have brought to their own version of implacable justice.

For Diana as much as for himself, he had to find the truth.

He had to understand.

"So there really was a killer?" Diana set her cup on the coffee table, frowning. After a hot shower,

a hot meal, and plenty of hot coffee, she was finally feeling herself again.

Or, rather, she was feeling stronger and oddly
focused, which wasn't like her usual self but was
certainly better.

Quentin gestured toward the legal pad he'd
filled with notes, and said, "From the info Nate's
people provided and what I was able to find in
newspaper morgues and other historical databases available, the disappearances began in this
area in the late 1880s. Maybe three or four a
year, on average. Considering how rough the
terrain was—and is—and the sheer difficulty of
travel in those days, it wasn't perceived as anything out of the ordinary. People got lost in these
mountains. Got hurt and died before anybody
could find them. It happened."

Diana nodded.

"The town of Leisure was barely in existence,
and didn't have a police force to speak of,"
Quentin continued. "They didn't think they
needed one; the people who settled around here
tended to be hardy and self-sufficient, and handled their problems without, usually, involving
anyone else. It's a mind-set that doesn't lend itself to calling the cops, but rather picking up the
family shotgun and . . ."

"Taking care of the problem themselves,"

Diana finished. "Which is what the men who built The Lodge did?"

Quentin nodded. "It's not entirely clear from what little I was able to find, but I gather that during construction a couple more people vanished—but this time bodies were found. Obviously murdered. The common belief was that robbery was the motive, especially since what we later called stranger killings and then serial killings were virtually unheard-of at the time. Then a child disappeared."

"And who would steal a child?" Diana said slowly.

"Exactly. There was enough fear and outrage that the men who were heavily invested in this land and in The Lodge decided to hire a Pinkerton detective to try to get to the bottom of things before their workers began walking off the job."

"I didn't know Pinkertons looked for killers."

"It was generally outside their area of expertise, but apparently the man assigned was what they called a good tracker. Now, the public record on all this is virtually nil, but I did find a couple of letters in the state historical databases written by people who were here when all this was going down. One of the construction workers, especially, wrote about the hunt for this killer in detail in a letter to his sister. It's pretty clear his conscience was troubled."

"Because there was no trial?" Diana guessed.

"No trial, no arrest, nothing official at all. The Pinkerton found enough evidence to trace the killer, he believed, to a shack up in the mountains." Quentin paused, frowning. "It's still there, I think, an old stone building; I saw it five years ago."

Diana didn't question him on that point. "So the Pinkerton found the killer there. And—"

"And he, along with a small group of trusted workers that included the project manager, went up there and grabbed the guy. Whose name, by the way, was Samuel Barton. They'd already decided that hanging him would draw too much attention, and the consensus was that shooting was too good for him."

"So they dropped him down that shaft?"

"Pretty much. The shaft had been discovered when excavation was going on for the stables, and the ladder put in place because somebody had the notion they might be able to use the caves for storage. But the tunnel was so long and narrow that transporting anything down there turned out to be too much trouble. It made a dandy prison cell, though."

Diana frowned. "Did they intend for him to die down there?"

"I don't know what they intended, but they must have known he would die. The men were so angry that in **catching** him they had pretty much beaten him to a pulp. Dropped him down the shaft and bolted that trap door shut. He must have known nobody within hearing distance was going to help him. Maybe he just followed the tunnel hoping there'd be another way out."

"But there wasn't one."

"Moot point. According to the man who wrote the letter, Barton only got as far as that big cavern we found. The man felt guilty enough that he went down there himself a week or so later, secretly, at night. Found the body in the cavern. And left it there."

Diana drew a breath and finished the likely story. "The Pinkerton and the project manager reassured the others that the . . . problem . . . had been taken care of. The killings stopped. And The Lodge was completed."

Quentin nodded. "That's pretty much it. Except that the killings didn't really stop, except for a while. At least that's what I think. Because people kept disappearing in these mountains. Not many, a few every year. Travelers, people passing through. Transient workers. People who wouldn't be missed, for the most part. The difference was, they didn't find any more bodies."

"Until Missy?"

He nodded again.

"Quentin...you're not saying it's been the same killer all these years. Are you?"

"You said it," he reminded her. "Down in the caves."

She remembered. Scary though it was, she remembered it all. But..."Whatever Missy knows, I only know what I said. I mean, I don't understand how it could be the same killer. How a dead man could still be killing more than a hundred years after his own death. And I don't understand why, if it is somehow true, his— its—behavior changed with Missy. Anything hunting and killing that long, successfully, wouldn't change. Would it?"

"Not likely." Quentin was too good a profiler not to have thought of that, and offered a possibility. "Unless something external forced the change."

"Something like what?"

"Diana, spiritual energy has its own plane of existence. It can only exist in our world temporarily, and only then if a doorway is provided, or if the energy itself is strong enough to force its way through."

"So you're saying the spirit of this killer was strong enough to cross over, strong enough to kill?" She was dimly surprised that she didn't sound more incredulous.

"My guess is that it killed by—for want of a better term—possessing a person. Most likely someone who was vulnerable to that kind of attack. Mentally or emotionally unstable, or physically weakened in some way. The killer took them over and . . . used their bodies for a while. Enjoyed their terror and confusion. Maybe even forced them to kill someone else."

"Quentin—"

"That would help explain the time between these disappearances and deaths. There would have to be an interlude of rest after expending so much of its strength, but the interludes wouldn't be consistent because the amount of energy necessary would depend on whether it was merely possessing someone or using them to physically kill."

"Merely?" was all she could manage.

"It's possible, Diana. It's possible that the spiritual energy left behind when Samuel Barton was virtually buried alive held enough rage, enough evil, to go on killing, and hiding his crimes, all these years. At least until he killed Missy. Until he killed someone capable of somehow preventing him from hiding her body the way he'd hidden or buried all the others."

12

H ow?" Diana asked. "How could a little girl have done that? What **could** she have done if he'd killed her?"

"I don't know. Yet. But I know that something changed when Missy died. I feel it."

Diana didn't know how to challenge his certainty. She didn't even know if she should. So all she said was, "We have a lot more questions than answers."

"Yeah, I noticed that."

"Correct me if I'm wrong, but we won't know anything new from Jeremy's remains, or the bones down in the cavern, for a while yet."

"Maybe quite a while. Forensics takes time, especially when it comes to skeletal remains."

She hesitated, then said, "I have the sense that something is going to happen here, and soon. Something bad. I—I haven't told you, but I've seen other ghosts. People who very obviously lived in another age. Two women, a man, two little boys. Not in the gray time, but here, looking flesh-and-blood real. Like Jeremy. Asking me to help them. And at least one said something about it being time. There was an intentness about them, an urgency I could feel."

Quentin didn't bother to ask why she hadn't told him until now. "I gather they didn't tell you how you could help them."

"No." Diana got to her feet. "But Becca told me there was something in the tack room, and she was right about that. She also told me there was something in the attic I needed to see. That it would help me understand."

Quentin smiled, wondering if she had any idea of how much stronger she was since waking up. He didn't know how, but it seemed that providing a voice for Missy down in those caves had somehow enabled Diana to turn a corner. She had stopped protesting the reality of her abilities; she wanted answers.

"I wondered why you asked Stephanie so pointedly about the attic," he said.

"Now you know. Shall we?"

Quentin took only a few moments to lock his laptop and notes away in his computer case, habit making him cautious. Then he walked with Diana back to the main building.

It wasn't until they were climbing the stairs toward the attic that he said, "I guess Rebecca wasn't very specific about whatever it is she thinks you need to see in the attic?"

"No. As you said, they never seem to be specific when it would be helpful."

"They?"

"The guides. Spirits, I guess."

"Nice to see you're coming to terms with their reality," Quentin said.

A little laugh escaped Diana. "Reality? I'm not sure I know what's real anymore. Actually, I'm not sure I ever did."

"You know. You just have to trust yourself."

"Forgive me, but that sounds a lot like the psychobabble I've been listening to for years."

"There's a major difference," Quentin said, taking her hand as they climbed. "I know damned well you aren't sick and you aren't crazy, and I'll never try to convince you that you are. You can trust me. And you **can** trust yourself, you know."

"Can I? How do you know that?"

"Diana, what you've been through just in the

past couple of days would have sent half the psychics I know into shock or into a coma." He nodded as she glanced up at him. "You're a hell of a lot stronger than you realize."

"I hope you're right," she murmured.

A few minutes later they reached the attic, and looking around the vast, cluttered space, Diana really did hope he was right. Because it was going to take plenty of strength and energy just to go through everything up there, never mind coping with anything unexpected they might find.

"Damn," she said with a sigh. "Why can't things ever be easy?"

"The universe frowns on that." Quentin sighed as well. "Want to flip a coin, or should we just start at opposite ends and work our way toward the middle?"

"You're the seer," she said, only slightly mocking. "Why don't you see where we should start?"

"It doesn't really work that way."

"Figures." Diana looked around, absently admiring the beauty of the stained-glass windows illuminated by the afternoon sunlight. There were shafts of colored light shining in, almost beaming in, she thought, so that a stack of old storage trunks in the fairly clear aisle down the north/south axis of the attic seemed to glow in a brilliant spotlight.

Spotlight.

"Or maybe," she murmured, "it can be easy, after all."

Quentin followed her gaze. "Well, well. Almost as good as a sign, huh?"

"You sound a bit doubtful."

"I mistrust signs, as a rule. They tend to point me in directions I probably should avoid."

Diana lifted her eyebrows and waited.

"This is your sign," he said. "Let's go."

As they worked their way toward the stacked trunks, Diana said somewhat ruefully, "I can't decide if I should blame you for all this or just be glad you're here to help me steer."

"I vote for the latter."

"I'll just bet you do."

"Like I said from the beginning, you and I are both here for a reason. We both need answers."

Reaching the trunks, Diana eyed them and said a bit tentatively, "Yeah, but what are the questions? You want to know who killed Missy, and I want to know if I'm nuts?"

"We've already established you aren't nuts."

"Then what answer do I need?"

"Maybe the one Rebecca told you was up here." Quentin reached for the side handle of the topmost trunk. "Hang on, and let's see if this is as heavy as it looks."

It wasn't, thankfully, and they were able to line

all three trunks up end-to-end along the aisle. None of the trunks was locked, and when all the lids were raised, Diana and Quentin found themselves contemplating semi-organized chaos.

"Lovely," Diana said with another sigh. "The one on this end looks like it has mostly old clothes inside." She pulled out a feather boa that more or less disintegrated in her fingers, and sneezed. "Mostly."

"Bless you. The one on this end and the one in the middle also have old clothes, but—" He knelt at the trunk on his end and pulled out a creased box filled with loose papers. "—we also have what look like letters, invoices, receipts. At least a couple of ledgers and journals. Jesus. It's going to take hours to go through all this."

"No kidding." Diana knelt at the middle trunk and pulled out a scrapbook that was barely holding together. She checked a couple of pages, and said, "You'll love this. Lots and lots of photos of The Lodge, some of them from when it was being built."

"Great. Set it aside to take downstairs, will you? We'll get Stephanie's permission to look over anything interesting somewhere more comfortable. The light up here is very color-ful, but not the best for studying this sort of thing."

"That's for sure." Diana set the scrapbook

aside, along with another one she found in the trunk. Then she pulled out an old box with LOST AND FOUND stamped on its lid. She opened the box, discovering bits of costume jewelry, several hair clips and combs, a beaded change purse, other small items, and a number of loose photographs.

She lifted up the photos to see what lay under them, and one slid out to the side. In the bright, colorful light spilling into the box, the old black-and-white image seemed to glow.

Diana reached for the picture, allowing the box to tumble back into the trunk. She saw her fingers tremble, and wasn't surprised.

"What is it?" Quentin asked. He shifted a bit closer, looking at the photo she held, and sucked in a surprised breath. "That's Missy."

She sat on what looked like the front steps of an unidentifiable house, dressed for summer in shorts, her long dark hair parted in the middle and caught up by ribbons beneath each ear. She was smiling, one hand stretched out to touch the big dog lolling beside her.

And on the other side...

Diana's finger lightly touched the image of the little girl on the other side of the dog. She too was dressed for summer, but her fairer hair was shorter and less restrained, her grin not so shy as Missy's.

"She looks familiar," Quentin said. Then he swore under his breath as he looked at Diana.

"My father carries this picture in his wallet," she said slowly. "But only half of it." She touched the image of the fair little girl again. "This half. The part with me in it."

"You might as well use this lounge," Stephanie told Quentin, adding, "It isn't used much even when the hotel is full, and with the early check-outs we've had since yesterday..." She looked across the beautifully furnished third-floor room at Diana, who was standing by one of the windows gazing out over the gardens, and added in a lower voice, "Is she all right?" All Stephanie knew about the photograph they had found was that it might indicate a familial relationship between Diana and one of the children killed here at The Lodge; she hadn't asked for details.

"I don't know," he replied honestly. "The last twenty-four hours have been...Christ, 'rough' isn't the word for it. Her entire life has changed." He shook his head. "I don't know what happens now."

Stephanie eyed him uncertainly. "Aren't you supposed to? I mean, isn't that your psychic thing, seeing the future?"

Quentin didn't bother to once again explain that he never **saw** anything. Instead, he merely said, "The irony hasn't gone unnoticed, believe me. With a couple of minor exceptions, my abilities have pretty much been absent since I got here. Maybe the explanation is that I've been so focused on the past, the future's been out of my reach. At least that's what my boss says, and he's usually right."

"I don't pretend to understand any of it," Stephanie said frankly. "Look, do you want me to have some coffee sent up? It looks like you guys are going to be here for a while."

"That'd be great, thanks."

"Okay. Good luck finding something helpful in that lot." She nodded toward the two boxes filled with stuff Quentin had transferred, with her permission, from the trunks in the attic.

The lounge could be closed off from the hallway outside by pocket doors, but Quentin didn't bother to draw those closed after Stephanie left. The Lodge really did feel practically deserted, and he doubted they'd be interrupted or disturbed by a guest wandering casually into the room.

He approached Diana warily, more than a little worried because she'd said next to nothing since they had found the photograph in the attic. The photograph she still held in one hand, though she had stopped staring at it to gaze out the window.

Before Quentin could speak, she said in a perfectly composed voice, "You were right, you know, about any magnetized cards I carry not working for long."

He knew she was going somewhere with this, so he followed without question. "Yeah, something about our electromagnetic field affects them."

"The keycards die faster than credit cards."

"Probably because they're rekeyed or remagnetized more than once in a process meant to be fairly temporary."

She nodded slowly. "So the magnetic information on credit cards is intended to be more permanent, and so is more resistant to interference."

"That's our theory."

"And cell phones? They only work for me a week or two and then just die. The cell phone companies can't explain it. I finally stopped trying to carry one."

"Same thing. Our electromagnetic field interferes with anything magnetic or electronic, especially those things that we tend to carry with us or on us most often."

"You carry a cell phone." It was clearly visible, worn on a belt clip.

"We've found a rubberized casing that seems to protect them, at least for a while. The batteries still tend to lose their charge faster than what's considered normal, but at least we have the use of the phones for a reasonable amount of time."

"Ah. I wondered." She paused. "May I borrow your cell phone, please?"

"Of course." He released the phone from its belt clip and handed it over, beginning to have an inkling what she meant to do. He didn't know if it was a good idea, but he also couldn't think of an argument she was likely to listen to right now.

Diana examined the casing protecting his phone for a moment with what seemed idle curiosity, then opened it and tapped in a number, murmuring, "Long distance, sorry. Really long distance, since I think he's at his London office. My taxpayer dollars at work."

Ignoring that, he said, "I can leave, if you'd rather be alone."

She looked at him for the first time. "No. I'd rather you stayed."

Quentin nodded, but he wasn't much reassured. The odd, flat shine that had been visible in her eyes when they were in the caves was back, and the very stillness of her face hinted at something frozen. Something that might shatter at the first wrong touch.

Diana returned her gaze to the window as she waited for the call to go through, then said into the phone, "Hi, Sherry, it's Diana. Is he busy? I need to talk to him. Thanks."

"He works this late?" Quentin asked, having rapidly calculated the time difference.

"He works all hours, seven days a week," Diana replied. "And pays his assistants double overtime to work six."

Quentin wondered if that had always been the case, or if Diana's father had taken refuge in his work when first his wife and then his daughter had tried and seemingly failed to cope with apparent mental problems. But before he could frame the question, Diana's father took her call.

Elliot Brisco, as it turned out, had one of those distinct, powerful voices that was clearly audible on cell phones, so much so that Quentin was easily able to hear both sides of the conversation.

Then again, maybe he was automatically calling on the spider sense to listen with unusual intentness.

"Diana? Where the hell are you?"

"Hi, Dad. How've you been?"

"I've been worried to death about you, Diana, and you damned well know it. That doctor of yours has refused to answer any of my questions, and—"

"I asked him not to tell you where I was, and I asked you to respect that. Besides which, the law agrees my medical information should be confidential. I'm thirty-three, Dad, not a child. And the judge decided I was capable of making my own decisions."

The one statement about a court decision told Quentin a lot. Clearly, Diana had fought for her independence, probably as soon as the medications were out of her system. And just as obviously, her father had not relinquished control over her life willingly.

"You've been ill most of your life," he said now, his voice taking on a hard edge. "Am I not supposed to worry when you suddenly go off all your medications and then disappear God only knows where?"

"I didn't disappear. I told you I was going to try another form of therapy."

"And I wasn't supposed to ask questions about that? Jesus, Diana, with all the crackpots and New Age nonsense out there, you could have been doing any kind of half-assed thing masquerading as therapy. They used to believe LSD was therapeutic, remember?"

"No drugs this time," she said. "I'm not smoking anything. I'm not drinking anything. It's an artistic workshop, Dad, that's all. I've been... painting my demons."

Elliot Brisco made a sound that, to Quentin, indicated either disbelief or withering impatience. "Painting? What the hell is that supposed to accomplish?"

"It accomplished quite a lot, actually. Certainly much more than I expected it to." Diana drew a breath and then let it out slowly, as if for control. "I'm at The Lodge, Dad. In Tennessee. Does that ring a bell?"

"The Lodge. You're at The Lodge." Abruptly, her father's voice was flat, and in that flatness Quentin heard or sensed something a lot like fear.

"Yeah." Diana tilted her head slightly to one side, as if she heard it too, then lifted the hand holding the old photograph so that she could see it. "And I found something here I wasn't looking for. An old picture of two little girls. They don't really favor... and yet they do. When you really look at them, you realize they could be... sisters."

"Diana—"

"It's the photo you carry in your wallet, Dad. Part of it, anyway. Tell me, is the other half torn away, or just folded back out of sight? Did you rip her out of your life, or just tuck her away where you didn't have to look at her?"

Silence.

Diana's voice was quiet but relentless. "Don't you think it's time you told me about Missy?"

Beau Rafferty dismissed his students for the day, and when they'd gone began to gather up charcoal pencils and colored chalks they had used and put them neatly away in boxes and cans. Then he moved from easel to easel, carefully closing the big sketchbooks to allow his students' work some privacy.

He glanced up with a brief frown as a low rumble of thunder sounded, then returned to his worktable to clean a few brushes and put away a much-used set of watercolors. He was still silently debating when he finished, but another distant rumble of thunder made up his mind for him. He searched briefly among the organized clutter on the worktable and found his phone.

The number was programmed into his speed-dial, so he only had to hit one button. And the call was answered before the second ring.

"Yeah."

"There's a storm coming," Beau said.

"Spring in the mountains. Typical weather."

"Uh-huh. I was just wondering if you knew. Ahead of time."

"I've spent time in Tennessee," Bishop said.

"That wasn't really an answer," Beau said judiciously.

"Wasn't it?"

Sighing, Beau said, "Well, I can't say I haven't been warned."

"About what?"

"About you, Yoda."

"According to Maggie, you're the Zen-like master, not me."

"Maybe, but there's something just a little bit spooky about how you do it, pal."

Instead of responding to that, Bishop merely said, "I've been meaning to ask if you're enjoying your first official SCU assignment."

"It has had its moments," Beau said, ruefully accepting the change of subject. "I think I've helped a few of the students, anyway. Do you consider that a plus?"

"It's what I expected." Amusement crept into Bishop's voice. "The whole point of someone like you joining the unit, Beau, is so that you can do what you're best at—painting, and helping others. Whatever you do for me on the side is just a bonus."

"Umm. So you weren't really counting on any of my psychic skills this trip, huh?"

Immediately, Bishop's voice changed. "Why? What have you seen?"

Beau walked around the worktable and headed for the back corner and the secluded spot where Diana's easel had always been. With her otherwise occupied today, he had set up his own "doodling" oil painting there, and had worked on it earlier before his students had arrived.

"Beau?"

"I thought it was me, at first," he said conversationally. "Because I was working on a painting here on Diana's easel. But then I remembered that her big sketchpad was still here, behind my canvas. And since that's where it's coming from, I don't think it's me."

"Beau, what are you talking about?"

The artist lifted his half-finished oil of The Lodge off the easel and set it aside, then opened the big sketchpad and began turning the pages. "The thing is, she tore that page off the sketchpad. I noticed later that it was missing. So it shouldn't be here at all."

"Her sketch of Missy?"

"Yeah. It's here again, Bishop. Or something that looks a lot like the original." Beau stood back, studying the open sketchpad and the drawing it revealed, all in charcoal—except for the vivid slash of scarlet marring the figure of the little girl and still dripping very slowly off the page and onto some rags Beau had earlier placed beneath the easel.

"And it's bleeding."

"Tell me about my sister, Dad," Diana said.

There was a long silence while she waited patiently, and then Elliot Brisco finally replied.

"I am not having this discussion with you over the phone. I'll be finished up here and head back to the States by Monday. Then we can talk. Go home, Diana."

Quentin felt as well as saw her slump a little, not in a release of tension but rather as though a new weight had settled onto her shoulders.

"Home to more lies? I don't think so. I'm staying here, Dad. I'll find the answers myself."

"You don't know what you're saying. What you're doing. Go home. Go home, and I promise we'll talk."

Diana drew another breath, and this one sounded ragged as the frozen stillness of her face began to shatter. "More than thirty years. You've had plenty of time to tell me the truth about Missy, about who she was. Makes me wonder what else you've been lying about, Dad."

"Diana—"

She snapped the phone closed, hanging up on

her father, and handed it back to Quentin without looking at him. But her words were directed to him when she murmured, "Somehow, I don't see this story having a happy ending, do you?"

He automatically returned the phone to its belt clip, and with his free hand grasped her arm, because he once again had that unsettling feeling that she could somehow drift away from him. "Diana, you don't **know** the story—neither of us does."

"He didn't deny Missy was my sister. If it wasn't true, he would have denied it."

"Maybe. But there could still be a reasonable explanation for all this."

She turned her head and met his intent gaze, her own not quite pleading. "Could there? What could that be, Quentin? Why would a father never mention the existence of another daughter? Why, in all these years, have I never found any pictures of her except for this?" She lifted the photo again. "Why don't I **remember** her?"

Quentin answered the last question, because it was the only one he could think of an answer for. "You don't remember a lot of things from your life, you told me that yourself. The drugs, Diana, the medications."

A frown flitted across her face as they both heard a distant growl of thunder, and he felt her tense, but her gaze remained locked with his.

"Yes, the drugs. Maybe that's something else my father has to answer for. Because if he could lie to me about Missy...then maybe he lied about other things. Maybe he lied about me being sick."

"It doesn't have to have been a deliberate lie." Quentin played devil's advocate because he had to, because he knew how dangerous it was for Diana to so suddenly lose all trust in her father. "With everything you've described about your childhood, he had every reason to believe you were going through something out of the ordinary. He just looked in the wrong place for answers, for treatments."

"Or he knew. He knew and did his best to keep me doped up and unaware."

"Why would he do that?"

"So I wouldn't remember Missy."

Another rumble of thunder, this one louder, made Quentin pull her away from the window and guide her to sit on one of the sofas near the boxes he had brought down from the attic. He sat down beside her, silently cursing the approaching storm because already he felt edgy and uneasy, and was all too aware that his senses were becoming untrustworthy. It was like someone turning the volume up and down on a stereo system randomly, so that one moment his senses were muffled and the next they were blasting "loudly" in his consciousness.

It was, to say the least, distracting, and he called on all the discipline he had learned and earned over the years to concentrate on her and what they were talking about.

"Diana, listen to me. As far as I've been able to determine, Missy and her mother came to live here at The Lodge when Missy was about three. You can't have been much older than that. When did you turn thirty-three?"

"Last September."

He nodded. "If Missy had lived, she'd be thirty-three this July. So, assuming you two **were** sisters, you were older by less than a year, and no more than four when—when she came to live here. How many of us remember much at all of our lives from those early years?"

"I should remember a sister." She stared down at the photo she held, frowning.

"It's not something we can be sure about, Diana. Not without more information."

Her gaze shifted to the nearby boxes. "Maybe we'll find something in there."

"Maybe. But don't get your hopes up. Most of Missy and her mother's belongings were destroyed in the North Wing fire years ago. It's sheer chance that this photo survived." Except that he didn't believe in anything as random as chance, didn't believe in coincidence. There was always a reason. Always.

Even as the scattered thoughts raced through his mind, Diana looked at Quentin, a sudden hope in her eyes. "Her mother. Quentin, what happened to her mother?"

He didn't want to deliver more disturbing news, but had no choice. "She left not long after the fire. I've never been able to trace her."

"And that was when? How many years ago?"

"The fire was less than a year after Missy was murdered. So, twenty-four years ago, give or take a few weeks."

"What did she look like?"

Quentin had to pause for only an instant. "A lot like Missy. Dark hair, big dark eyes, oval face. Average height. On the thin side, as I recall. Maybe even fragile."

"Are you sure?"

"I remember her, Diana, vividly." He watched the hope in her eyes turn to confusion, and added, "What is it?"

"That isn't my mother."

13

M y mother was a redhead, like me," Diana
said. "Tall, athletic. There was nothing
fragile looking about her; that's one of the
reasons I always wondered about her illness, because in all the pictures, she looked so healthy.
So strong."

After a moment, Quentin suggested, "Same
father, different mothers?"

"A half sister?" Diana thought about it, absently drawing her arm free of Quentin's grasp so
she could rub her temple. Her whole head was
throbbing, making it difficult for her to think.
"Maybe. As far as I know, he never married
again after my mother died. But there could

have been some sort of relationship along the way, I suppose."

Quentin hesitated, then said, "You told me you were very young when your mother died. How young?"

"I was four." She nodded before he could point out the obvious. "Yeah, I've already thought about that. If Missy was less than a year younger than me, it means she was born while my mother was still alive. She was in and out of hospitals even before I was born, but it got worse with every passing year. Which means my father was involved with another woman while my mother was probably ill in a hospital."

"Diana, we don't know that. We don't really **know** anything. Except that we've found a photograph of you and Missy together and that your father—caught completely off guard—didn't deny she was your sister when you asked him about it. That's all we know."

"You sound like a lawyer," she murmured.

"I am a lawyer, technically. And I'm a cop. Look, all I'm saying is that we can't assume anything. If there's one thing I've learned in my life, it's that any situation is **always** more complicated than it looks at first. Always."

Diana felt as well as heard the thunder rolling down from the mountains, and rubbed her temple harder, wishing the pounding would stop and wondering why his voice sounded distant all of a sudden. "We probably won't have to assume for long," she said. "If I know my father, he'll be here by Sunday evening, Monday at the latest."

"Are you okay with that?"

"I don't have much choice, do I? It's a public hotel."

"That's not what I meant."

She knew that. "If I have to face him, it might as well be here, and might as well be now. I want the truth. I'm tired of . . . not remembering. Not knowing."

"You'll get there. We'll get there."

"Yeah." She looked away from him finally to stare at the photo in her hand, still rubbing her pounding temple. "In the meantime, I feel like I'm in the middle of a bad soap-opera plot without a rudder. Sisters separated in childhood, one of them murdered and now a restless ghost. A mother who died in a mental hospital. A lying, cheating father. An old Victorian hotel where ghosts walk. And an FBI agent who believes I can somehow make sense of it all."

"I do believe that."

Thunder rumbled and boomed, loudly now, and lightning flashed.

The photo blurred a little and then cleared. And Diana caught her breath as she could have sworn that the image of Missy took her hand off the dog and held it out as though beckoning. To the person holding the camera. Or to her older sister looking on.

"Diana—"

Before he could touch her, she flinched away from the movement she felt more than saw, murmuring, "No. Don't." She didn't take her eyes off the picture.

"What is it?" he demanded, his voice strained.

Don't let him touch you. Not now. Not this time.

The voice was too familiar, its urgency too real, for Diana to be able to disobey, and without even considering the matter she heard herself tell Quentin tensely, "Don't touch me. There's something I have to— Just don't touch me. Wait."

Lightning flashed brilliantly seconds after she uttered the command, and abruptly Diana found herself in the gray time.

Alone.

Ellie Weeks hadn't believed she could be more nervous than she had been making that phone call, but with everything happening in and around The Lodge, she was convinced she'd jump out of her skin if somebody so much as said boo in her general vicinity. Of course, being watched like a hawk by that old bat Mrs. Kincaid was enough to make anybody jittery, and she expected that pregnancy hormones could account for the rest, but still.

She was beginning to think getting kicked out of this place might not be such a bad thing. Assuming she had someplace else to go, of course.

She checked her cell phone for the tenth time, just to make sure she had a strong signal and hadn't missed a call. And like the other nine times, the indicator promised a strong signal and no missed calls.

"Shit," she murmured softly.

"Ellie!"

She jumped and then turned to face Mrs. Kincaid, knowing she looked guilty as hell but unable to do anything about it. As unobtrusively as possible, she slipped the cell phone back into the pocket of her uniform. None of the staff was supposed to carry their phones on duty. "Yes, ma'am?"

"I thought I asked you to get the Orchid Room ready. We have a Very Important Guest arriving tomorrow."

There were always Very Important Guests checking in, Ellie thought. But her mild curiosity as to who might be checking in became something else as she wondered suddenly whether this guest might be the result of her phone call.

Could he have gotten here so fast? Would he?

"Yes, ma'am." She tried to keep the hope out of her voice, asking as casually as possible, "A returning guest, ma'am?"

Mrs. Kincaid frowned at her.

Quickly, Ellie said, "I just wondered if it was somebody we knew liked a certain kind of soap or extra towels or—or something like that."

Still frowning, the housekeeper said, "As a matter of fact, it is a returning guest. Check your worksheet, for heaven's sake, Ellie. His preferences are noted, as always."

"Oh, yes, ma'am. I'm sorry. Sort of scatterbrained today."

"I noticed," Mrs. Kincaid snapped. "Keep your mind on your work if you want to keep your job."

Ellie nodded and went hurriedly to get her cart, her heart pounding in sick excitement. Was it him? Was he coming here after getting her message, perhaps because he knew or had guessed what she had to tell him?

Her worksheet was, as they usually were, maddeningly enigmatic. No names. The guest due to check into the Orchid Room the following day preferred no fresh flowers or scented soaps due to allergies, and required both extra towels and pillows.

Which told her nothing. Ellie hadn't prepared his room before his last visit. But her friend Alison had.

It required only a few minutes for Ellie to push her cart into the service elevator and take it up to her floor—which was mostly deserted due to check-outs. Whether it was the fairly unobtrusive presence of the police or general unease about what the hell was going on, quite a few guests had decided to cut short their stays.

Not that Ellie minded that. She unlocked the door to the Orchid Room and pushed it open, forgetting in her haste the automatic knock-first-even-if-you-know-the-room-is-empty rule drummed into them all by Mrs. Kincaid.

At The Lodge, privacy and discretion were guaranteed.

She quickly stripped the bed and dragged the vacuum out into the room, just to make it look as if she had been working in here. And it was sheer chance that as she turned for the door, she noticed a flicker of lightning from outside the window catch something metallic that was otherwise hidden in the deep pile carpet.

Ellie hesitated, but she was too curious not to look, to search for what the flash of light had revealed.

A locket.

The locket.

The same damned one she had found before, in this very room.

"You're in the Lost and Found," she murmured, staring down at what lay in the palm of her hand. "I took you there. I put you in an envelope and left you in the Lost and Found. So . . . how did you get back here?"

It was a puzzle, and baffling, but Ellie had more important things on her mind at the moment and was easily able to shrug it off for now. She slid the locket into the pocket of her uniform, disobeying yet another of Mrs. Kincaid's iron rules because she didn't have time to stop and do the envelope thing.

Besides, it apparently hadn't worked the last time.

She checked the empty and very quiet hallway, then went in search of her friend.

Despite the earlier flash of lightning, Ellie was only vaguely aware that another storm was crackling and groaning outside. She'd been here long enough to be familiar with the way spring storms rolled down from the mountains, and since she didn't have to be out in this one, she didn't pay attention to the increasing violence in the sounds.

Where was Alison working today? Hadn't she

said something about the North Wing? Yes, because she'd been unhappy about the assignment; she was one member of the staff who was easily spooked, and was convinced The Lodge was haunted. Particularly that wing.

Ellie had never shared that conviction, largely because she was singularly uninterested in ghosts. Even if they existed, they were dead, so why worry about them? It wasn't as if a ghost could hurt anybody, after all.

Still, as she slipped through corridors and crept up stairways, Ellie was conscious of a weird impulse to look back over her shoulder. She'd rarely seen The Lodge so seemingly deserted, maybe that was it. Or maybe it was just because she was unusually jumpy today, unusually anxious.

Those pregnancy hormones, probably.

She had searched two floors of the North Wing without success. Not that she knocked on every door, of course; she was just looking for Alison's cart. But it was nowhere to be seen, and by the time Ellie climbed yet another set of stairs, she was getting as weary as she was impatient.

She got tired so easily these days, dammit. And that hardly boded well for her ability to hide her condition from the eagle eyes of Mrs. Kincaid.

"He has to come," she murmured as she rounded another corner. "He has to."

"Who has to?"

Almost jumping out of her skin, Ellie stared at someone else who wasn't supposed to be here. "Just—talking to myself," she said hastily, and before that could be questioned, added, "What're you doing up here?"

"Waiting for you," he said.

Diana looked around the still, silent lounge, vaguely interested as always in the peculiarity of this. The strong Victorian colors were gone, the patterns of fabrics and wallpaper muted and blurred now. No lightning flashed outside the blank, silvery sheen of the windows. No thunder rumbled. Everything was gray and silent and cold.

Diana knew Quentin was still sitting beside her, but when she turned her head, he wasn't there. And for a moment, she felt a rush of terror as she wondered if she would be able, this time, to find her way out of the gray time.

"It'll be harder," a sweet voice said. "You're deeper in now. I'm sorry. It has to be this way."

Diana looked toward the door and felt only a little shock to see the sister she had never known. Every bit as thin, pale, and haunted as she had appeared on the veranda, this time she was speaking aloud in a voice much older and wiser than the years she had lived. Her oval face was solemn.

"Missy." As always, Diana's own voice sounded strange and hollow to her ears. She wished she could feel something other than sadness for this unknown sister, but that's what she felt. Sadness. Because Missy had been cheated of her life, and because Diana had been cheated of her sister.

Nodding, Missy said, "We don't have much time."

"There's **no** time here," Diana said. "I've figured out that much."

"Yes, but he's with you. On the other side of the door you opened. He won't wait very long before he...interferes. He's afraid for you."

"Afraid I'll get...stuck...here."

"Yes."

"Will I?"

"I don't know. I only know that you need to be here, and that now is the best time. While it's storming. There's a lot of energy while it's storming, energy that helps you. Please, Diana, come with me."

Determined to control some part of this rather than be pulled along like a puppet, Diana said, "Tell me one thing. Are you my sister?"

Missy didn't hesitate. "Yes."

"Then why don't I remember you?"

Missy took a step back, then turned toward the door. "Come with me, Diana."

Diana wasn't surprised her second question had gone unanswered; she was only surprised her first question hadn't as well. She got up and followed Missy from the room. "Am I really moving?" she wondered aloud. "Or am I still sitting back there with Quentin?"

Walking without a sound down the gray hallway toward the stairs, Missy said, "You're here only in spirit this time."

Which was the more common way she visited the gray time, Diana knew. She had "awakened" too often in her bed or sitting up in a chair after such a "journey" not to know that much. Still, she had a question.

"Why? This morning was different."

"This morning, I needed to speak through you. I needed him and the other policeman to hear me. Bringing you through the door physically was the first step. You were sort of . . . connected after that. You felt it, the difference."

"I was cold. I couldn't get warm."

"Yes. I'm sorry about that, but I needed the connection for later. For the cave. So I could speak through you. But it took a lot out of you. More than I expected. I really am sorry."

Diana accepted the apology, but the farther

she moved from Quentin, the more uneasy she became. "Where are we going?"

"There's something I have to show you."

Recalling Quentin's wry comment about the curiously unhelpful role spirits often played when there were too many questions and too few answers, Diana said, "Why can't you just tell me who killed you?"

To her surprise, Missy offered an answer. Of sorts.

"Because knowing who killed me wouldn't help you. Or Quentin."

It was the first time she had said Quentin's name, something that caused Diana a curious pang she couldn't have explained. "It would help him. It's—haunted him all these years."

"I know."

"Then don't you want peace for him? Don't you want him to put all this behind him and get on with his life?"

"Yes." Missy stopped and turned to face Diana in the cold, gray hallway. "I couldn't get through, all the times he was here before. I couldn't reach him. Even though he brought another medium at least once to try."

"He didn't tell me that."

"It was a long time ago."

"How do you know that? Time doesn't pass here."

Missy smiled faintly. "Because he was younger. Younger and very impatient and determined. I've always been able to see him from here. I just couldn't reach him." Her thin shoulders rose and fell in a shrug.

"You can reach him now. Through me. So why don't you tell him what he needs to know? Why don't you give him peace?"

"It's not mine to give him."

"That's not true."

"Diana, Quentin blames himself for not protecting me. For not saving me. But, most of all, he blames himself because, deep down inside, he knew what was wrong here. Or at least that something was. He could feel it, just like I could. Being psychic, being a seer, is something he was born, not something created in him the day he found me. The shock just woke him up, that's all."

"Missy—"

"He could feel what was wrong here, but he couldn't believe in it. He was older, maybe that was part of it. Maybe it was just that no one had ever explained why he was different, and so he decided not to be. Decided to be like everybody else. Decided not to pay attention to those feelings he couldn't explain. His mind told him to ignore what he felt, to doubt his senses. He listened to his mind, just the way you listened to the doctors all these years."

"That was different."

"No, it was the same. You knew you weren't crazy. You knew you weren't sick. But you listened to them anyway. Because, deep down, you were more afraid of the truth."

"I don't know what you mean."

"You know, you've always known, that the wall between the living and the dead isn't something solid. You've known that you could make doors and let us cross over. You've known that you could come through those doors to our side. You've known you could walk with us."

Missy paused, then added, "You've always been afraid of being trapped here, like those people you saw in the hospital when we visited Mommy. You knew what I knew. That they were just living bodies without souls."

Diana felt her throat tighten, felt the familiar tendrils of icy terror coiling deep inside her. The memory triggered by Missy's words was sudden and incredibly vivid. She was transported back nearly thirty years, her small hand held in her father's grasp, her short legs trying to keep up as he led her down a long, long hallway. A hallway with doors on either side, some open, some closed. Behind some of the closed doors was silence; behind others she could hear an occasional laugh or sob, and behind one a strange, sad wailing. Through the open doors she could see beds, some of them holding people who were sitting up, reading, watching TV.

But in other beds, people lay still and silent, with machines beeping quietly nearby. Most were just sleeping or unconscious, she knew that. Even then, she knew that.

Some were gone. Their bodies lay there and breathed, their heartbeats recorded by those beeping machines, but the people who had once been inside those bodies were gone.

And they were never coming back.

Diana had known that, with utter certainty. Beyond a small child's ability to communicate the knowledge, beyond words, beyond reason, she had known exactly what had happened to those people.

Someone had opened a door, perhaps even they themselves. And now they were trapped on the other side, unable to return to their physical selves.

Diana's terror had been deep and wordless, but it had been nothing compared to what she had felt when her father led her into one of the rooms. When she saw her mother lying still and silent in a bed. When she heard the machines beeping quietly.

When she understood.

"Diana?"

She blinked and stared at Missy's young, solemn face. "My God. It happened to her. She was . . . gone. Before Daddy or the doctors ever realized, a long time before they said it, before her body finally stopped, she was gone."

"Yes."

"I didn't . . . why didn't I remember that?"

"You were too afraid to remember."

This time, Diana understood. "Because I knew I could do what she'd been able to."

Missy nodded. "You were afraid you couldn't control it, that you'd be lost on this side just like she was. And you couldn't control it, then. You were too little, you didn't know how. And she wasn't there to help you understand. No one was. Not then."

"Until now."

"There are no medicines fogging your mind now. And he's here to push you to see what is. To help you understand. You needed that. But you're still afraid. That's why you argue with him when he wants to talk about it."

"I have reason to be afraid, don't I? You said yourself you didn't know whether I could be trapped on this side. But we both know it's possible, so—"

"There are worse things than being trapped here, Diana."

Tha-thum.

Tha-thum.

It wasn't a sound so much as a sensation, and shocking in this gray place of stillness and silence.

Quentin had asked her if she had ever felt or heard something like a heartbeat inside her, and Diana had denied it because she hadn't remembered. But now she recognized it instantly. She remembered it, an echo from her childhood and from somewhere inside her, someplace deeper than instinct.

She knew this.

Tha-thum.

Tha-thum.

It was vast and dark and smelled of damp earth and rotten eggs. It was so cold it burned, and the blackness of it stole every flicker of light. And it was...inevitable. Ancient. Beyond powerful. So overwhelming she felt weak and terrified.

Tha-thum.

Tha-thum.

"It's coming," Missy said. "It's ready to kill again."

"You mean him, don't you? That murderer."

"He stopped being a person even before they buried him alive. Now there's only...it. And you know what it is."

Diana did. That was the terrifying thing. She did.

"What will it look like this time?" she whispered. "Who will it take over?"

"It almost always looks like someone we trust, doesn't it?" Missy turned and again led the way down the long, gray corridor. "This way. Hurry, Diana."

Because she couldn't do anything else, Diana followed, frightened of what was coming and uneasily aware of the growing distance between the part of her taking this journey and the part of her left behind with Quentin. An anxiety that only increased when she realized this corridor was unfamiliar and that she had no idea how to find her way back to him.

Quentin prowled the lounge restlessly, his gaze returning again and again to Diana's face. Her eyes were closed, her face peaceful, and if he hadn't known better, he would have believed her to be asleep.

She wasn't sleeping, though.

A room service waiter had come and gone,

but the coffee Stephanie had sent up sat untouched on the tray. Quentin didn't want coffee, though he could have done with something stronger. Something a lot stronger.

"Don't touch me. There's something I have to— Just don't touch me. Wait."

Wait. Just wait. How long was he supposed to wait? How long was it safe for her to be . . . wherever she was?

She was in the gray time, he assumed. He wasn't certain what had triggered the event, unless it had been a combination of Diana's troubled emotional state after finding out about Missy and the storm rumbling outside. Probably that, he thought. The storm was certainly scrambling all his senses, and given what had happened during the last one, this one had undoubtedly enhanced hers.

It was his own undependable senses that kept him from reaching out to her now, touching her, anchoring her. Even more so than usual during a storm, he felt almost disconnected from the sensory input his body and mind were accustomed to. Everything was muffled, distant, beyond his reach.

All he knew for sure was that what Diana was doing was dangerous. And necessary.

That was what he couldn't get past, that strong certainty that she had to do this, that it was important. And that if he interfered, if he yanked her back from wherever she had to be right now, he would regret it.

The question was, could he trust even his own deepest certainties? Could he trust his instincts?

Because if he couldn't, and he waited too long before trying to draw her back... she could be beyond his or anyone's reach.

"She's done this before," he heard himself mutter as he paced and watched her. "For years, she's done it, decades. I wasn't there then, and she got back without my help. Without anyone's help. She can get back now."

If she was as strong as he believed she was.

If she was strong enough.

Quentin hated this. He hated waiting, hated standing by with nothing to do except worry. He'd been forced to do it more than once in the past and, in fact, suspected that Bishop had from time to time put him in that position quite deliberately in order to teach him some patience.

Confronted with Quentin's suspicion, Bishop hadn't denied it. But he hadn't confirmed it either.

Par for the course.

In any case, if a lesson had been intended, Quentin had yet to learn it. It went against his deepest instincts, his very nature, to allow someone else to take the active role while he waited around twiddling his thumbs. Especially when that person was, despite her strength, damaged and fragile and someone he cared about—

A loud crash of thunder sounded almost deafening in his ears, the brilliant flash of lightning so blinding that for an instant he was totally in the dark and abruptly alone inside his own head. Except for . . .

Now. Hurry. Before it's too late.

The storm had his senses so scrambled that he thought it was a wonder he could even hear that whisper in his mind. Or maybe it had been whispering for a long time now, and he'd been unable to hear it.

Suddenly afraid he had waited too long, Quentin hurried back to Diana's side and took her cool hand in his, holding it strongly.

Nothing. No reaction, no response. She sat there, still and silent, her eyes closed, face peaceful.

He had never been called upon to be someone's lifeline, but Quentin had learned long ago that the mind could do remarkable things if properly motivated and harnessed.

Concentrating, fiercely closing out the distraction of the storm, he fixed all his will on reaching Diana and pulling her back to him.

14

Missy, where are you taking me?" The uneasiness Diana felt was increasing, building, and she had the sudden, frightened notion that this spirit of her supposed sister might be far less benevolent than Diana had assumed her to be.

"There's something I have to show you."

"Why can't you just tell me whatever it is you want me to know?" Diana was looking around, trying to figure out where in the hotel they were. But the corridor was peculiarly featureless in the gray time—even more so than usual—and seemed to stretch ahead of them forever. "This isn't right," she added before Missy could reply. "This looks—"

"There's something Quentin's forgotten," Missy said, ignoring both the question and comment.

"What?"

"Because of what happened to me, he thinks it's about children."

Diana only partly heard, because Missy had turned a corner as she spoke, and to her surprise Diana found herself looking at a green door. It was the only spot of color she had ever seen in the gray time.

"You have to remember this place, Diana. This door."

"Why?" Diana was doing her best to think clearly, but it was becoming increasingly difficult.

"Because you'll be safe here. When it's important, when you need a safe place, come here."

"I thought . . . all places were the same in the gray time."

"Not this place. It's a special place, in your time as well as here. It's protected. Don't forget."

Diana wanted to ask more questions, but before she could, Missy was going on.

"Diana, listen to me. Quentin always believed it was about children, but it isn't. Children are easiest because they're so often vulnerable, un-

protected. Easy prey. It feeds off fear. You remember the terror of a child, don't you, Diana?"

Her lips felt oddly stiff and very cold when
Diana murmured, "Yes. I remember."

"It isn't about the children. It isn't even about
me. It's about punishment. It's about judgment.
He was judged. And punished."

Again, Diana wanted to question, wanted to
understand all this more clearly. But before she
could speak, they both heard/felt it.

Tha-thum.

Tha-thum.

Tha-thum!

Missy's face changed, and she said quickly,
"You have to go back. Now. It can cross over too,
Diana, don't forget that. And a medium's mind
can be the most vulnerable of all. If it finds
you—"

"Missy, I don't understand."

"You will." Missy reached out and took
Diana's hand, her small one surprisingly warm
rather than cold. "Don't forget the green door.
But go back now. Reach for Quentin."

Diana wasn't sure she could, because her mind
felt sluggish and cold, and doing anything at all
required too much effort of her. But the warmth
of Missy's small hand seemed to chase away part
of the chill . . .

Tha-thum!

Tha-thum!

She could feel the floor underneath her vibrate, as though under the steps of something immeasurably heavy, and the grayness around her seemed to be darkening, shading toward black. She tried to reach out mentally, thinking of Quentin, needing to be with him.

There was a bright flash of light, then another, and between them the gray was getting darker and darker.

"Hurry," Missy said. "It's—"

"—here," Diana said, opening her eyes.

"Jesus, don't do that to me again," Quentin said.

She turned her head and looked at him, a little dazed and more than a little confused. He was holding her hand, and his felt warm and strong, and she was once again conscious of that unfamiliar sense of security.

Safe. She was safe. Now.

"Are you all right?" he demanded.

"I think so."

He drew a breath and released it, clearly relieved. He didn't let go of her hand. "Another visit to the gray time?"

Diana nodded slowly.

"Another guide?"

"Missy."

That caught him off guard. "You talked to her?"

"Yes."

"And?"

Diana told him, about the green door and Missy's warning that "it" wasn't about hurting children but was about punishment and judgment.

"I don't remember a green door in this place," he said.

"Me either."

"But it's a safe place for you."

Trying to remember exactly what she'd been told, Diana said, "I think so. Something about it being a protected place here and in the gray time."

A bit grim, Quentin said, "If she offered you a safe place, it must mean she believes you'll need one."

A cold finger glided up Diana's spine. "I guess so."

"And she said it's about judgment, about punishment."

"Yes. Because he was judged and punished. That killer."

"Samuel Barton."

"Yes."

Quentin digested that for a few moments, frowning, then said, "What else?"

She didn't know if he was using any of his extra senses or if her face was an open book to him, but she knew she had to answer. So she did, telling him what Missy had said about her deepest fears of being unable to handle her abilities and becoming trapped between two worlds, about her terror over what had happened to her mother. And it was only then that Diana remembered something else.

"My God. She said 'when we visited Mommy.' That I was frightened by the people in the hospital, the people without their souls, when **we** visited **Mommy**. Quentin...Missy wasn't a half sister. We had the same father **and** mother."

Stephanie wouldn't have admitted it aloud, but the major reason she asked Ransom Padgett to accompany her down to the basement wasn't to help carry any files or boxes she decided to bring back upstairs. It was because she didn't want to be alone down there.

Not that he asked, of course.

He used one of the many keys on his ring to unlock the basement access door, then led the way down well-illuminated stairs, saying over his shoulder, "I'll give you fair warning, Ms. Boyd—it's hell trying to find anything down here. I told Management years ago that the place ought to be cleared out, at least of the junk, but they didn't listen to me. Don't have to, mind you, 'cause I just work here. But still."

Stephanie only half listened to him, looking around as they reached the bottom of the steps and feeling a bit sheepish now. The basement was as well illuminated as the stairs had been, and though the vast space was undoubtedly cluttered with what Padgett termed "junk," there was a kind of order to it all.

She could see a dozen big filing cabinets in a smaller, partially walled-off area near the stairs, the bulging cardboard file boxes stacked on top of them mute evidence that all of the cabinets were undoubtedly stuffed to capacity and that more storage space for paperwork had been required.

Great. That's just great. I'll be down here for weeks.

Sighing, she looked around the rest of the basement space visible from the foot of the stairs.

One section held unused furniture, presumably in need of repair or perhaps just abandoned due to changing styles and tastes, with chairs stacked atop tables and an occasional dust cloth draped over upholstered pieces to protect them. Another section was filled with boxes, most of whose big labels indicated old linens and draperies.

In yet another area, shelves held an amazing assortment of outmoded kitchen gadgets, cheek by jowl with what looked like stacks of old magazines and newspapers. And leaning against the shelves were dozens of large framed prints, again, presumably, moved down here due to changing tastes.

"My God," she muttered. "Did they throw **anything** away?"

"Not so's you'd notice," Padgett said in mild disgust. "Ought to, though. There's plenty of charities would love some of this junk, and God knows the textiles they saved are likely rotten or moth-eaten after so many years. There's a whole stack of rugs in one of the back corners that were probably worth a fortune in their day. Not much left of 'em now." He shrugged. "Anything's needed up in the hotel, they always buy new, so I don't get why the old and broken stuff ends up down here."

"Saving for a rainy day, I suppose."

They both listened to a rumble of thunder so low and long that they could feel the vibrations of it beneath their feet, and Padgett lifted an eyebrow at her.

Stephanie had to laugh, but said, "Well, I'm not going to be the one to tackle this, that's all I know. Or at least, I'm not planning to go through anything except the paperwork. I have to say, though, this space is a lot more inviting than I'd expected, even with all the clutter. At least the paperwork seems to be filed fairly neatly, and all in one place."

Padgett gave her a pitying look, then beckoned her to follow as he headed toward the section piled high with furniture. "Couple managers back, somebody had the bright idea to get all the old Lodge records and other paperwork in its own space, nice and neat and organized instead of just stacked wherever there happened to have been a bit of clear floor or an empty shelf. Most of it got moved, eventually, out of all the scattered corners of this place. But not all."

Stephanie followed him around the furniture, and bit back a groan when she saw a rather dark corner piled high with obviously old ledgers and file boxes and even several old banded trunks.

"Jesus," she muttered.

"The light's not great here," Padgett said. "Why don't I start dragging all this stuff back toward the stairs? At least then you'll be able to see what you're looking at. That's assuming you want to start in on this stuff." His face said clearly enough that he hoped she'd return to the file cabinets, which would obviously keep her busy for a long time.

Stephanie hesitated, then said, "I guess this

stuff here would have contained some of the oldest records, right?"

"Yeah, probably. It all used to spill out a lot farther in this corner, with boxes stacked right up against the furniture, so I'd expect the oldest stuff to be back in that corner against the walls." He eyed her. "I've been here about as long as anybody, so if I knew what you were looking for, I might be able to shorten the search."

Briskly, she said, "Well, I don't really know myself. But since you offered to help, why don't you grab some of that stuff and start bringing it closer to the stairs? I don't know how much time I've got before the next crisis erupts, so I might as well do what I can in the meantime."

"Yes, ma'am."

Leaving him to it, Stephanie retreated to the "organized" area near the stairs and, drawing a deep breath and flipping a mental coin, opened a file drawer at random to start her search. She didn't have a clue what she was looking for.

But she had a hunch she'd know it when she found it.

"That's the last of this lot," Quentin said, setting aside the largest of the two boxes.

"Anything helpful?"

"Not as far as I can see. A few interesting letters from around the early 1900s, written to guests and staff, but nothing to indicate unsolved disappearances or other mysteries here."

Diana gestured toward the old photographs stacked on the coffee table before her and said, "Same here, more or less. I've gone through all the photo albums and all the loose photos we found. Interesting pictures, most without even a date on the back, but nothing that sends up a red flag."

"Well, the universe never makes things easy."

"So I've noticed." She shook her head. "Maybe there's nothing else here, and all I was meant to find was the one picture."

It lay alone on the coffee table within easy reach of Diana, and she glanced at it often. That picture of two little girls and a dog, a moment frozen in time.

"Could be," Quentin agreed. "Signs and portents."

"Is that what we're looking for?"

"God knows. Bishop calls them signposts, and says too many of us walk right by them without noticing. That's probably true. I mean, most people are too busy just getting through the day to pay much attention to hints from the universe."

"So what do these signposts look like, according to Bishop?"

Since Diana had asked him to talk about the Special Crimes Unit while they went through the stuff from the attic, Quentin had obliged. She hadn't wanted to talk any more about the experience the storm had triggered, obviously needing time to come to terms with it, and he was reluctant to push her even though questions and thoughts were still swirling in his mind.

Instead, he had talked about the SCU as the storm had gradually faded away outside and they had worked their way through most of the stuff brought down from the attic, offering thumbnail sketches of some of his fellow team members as well as a few of the more interesting war stories involving the unit.

He wasn't at all sure she had even listened to him, and half suspected she'd only wanted the sound of another voice in the room, the sense of another person, while her own thoughts were miles away. But he had jumped at the chance to talk about the unit, feeling it was important for her to hear about things that would make her own paranormal experiences at least sound fairly ordinary by comparison.

She had, it seemed, heard at least some of what he'd told her.

"Signs and portents. They can look like anything, that's the hell of it," he answered her.

"The more ordinary, the more likely they are to be anything but. For instance—" He reached for the last box he had to go through, and from the jumble of its contents produced a very old cigar box. "—this. This is, what, the third lost-and-found box we've come across?"

"At least."

"And the same sort of stuff inside." He opened the box and inspected its contents. "Bits of jewelry, a cigarette lighter, assorted keys, hair combs and clips, a fountain pen, a rabbit's foot, nail clippers, coins—junk, mostly. Stuff the original owners have long, long since forgotten about. But who knows if there's a signpost in here? A sign or portent just lying in this ordinary little box for somebody paying attention? There could be."

"In a cigar box filled with junk?"

"You know what they say. One man's junk is another man's treasure." Quentin shrugged. "Though it's not intrinsic value that matters, of course. Like I said—any sign tends to be something ordinary. At least at first glance. Or even at second glance."

Diana held out her hand and, when Quentin gave her the box, began going through the contents almost idly. "I'd say this stuff was pretty ordinary, all right. How are we supposed to recognize signs and . . . portents . . . if they're just average, everyday things? What does your Bishop say about that?"

"Well, to me he said something typically cryptic. He said to pay attention to everything, and the important bits would make themselves conspicuous at some point along the way."

"I guess the universe doesn't like to be obvious."

"Apparently not." Quentin hesitated, then said carefully, "If you're right about your father coming here, he should be able to give us at least some of the answers."

Diana was frowning slightly as she continued to gaze into the box on her lap. "But will he? That's the question. And even if he does, will his answers be the truth?"

"You think he'd try to keep a lie going even in the face of this?"

"That depends on why he started the lie in the first place, doesn't it? And we don't have so much, after all. A photograph of two little girls. As far as you've known all these years, Missy lived here with her mother. We can't prove otherwise, can we?"

"No," Quentin admitted. "At least not with any information I've found to date. There was never a hint, from Missy or from anything I've found since her death, to indicate that Laura

Turner wasn't her natural mother. In fact, in the police files of the original investigation is a photocopy of Missy's birth certificate. Supposedly, anyway. Born Missy Turner, daughter of Laura, in Knoxville, Tennessee. Father unknown."

"You never thought that could have been a fake?"

"About ten years ago I went as far as checking original hospital records, and there was a child named Missy Turner born to a Laura Turner on that date, just as the certificate noted. I had no reason to dig any deeper."

Diana nodded, but said, "The way Missy spoke when I was with her, when she said 'we visited Mommy,' was so natural that I'm positive she meant exactly what she said. That the two of us went to visit **our** mother."

"I believe you," Quentin said. "And I can't think of any reason why she would lie to you. But proving that you and Missy had the same father **and** mother won't be easy if your father has, for whatever reasons, covered up that fact. That is what you suspect, isn't it? That he did it deliberately?"

Choosing her words carefully, Diana said, "My father is a very powerful man. It's not just money, although he has plenty of that. It's real power. Political connections, even internationally; both his father and grandfather were ambassadors. And his company, the family company, has interests in everything from cutting-edge technology to diamond mines. And offices all over the world."

Quentin nodded. "So . . . if he wanted to hide a secret . . ."

"He could pretty much move heaven and earth to hide it. And it would stay hidden."

"Realistically, we wouldn't have much of a shot of digging up that secret, if he buried it deep enough."

"No. And convincing him to talk now won't be easy, not after all these years. He's hardly likely to listen to my . . . experiences . . . let alone believe them. In fact, if I tell him what's happened to me here, he's entirely capable of using it against me. The delusional ravings of someone in need of medical care, obviously. He wants me back under the thumbs of his handpicked doctors, medicated until I stop thinking for myself."

"Why?"

She looked up at Quentin, honestly startled. "Why?"

"Yeah. Why would he want that now? What secret would demand such extreme measures?"

"The one that kept me from knowing I had a sister, maybe?"

Quentin chose his words carefully. "Obviously, there's a lot we don't know about this. All

I'm saying is that we can't assume anything until we have more information. That Missy's existence was kept from you and that you were under medical care for so many years may have been due to different situations completely unrelated to each other."

"You don't really believe that."

With a sigh, Quentin said, "No, I don't. But I still say we can't assume without more facts."

Diana looked back down at the old cigar box in her lap, absently fingering a rather gaudy costume earring. "Quentin . . . my mother died in a mental hospital, and if Missy and my own memories are right, both her illness and her death had something to do with paranormal abilities she couldn't control."

"We've always known it was possible," he admitted reluctantly.

"Abilities my father probably believed were simply . . . manifestations of mental illness."

"Also possible. Maybe even likely. Medical science, especially twenty-five or thirty years ago, tended to view anything it couldn't explain as an illness."

"So what am I supposed to tell him when he gets here? That I can . . . walk with the dead, and encountered the spirit of my sister on one of those journeys? How do you think he's going to react to that?"

Madison was glad the storm had finally died away. They seemed to bother her more every time, and as for Angelo, he just shook like a leaf, poor little thing.

"It's over now," she told her dog reassuringly.

He whined softly as he stood gazing up at her. Storms always bothered him, but his anxiety had been growing steadily for quite a while now.

"It **is** over," she told him. "The storm, anyway. And the rest . . . will be over soon. I promise."

Angelo sat down with a peculiarly human sigh, managing to express even more uneasiness along with his frustration.

Madison looked around the game room, where she and Angelo had waited out the storm and which was, except for them, empty. The whole place was awfully empty, really; it practically echoed.

"It's here," Becca said from the doorway.

Madison wasn't really surprised, but she was worried and didn't try to hide her shiver of fear. "You said Diana wasn't ready yet."

"She'll have to be, won't she?"

"But what if she isn't?"

"I expect he'll help her."

Madison bent down to pick up her little dog, and held him, stroking him to soothe his uneasy whining. "Still, if it's here...bad things will happen, won't they?"

"Usually do. When it's here, I mean."

"Will they find more bones, Becca?"

Becca turned her head slightly, as though listening to some distant sound. Softly, she said, "No, it won't be bones this time. It won't be bones."

"Diana, no one is going to haul you to a mental hospital or put you under medication against your will, no matter how your father reacts. I promise you that."

Her mouth twisted. "Are you going to tell him you're a seer? That the FBI has a whole official unit made up of psychics?"

"It's not a secret." He smiled faintly. "We do our best to avoid undue publicity, but plenty of people in this country know about the SCU. Some very highly respected, powerful people. If he doesn't want to believe you or me, I can offer your father quite a few unimpeachable references, people who will willingly talk to him about their paranormal experiences. Whether or not he believes what they say, he'll have to take it seriously."

"At least seriously enough not to call the guys with the butterfly nets to catch his daughter?"

"That is not going to happen."

"You sound so sure."

"I am sure. Believe me."

Diana almost did. But she knew her father, and her anxiety level hardly diminished. Still, she was able to push the question aside for the moment to ask Quentin another one.

"Anything of interest in that last box?" With nothing else to show for their efforts so far, she had to wonder if the only "signpost" either of them had been intended to see was the photograph of two seemingly ordinary little girls.

Though heaven knew **that** signpost was sending Diana in a completely unanticipated direction in her life, one she would have thought unbelievable even a few days ago.

Quentin reached into the box and produced what looked like an old journal of some kind, and began flipping through the pages. "Well, well. I'd call this of interest."

The very matter-of-factness of his tone alerted Diana. "What is it?"

"Unless I miss my guess, it's somebody's account of at least a few of this hotel's secrets."

"What?" Diana left her chair and went around the coffee table to join him on the sofa.

"Look at this. The dates aren't in any particular sequence; one page has an entry dated 1976, and the facing page is dated 1998." He indicated the former page, and read aloud, " 'Senator Ryan brought his mistress this trip. We're all under orders to call her Mrs. Ryan, but we know better.' And more of the same. Sounds sort of . . ."

"Bitchy," Diana supplied.

"I was going to say 'resentful.' "

"That too." Diana was studying the page dated 1998. "And more of the same on this other page. An actress came here to dry out . . . a senator with a cocaine problem . . . And what looks like an account of an overheard argument between a wife and her cheating husband."

"I'm guessing someone from the housekeeping staff wrote this."

"Or reported it to whoever wrote this." Diana reached over and turned a few more pages, pausing long enough for both of them to silently read the few lines on each page. "And these are the sort of secrets the housekeeping staff could easily know about just because maids and maintenance personnel are so often present and so seldom noticed. They'd see what was there, even behind closed doors. Mistresses, alcoholism, lovers' quarrels, gambling problems. The underage daughter of a politician sent here to secretly give birth. And look at this—a European prince apparently spent the better part of a month here twenty years ago while his parents worked quietly to extricate him from some very messy legal problems."

"Those were the days," Quentin murmured.

"Yeah, a lot of this sort of thing would hardly cause a ripple now. Except in the tabloids, I guess. But setting aside what's written here, look at how it's written. Look how the handwriting changes. What—it was a round robin kind of deal, with one person passing the journal on to another, taking turns to write what they knew? I'm a big fan of conspiracy theories, but what kind of sense does that make?"

"It doesn't."

"No, it doesn't. And here's a date of 1960. More than forty years? What would be the point of keeping this journal that long? Has anybody **been** here that long?"

"The housekeeper, Mrs. Kincaid, has lived here her whole life," Quentin answered. "Her mother was housekeeper here before her. In 1960, she wouldn't have been much more than ten, I'd guess."

"None of this was written by a child."

Like most of Bishop's team, Quentin had at least a bit of expertise in numerous diverse fields, and was able to say with some confidence, "I agree. I know enough about handwriting analysis to be pretty sure of that. Not written by a child and not written by a single individual. But at least some of these entries show some fairly clear indications of individuals with a few problems."

"You said 'resentful' before."

He nodded, frowning down at one page in particular. "I'd say so. Envious, resentful, judgmental."

After a moment, Diana said quietly, "It's about judgment. It's about punishment. Maybe whatever's left of Samuel Barton set himself up as judge and jury."

15

"Yeah, except..." Quentin leafed through the pages, his frown deepening. "As far as I know, none of these names connect to any of the missing or dead people."

Diana leaned back on the sofa with a sigh. "Dammit, I was hoping we were getting somewhere. Somehow. But it's just another puzzle piece, isn't it? A journal filled with secrets, written by God knows how many different people over a span of more than forty years."

"If it's a signpost, it's a damned enigmatic one," Quentin agreed.

"And why was it in the attic?" Diana wondered. "The most recent entry was that one for

1998, and if it was written when it was dated, then the journal must have ended up in the attic only a few years ago."

"Unless it was kept in the attic all along," Quentin suggested. "It was in one of the old steamer trunks that have to be over a hundred years old, so it would have been easy to find up there. Easy to keep track of. From what Stephanie said, the attic is aired and dusted maybe once or twice a year, but otherwise is left undisturbed, so whoever kept it there could be reasonably sure it would remain hidden."

"It's as good a possibility as any," Diana said with a sigh of agreement. "But I still don't get how—and why—so many different people would have kept up the entries."

"Because," Stephanie said from the doorway in a rather grim tone, "they were paid money to do it. A lot of money."

Alison Macon would have been the first to cheerfully admit that she wasn't the best maid in the world. Or even the best one in The Lodge. Work wasn't her favorite thing, and being a maid was hard work—especially when she was expected to follow Mrs. Kincaid's exacting standards.

Being a reasonably bright girl, Alison had developed a number of shortcuts to make her job a bit easier and even more pleasant. Most were harmless, depriving no one of a clean or comfortable room. So what if she didn't change the unused towels for "fresh" ones as Mrs. Kincaid demanded; the towels were still clean, after all.

And there was no need to throw out perfectly good flowers when all that was needed to freshen them was a change of water in the vase. And what was the sense of scrubbing a tub that had clearly not been used since she had last cleaned?

The result of all her little shortcuts was that Alison often had a bit of extra time to herself now and then. Time to slip out and enjoy one of the rare cigarettes she allowed herself. Time for an extra half hour of sleep in the mornings, and perhaps even an occasional very refreshing afternoon nap.

Most importantly of all, time to sneak out and meet her boyfriend, Eric Beck, whenever he could get half an hour or so away from his own boss down at the stables.

Like her friend Ellie, Alison carried a forbidden cell phone, making it easier to arrange their meetings.

On this late Friday afternoon, Alison finished her work in record time, helped along by the fact that nearly every room on her floor was empty and only a few due to have guests to check in over the weekend. So when her silently vibrating phone announced a call, she was able to happily arrange a meeting.

But she was startled to encounter Eric just outside the side door she always used.

"Why are you up here? If Mrs. Kincaid sees you—"

"She won't. Look, I don't have much time, because that damned storm earlier postponed one of my classes." Eric often led the trail rides into the mountains, but also taught the occasional beginning rider classes The Lodge offered.

"People want to ride this late?" she asked, allowing herself to be led around the corner and along a narrow path through the shrubbery toward one of their favorite meeting places.

"Maybe three," he grunted. "I told Cullen it was hardly worth the bother of saddling the horses, but he gave me the old company line about always entertaining the guests."

"Well, it **is** what The Lodge is famous for, after all," Alison said. Suddenly uneasy, she added, "Maybe we'd better not do this, Eric."

"My work's caught up, and I'm on a break."

Alison hadn't told him that her own "breaks" were slightly on the unofficial side, and she didn't want to confess now. Eric was the best-looking single man under thirty employed at

The Lodge, and she was still astonished that she'd caught him.

Well, sort of caught him. That wasn't exactly official either.

"Nobody's going to give us grief for taking our breaks," he added, still pulling her along.

His eagerness sparked her own, helped along by her usual gleeful awareness of having pulled one over on Mrs. Kincaid. No fraternizing among the staff—yeah, right.

"Okay, but we'd better be quick," she told him.

He grinned at her over one shoulder. "When weren't we quick?"

Alison was about to offer a witty response to that when Eric suddenly stumbled and lurched forward, pulling her with him. They ended in a tangle on the ground, and her breathless laugh was cut off with brutal suddenness when she looked to see what they'd fallen over.

Once she started screaming, she couldn't stop.

The body of Ellie Weeks lay sprawled just past the overgrown arbor, one outflung hand resting among a few bright flowers that had probably been planted long ago and just as long ago forgotten.

Her maid's uniform was neat, her hair still in

its accustomed and girlish high ponytail. But a braided leather strip cut deeply into the flesh of her neck, and above it her face was mottled, her eyes wide and tongue thrusting between her parted lips.

The big, bright lights illuminating the area so that the police could work as darkness fell lent the area a garish, almost stagelike glow. The young woman might have been posed, as though playing the part of murder victim only to rise unhurt when the curtain fell.

Except that she wouldn't do that.

"It's here," Diana said softly.

Quentin reached for her hand. "This time we'll stop it," he said.

"You don't know that."

"I believe it."

"I wish I did."

Nate looked at them both rather curiously, but said, "Apparently, this was fairly popular as a meeting place for young lovers. Not far from the main building but more or less isolated, at least from the areas used by guests. It was a part of the original garden, but they'd allowed the hedges to overgrow and hide the two garden sheds."

"That isn't a garden shed." Diana was gazing at the nearby small building that seemed clearly intended to have a different life than the prosaic one of storage. It was rather sadly pretty even with its paint peeling and the few faded plastic flowers that had survived, drooping, in its cottagelike window boxes.

Diana felt cold just looking at it, even more so than when she'd seen the young maid's body. Every sense and instinct she could claim said there was something wrong with this place, something dark.

It was Stephanie, still pale and obviously shocked by the murder, who said, "According to what I was told, that was once a playhouse. For the children of guests. I don't know why it fell into disuse."

"I do," Diana murmured.

"So do I," Quentin said.

She looked up at him, a little surprised. "You remember?"

"I do now." He glanced at Nate, who was waiting with brows lifted. "The summer Missy was murdered, weeks before she died, we had all gotten into the habit of using the playhouse as a sort of clubhouse, a meeting place. This area wasn't so overgrown then, but it wasn't commonly used by the adults and we liked the illusion of secrecy."

Nate nodded. "Okay. And?"

"And ... we were all heading here one morning, sort of in a loose group. Missy ran ahead and was the first one through the door. We heard her scream and came running." He shook his head slightly. "The inside of the playhouse was a bloody mess. Someone had butchered a couple of rabbits and a fox, scattered pieces of them everywhere."

"I don't remember seeing a report about that," Nate said.

"I don't remember seeing a cop." Quentin shrugged. "I assume The Lodge management at the time decided not to call the police, and I guess our parents agreed. They probably all chalked it up to some kind of sick joke or prank. The playhouse was cleaned up, even repainted. But none of us wanted to go near it again. Maybe the kids who came after us felt the same way about the place."

Still frowning, Nate said to Diana, "Quentin was here; how do you know what happened?"

She answered readily. "I dreamed about it. When I first came here, before I met Quentin, I was having nightmares just about every night. I could never remember much about them after I woke up. But as soon as I saw the playhouse a few minutes ago, I remembered one of them. It's like I was... Missy. Happy, running toward the playhouse, opening the door. And then seeing. All the blood, the... pieces. Trying to scream and not being able to at first."

Quentin's fingers tightened around hers. "Diana—"

"There was a little table and chairs inside," she went on steadily, gazing toward the playhouse. "Whoever had done it . . . had put the severed heads of the rabbits and the fox in the middle of the table. Carefully arranged. Like a center-piece."

"Christ," Nate said. "Quentin, was that—?"

"Yeah. That's exactly the way it looked. Almost ritualistic. Probably what spooked the parents even more and kept everybody quiet about it, reluctant to investigate. I've seen that kind of thing before." To Diana, he added, "Missy took it hard. She was never the same after that morning."

Nate seemed to grope for words, then said, "So, Diana, you're saying you dreamed about this because Missy, who might have been your sister, experienced it?"

"I guess so," she replied. "Maybe a lot of my nightmares here were actually Missy's. If she was as scared that summer as Quentin remembers."

Quentin said, "It's not that uncommon, Nate. These sorts of abilities often run in families, and a blood connection between Missy and Diana could have helped form a psychic bond that survived separation."

"And survived the death of one of them?"

"Stranger things have happened, believe me." He wasn't quite ready to confide that he and Diana believed a far stranger thing was happening here and now, not when they had no more than the century-old story of a murderer caught and punished.

Nate shook his head, but said, "Look, guys, I know we've all seen a lot of weird stuff here in the last few days, and I get that you two believe most of it is somehow connected. But this"—he gestured toward the sprawled body only a few yards away—"is a murder. Not a nightmare memory. Not buried bones ten years dead, not remains that may or may not have been left by some animals in a cave, but a victim of a flesh-and-blood killer, a victim who was still breathing a couple of hours ago. Somebody choked the life out of this girl, and my job is to find out who and catch the son of a bitch. With all due respect, that's really the only thing I'm thinking about right now."

And all I want to think about, his tone said.

No one argued. No one could.

Calling on his more mundane experiences as an investigator, Quentin asked, "Did you get anything helpful out of the couple who found the body?"

"Hysterics from her and shock from him,

mostly. They literally fell over the body. I don't think either of them knows anything. They didn't see or hear anyone else in the area, they said."

"Probably a fairly reliable statement, I imagine; if they were being secretive, they would have paid attention to their surroundings."

Stephanie said, "No fraternizing among the staff. It's one of Mrs. Kincaid's rules." She looked at Nate, clearly trying to avoid another look at the body of Ellie Weeks. "For what it's worth, Mrs. Kincaid was watching Ellie. She believed the girl was up to something."

"What kind of something?"

"I have no idea, and if she knew, she wasn't willing to come right out and say it."

"I'll talk to her." Nate made a note, then looked toward the body, watching for a moment as his two crime-scene technicians worked. "I have several of my people taking statements from the rest of the staff and the few guests left here. So far, the only thing that might prove helpful is that one of the other maids is pretty sure she saw Ellie talking to a man inside The Lodge. It was at least a couple of hours ago, so the timing is right. And from the description, it was Cullen Ruppe."

Quentin said, "Interesting, how he keeps coming up."

"Yeah, I noticed that. Time for a talk, I think."

Quentin nodded, and frowned slightly. "He was seen with her during the storm. But her clothing is dry, isn't it?"

"Yeah, except for where the material touches the ground."

"Then she was carried out here no more than an hour ago, after it stopped raining."

"You think she was killed somewhere else?" Nate demanded.

"I'd say so. The ground is almost completely undisturbed, and she likely would have struggled." Quentin's voice was detached, but a muscle tightened in his jaw. "The grass is so thick here, there's no way your CSI team will find any footprints. So unless he was real stupid or careless and dropped something to help identify him..."

"She was strangled inside the main building and then was carried outside and no one saw it?" Stephanie shook her head. "Is that even possible?"

"You'd be surprised what's possible," Quentin said.

"I'm looking for a motive," Nate told her. "What reason could someone have had to kill this girl? Maybe your Mrs. Kincaid can point me in the right direction."

"Maybe she can. She seems to know just about everything that goes on here. Which brings me to this other wrinkle." Stephanie looked at Quentin and waited for his nod before telling Nate, "Apparently, most of the previous managers of The Lodge were paid to keep a record of all the...um...indiscretions taking place here and being hidden here. While the guests thought their secrets were being discreetly kept safe—and while they were paying through the nose to supposedly ensure that—it was all being written down."

Nate frowned, not sure this had anything to do with his murder investigation, but interested despite himself. "And used?"

"That," Quentin told him, "is what we're all wondering. There's no sense keeping a record unless you mean to use it. So the question is, what was the plan?"

"Blackmail?"

"Could be. Or insurance in case clout was needed somewhere along the way. Sometimes, knowledge is worth more than gold."

Cullen Ruppe was not, at the best of times, a cheerful man. He worked with horses for a reason: because he didn't like to deal with people. Unfortunately, he hadn't yet been able to find a job that took people out of the equation.

Especially when there was trouble.

"I told you," he said to the cop, "that I didn't go near the main building today. Until you called me up here, anyway." They were in one of the first-floor lounges that was serving as a rather ludicrously comfortable interrogation room.

Hard to feel threatened or even defensive when you were sitting on an elegant sofa with coffee in a silver pot on the table before you.

McDaniel made a show of consulting his notes, and said mildly, "Funny. I have a statement from a witness who saw you up here. In fact, she's pretty damned sure she saw you talking to Ellie Weeks. And that would have been just a few minutes before Ellie was strangled. With a braided leather lead rope from one of the barns."

Cullen kept his face expressionless and his gaze on the cop. He didn't so much as glance at the other two sitting off to the side, though he was keenly aware of them. He'd been aware of them, in fact, long before they'd invaded his tack room at dawn to uncover an old secret.

Calmly, he said, "Your witness made a mistake. I wasn't up here."

"She's sure it was you."

"She's wrong. It happens."

"I haven't been able to place you down at the barns when you said you were there, Cullen."

"Horses don't make for talkative witnesses. Sorry about that."

"Which means you don't have an alibi."

Cullen shrugged. "If you can find a reason for me to have killed that girl—and believe I would have been stupid enough to use one of my own lead ropes to do it—arrest me."

McDaniel ignored that and instead switched gears. "Another funny thing. That trap door in your tack room."

"Tack room's not mine, it belongs to The Lodge. And we both know that door was made a long time before either one of us was born."

"And you've never been down that ladder? Never been down in those caves?"

Cullen hesitated and swore inwardly. Everybody knew about trace evidence these days, about DNA and such. The human body had a nasty habit of shedding skin cells and hairs and God only knew what else with every step.

And something other than God knew he'd gone down into the earth more than once.

He wished he dared look at the two off to the side, wished he dared ask them if they knew what was going on, if they **understood**. Because this cop didn't, that was plain. He didn't understand, and not understanding could get a lot of people killed, and worse.

Far worse.

"Cullen? Have you been in those caves?"

He couldn't risk an outright lie that might trap him later, and so answered casually, "Maybe a long time ago. I worked here once before, you know."

"Yes, I do know. You worked here twenty-five years ago. You were working here when Missy Turner was murdered."

He'd been ready for that one. "I was. And I was in the training ring working with a young horse all that afternoon and well into the evening. Along with an assistant trainer and two of the guests. The cops found that out quick enough. I didn't even know the little girl had been killed until I heard all the sirens."

McDaniel consulted his notes, lips pursed.

Cullen wanted to tell him to cut the bullshit but, again, didn't dare. He had no way to be sure he was right, not really, not swearing-on-the-Bible sure, and if it turned out he was wrong, well, he wanted a way out of this mess. Alienating a cop—either of these two cops, especially the fed—could turn out to be a mistake. A big mistake.

It was getting late. Late in the evening and just...late. He could hear his watch ticking, and he hadn't worn a ticking watch in years.

"You left The Lodge not long after, I believe."

"Months later."

"After the fire."

Again, Cullen concentrated on keeping his breathing even. Normal. "Yeah. After the fire."

"We never really knew what started that fire," McDaniel mused. "Any ideas?"

"No. Which is what I told the cops at the time. It was obvious they suspected arson, but I'd no reason to burn the place."

"I suppose not. And you left because...?"

"Because I was ready to move on." He stopped it there and stared McDaniel in the eye defiantly.

The cop didn't blink. "I see. Well, let me ask you something else, Cullen. How well did you know Laura Turner?"

He shrugged. "She was house staff, I was stable staff. We don't mix much now and didn't at all then."

"You'd both been here for several years; are you trying to tell me you didn't know her at all?"

"Didn't say that. Said we didn't mix in those days. I knew her name, knew her to speak to, to say hello. Knew she had a kid. That's about it."

"Did you go to her daughter's funeral?"

That one caught Cullen unprepared, and he had to settle himself before answering evenly, "All the staff went."

"Just a matter of paying your respects, I guess."

"Yeah. Yeah, it was like that."

McDaniel nodded, and as if it had been a signal, the fed left the silent redhead's side and came to sit in the other chair across from Cullen.

"Still paying your respects?" he inquired casually.

"I don't know what you're talking about."

"Sure you do, Cullen. On a hunch, I asked Captain McDaniel to check something for me before we called you up here. And it turns out that the caretaker at the cemetery definitely noticed your visits. Once a week, ever since you came back to work at The Lodge. You visit Missy's grave, and you leave a single flower there."

Some hunch. Some goddamned hunch, Cullen thought.

He found himself gazing into a pair of extremely sharp blue eyes, and debated silently before deciding once again to hold his peace. He couldn't afford to be wrong, couldn't take the chance they'd lock him up before this was finished.

Because it had to be finished. This time.

Still, he had to say something, had to at least appear to cooperate, else they'd lock him up anyway. Part of the truth, he thought, was better than none.

"Okay, so I pay my respects. So I knew Laura

Turner and her daughter a bit better than I let on."

He could see he'd surprised the fed, and pressed his advantage to lead the "conversation" in the direction he wanted it to take.

"I knew that little girl didn't belong here. Never should have been here. And sure as hell never should have died here. There's nobody from this place ever visits her. The caretaker told me that. So I visit. And put something pretty on her grave."

Slowly, the fed said, "What do you mean, she never should have been here?"

Cullen hesitated visibly, striving to look reluctant. "I overheard something, okay? Something that made me realize Laura's own little girl had died—and she had stolen Missy away from her rightful parents."

The silent redhead moved suddenly, leaving her chair and coming to join Cullen on the sofa. Her face was pale, those green eyes anxious, and when he turned his head to meet her gaze, Cullen felt an instant, surprising certainty.

So that's it. That's why she's here. He felt his heartbeat quicken and had to fight once again to remain calm.

"Are you sure about that?" she asked unsteadily. "Sure she had been abducted from her real parents?"

"Sure enough."

The fed said, "Missy never said a word to even hint that Laura might not be her real mother."

Cullen managed a shrug. "She wasn't but about two when Laura took her. By the time you came here that summer, I imagine she'd forgotten she belonged anywhere else."

The fed's eyes narrowed. "You remember me?"

"Of course I remember you. You could ride any horse we had, even the mean ones, and you didn't mind grooming them afterward. Not such an arrogant little shit as most of 'em were. And I'm thinking you were the one the others followed that summer. The bunch of you spent more time down at the stables than anywhere else." Cullen shrugged again. "And left Missy to play alone, more often than not."

He half expected to get a rise out of the fed with that one, but it was clear the younger man had been a cop too long to let something like that get to him. Then again, maybe he just knew Cullen had said it deliberately.

"Yeah, she didn't care for horses. Which makes me wonder how you spent any time with her."

"I'm wondering something else," McDaniel said suddenly in the slightly-too-loud tone of a man who'd been forcing himself to be silent against his will. "I'm wondering why in hell you didn't say a word after she was murdered about Missy having been abducted. Didn't it occur to you that it might be important information?"

Cullen looked at him and, coolly, said, "Fact is, I did say something about it. To the chief of police. And signed my statement, all right and proper. So they knew then. They knew Missy was a stolen child."

It was nearly midnight when Nate hung up the phone in the lounge and turned to face Quentin. "Well, the chief isn't happy with me. I woke him up."

"How can he possibly sleep with all this going on?" Stephanie demanded. She had come into the room as Cullen was leaving, and had been filled in by the others.

"Easily. He's six months away from retirement."

Keeping to the point, Quentin asked, "What about Ruppe's statement?"

"The chief denied it ever happened." Nate sighed heavily. "But either you've infected me with your conspiracy theories and I imagined it, or he was badly rattled by my question."

"Which do you believe? Gut instinct."

"He was rattled. If I were a betting man, I'd bet that Cullen Ruppe made exactly the statement he says he made—and for some reason that statement and any information supporting it were expunged from the record."

"Why on earth would they have done that?" Stephanie asked.

"Secrets," Diana said. She was still sitting on the sofa where she had earlier gone to join Cullen. "Someone wanted the secret of Missy's abduction kept under wraps."

Frowning, Stephanie said, "I suppose someone connected with The Lodge might have wanted that. I mean, if Laura Turner was unbalanced enough to have stolen a child, her living here all those years didn't exactly reflect well on whoever had hired her. But to suppress a statement...even if it had nothing to do with Missy's murder, the information in that statement was important to the investigation. It must have taken a pretty big stick or a hell of a carrot to persuade the chief to bury it."

"My father could have done it."

16

They all looked at Diana, and it was Nate who said, "If we believe Missy was abducted from your family, Diana, then I'd think your father would be the last one we could suspect of suppressing that sort of evidence. They can't have known who took their child, let alone where she was, or they would have gotten her back."

"That's true enough. But suppose my father only found out **after** Missy was murdered."

"How?" Nate shook his head. "Cullen claims he never knew who Missy really belonged to, so even if his statement wasn't initially suppressed, no one else would have been notified of her death. And as Quentin has pointed out more than once, there was precious little media coverage. Never a picture run in the press that your parents might have recognized, even if the story had made the news outside this area."

Diana was afraid she sounded paranoid about all this, but Quentin kept telling her to trust herself, her feelings and intuitions, and that's what she was trying to do.

She didn't know who had murdered Missy, but she was utterly certain her father had had a hand in the subsequent investigation, and that he was responsible for the suppression of facts and information.

No wonder Quentin had found the trail to Missy's killer so cold for so long.

Holding her voice steady, she said, "I don't know how it happened. But there is something I do know." She looked at Quentin. "When I talked to Dad on the phone, when I told him where I was, he reacted. He was surprised, unsettled, maybe even afraid. Because I was **here,** at The Lodge. That's what shook him. And why would it have, if there wasn't something **here** he didn't want me to find out about?"

"Secrets," Quentin said. "At the very least, your father knew of The Lodge. Had he ever stayed here?"

"We can check the records," Stephanie said.

But Diana was shaking her head. "Dad hates resort-type hotels, always has. He stays in one of two types of places when he travels: downtown penthouse hotel suites in the city, or houses or apartments he rents for the duration. Staying at a place like The Lodge, miles from anywhere, surrounded by mountains and scenery, would be his idea of hell."

Quentin accepted that with a nod. "The Lodge is very well known, though, so he could easily have heard of it. But, as you say, he reacted very strongly to the knowledge that you were here, and there has to be a reason for that." He frowned. "Cullen said he'd overheard enough to know that Laura's own child had died and she'd abducted Missy. My question is, who was she talking to when he overheard the conversation?"

Nate grimaced. "Yeah, I sort of interrupted you, didn't I? Sorry about that."

"It's okay. The way he shut down after telling us about his statement, I have a hunch he'd told us everything he meant to, and no amount of questioning would have gotten anything else out of him. Not tonight, anyway."

Diana said, "I wonder if he overheard that conversation before or after Missy was killed. He didn't say."

"Does it matter?" Stephanie asked.

"It might," Quentin said. "If Laura was unbalanced enough to have abducted someone else's child to raise as her own, Missy's murder may well have pushed her even farther over the edge. In that state, she could have told anybody the truth about Missy's parentage."

Nate asked, "You don't remember how Laura acted after the murder?"

"Not really. In those days, there was a doctor on staff here, and I have the vague recollection that he kept her under sedation at least through the funeral. We left just a few weeks later. I remember seeing Laura at the funeral, but not after that."

Somewhat tentatively, Diana said, "She'd kept the secret of Missy's abduction for a long time, years. It makes more sense to me that she might have talked about it only after Missy was murdered."

Nate was making a note in the small black notebook he carried. "I'll ask Cullen. I definitely want to talk to that guy again."

Stephanie sat on the arm of a chair and said, "What creeps me out is the bit about him putting flowers on Missy's grave. Isn't that the sort of thing a killer might do?"

"It's possible," Quentin said. "But not in this case, I think. Besides, what he said about his alibi was right. He couldn't possibly have killed Missy."

Nate looked at Quentin. "Been meaning to ask you, by the way, about that **hunch** of yours. It seemed to come out of nowhere. Far as I can remember, you've never asked anything about Missy's grave before now."

"I know. A little voice told me now was the time. I've learned to listen to that little voice." He shook his head. "It was when you told us the other maid had identified Cullen as the man she'd seen talking to Ellie Weeks. Up until then, I was interested in Cullen only because he'd been here that summer twenty-five years ago. And because we found that trap door in his tack room."

"And you still believe all this is connected?"

Quentin nodded without hesitation.

Grimly, Nate said, "Well, whether it is or isn't, this is one murder that is damned well **not** going to go unsolved." He checked his watch. "Shit. After midnight. Once Sally and Ryan finished processing the scene, I okayed the removal of the body; it'll be in the hospital morgue by now. Doc said he'd do a preliminary check, but I want the post done by the state crime lab."

"And I bet they're backed up," Quentin said.

"It won't be fast," Nate conceded. "But it'll be thorough. And that's what I want. In the meantime, we have whatever forensic evidence my CSI team found, and God knows we've got plenty of questions."

"Yeah," Quentin said. "We've got plenty of those."

"Captain, you do realize I have to be up in a few hours?" The housekeeper's voice was frosty.

Nate wasn't intimidated. "One of your maids was brutally murdered not twelve hours ago, Mrs. Kincaid; I would think you'd want to help in any way possible to find out who killed her."

As unaffected by his tone as he was by hers, she snapped, "In the morning would be soon enough for your questions; no one here is going to be running away."

"Still, I'm sure you won't mind answering a few questions tonight." Nate deliberately placed his notebook on the spotless butcher-block work island in the huge kitchen, turning the pages until he found the notes he'd made earlier.

Mrs. Kincaid crossed her arms over her ample bosom and waited, standing on the other side of the island. She hadn't suggested they adjourn to another room nor try to make themselves more comfortable in this one.

"Well?"

Nate didn't allow himself to be rushed, and refused to admit even to himself that he found the big, empty kitchen very cold and more than a little spooky somehow, especially so late at night. He checked his notes, then said to her, "You informed Ms. Boyd that you believed Ellie Weeks was up to something, did you not?"

"I did."

"What was it you suspected?"

"I'm not a mind reader, Captain. But I've worked with young girls long enough to know when one of them is up to no good, and Ellie was."

"So you were watching her?"

"I was keeping a close eye on her, of course."

"Was there anything in particular she did to alert you that something was going on with her?"

"I saw her hanging around Ms. Boyd's office. Her duties took her nowhere near that area."

"She could have just been passing through on her way to another part of the hotel."

"That's what she said."

"You didn't believe her?"

"I know when I'm being lied to."

Nate wondered, but didn't question her on that point. "What else?"

"She kept slipping out to the smoking porch every chance she got, for one thing."

"That was suspicious?"

"She didn't smoke."

"So what do you think she was doing out there?"

"Probably using her cell phone. The maids aren't allowed to carry the things while on duty, but some of them sneak and do it anyway. To call their boyfriends."

"That seems innocent enough," Nate observed, making a note to look for that cell phone.

"Ellie didn't have a boyfriend." Mrs. Kincaid smiled thinly. "Here, anyway."

"Meaning?"

"Meaning she might have been stupid enough to get involved with one of our guests. That was, of course, forbidden. She would have been dismissed the instant I had proof."

"That's what you were watching for? Proof?"

"She would have betrayed herself sooner or later. They all do."

Nate frowned. "You've had that problem before? Maids getting involved with guests?"

"Well, men will be men, won't they, Captain?"

Thinking about the old double standard, Nate said, "Then why blame the maids?"

"Because they aren't being paid to provide... entertainment... for guests. The Lodge is not that sort of place." Mrs. Kincaid drew herself up even more stiffly. "I've told you when I last saw Ellie and what I said to her when I did. If you have further questions, Captain, I'm sure you can ask them in the morning. I'm going to bed."

Nate didn't try to stop her. He gazed after her for a moment, then looked around the spotless, curiously sterile kitchen, and felt a shiver for no reason he could explain.

Though he couldn't help wondering if the ghost of a murdered maid was trying to get his attention.

"Bullshit," he murmured, but without much force. Without much force at all.

"She wasn't very big, was she?"

Quentin turned a bit on the sofa to better look at Diana where she sat at the other end. She was leaning forward, elbows on her knees as she gazed into the cold fireplace nearby.

The lounge was empty except for the two of them, and though it was nearly one in the morning, neither of them had suggested they call it a night.

"Ellie, you mean?"

Diana nodded, still without looking at him. "She wasn't very big at all. And couldn't have been more than . . . what? Twenty-two? Twenty-three?"

"About that."

"We didn't talk about her much. I mean, she was lying there, dead. Murdered. Just a few yards away. And we hardly talked about **her**."

"We were all thinking about her. You know that."

"I guess."

Quentin drew a breath and let it out slowly. "Without a certain amount of detachment, cops couldn't do their jobs. Not for long, anyway."

"But what was my excuse?"

"It isn't an excuse, Diana, it's just the way things are. Death is always around us. We all learn to deal with it the best way we can, sometimes just moment to moment. But you of all people know it's not an ending. Or at least not an absolute ending."

She turned her head then and looked at him, frowning. "I hadn't thought... but that should make me feel differently about death, shouldn't it? That I know there's some kind of existence beyond it. That I know we don't just... stop."

"Maybe you will feel differently about it one day."

"But not today?"

Quentin hesitated. "A lot's happened in a very short time. You probably haven't even begun to process it all."

"Have you?"

He found the question surprising at first, but then not so much. "You're wondering why I haven't asked you any details about Missy."

"You've spent so many years thinking about her. Working to solve her murder. Going over the facts again and again. It's been an obsession."

"Yes. It has."

"So, yeah, I guess I'm surprised you haven't asked me more about her."

"What could I ask? If she looks the same? I know she does. If she's happy? I know she isn't. If she'll help me solve her murder? I know she won't."

"She said . . . it wouldn't help me to know who killed her. That it wouldn't help you. I don't know what she meant by that. I'm sorry."

"It's all right."

Diana shook her head. "It isn't all right. Because now you're here. And Missy's here. Not so far away, in one sense, not with me here too. Almost close enough to touch. I touched her. I touched her hand, and it was . . . surprisingly warm. And then I opened my eyes, and it was your hand I was touching."

Quentin didn't say anything, just looked at her.

"We're connected, aren't we, the three of us? I'm connected to Missy by blood, and you're connected to us by what happened twenty-five years ago."

"It's a little more complicated than that," he said finally.

"Is it? Why is it?"

"Because we're alive, and Missy's dead."

Diana turned that over in her mind. "I don't understand."

"I know you don't. It's another thing you haven't really had the time—or the emotional energy—to process."

Her frown returned. "Is there something between us? You and me?"

"What do you think? No—what do you feel?"

A little laugh escaped her. "I feel . . . raw. Overloaded. Numb one minute and incredibly aware of everything around me the next. I feel afraid a lot. And anxious. Confused. But not in the gray time. Isn't that strange? In the gray time, I feel calm and sure of myself. It's like pulling on a comfortable pair of jeans I've worn so long they're almost a part of me."

Quentin nodded. "That's when you're tapped in, connected to your abilities. When you're centered, balanced. Whole."

"And when I'm here? In the everyday world of the living? Why can't I be centered here? Why can't I be balanced and whole?"

"You can be. You will be. But it takes time,

Diana. You might have learned to do it by now, but they cheated you out of that time with the drugs and the therapy. You...have a lot of catching up to do."

"Consciously."

Again, Quentin nodded. "Your subconscious has been learning for years, obviously. Maybe all your life. In dreams. During those blackouts."

"I thought of the dreams and the blackouts as me being...out of control," she murmured, half to herself. "But I was most in control then, wasn't I?"

Quentin sensed danger in that question, though he couldn't have said just why. "Maybe. On some level. But as gifted as you are, that isn't your natural state, Diana."

"Isn't it?"

"No, of course not. We exist in the...everyday world of the living. Physically and emotionally, this is where we belong. What we tap in to in order to use our abilities is a place we visit, not a place we live."

She looked at him as if she would have asked another question, but instead said, "I suppose you're right."

Again, Quentin felt uneasy without knowing why. The little voice he sometimes heard was silent, and yet he had the sense of something being slightly off, even wrong.

"Are you okay?" he asked.

"I'm tired." She smiled faintly. "It's . . . been a long day."

"Yeah. Look, until we know what's going on here, I'd feel better if you didn't spend the night in your cottage. Why don't you take my bed, and I'll bunk down on the sofa bed in the sitting room?"

She didn't exactly protest, but said, "Nate has officers patrolling the grounds."

"I know. Still."

"There are plenty of empty rooms here in the main building."

Steadily, he repeated, "I know."

Diana looked at him for a long moment, then nodded. "Okay. Thanks."

And it wasn't until a few minutes later, when they were in his suite and she was about to close the door of the bedroom, that Diana went back to a subject they had touched on earlier.

"There is something between us."

At the moment, there was a door between them. A door she was about to close.

He stood there looking down at her, wanting to say more than he knew he should.

Not now. Not yet. She had been through so much, and her own words told him she was too confused and unsettled to be able to handle any-thing more right now.

So all he said was, "There was always something between us, Diana. Try to get some sleep."

At first it seemed she'd question that, but finally she just nodded, and murmured, "Good night." And closed the door.

Diana didn't know if it would work. Whatever control she sometimes managed to have while in the gray time, the fact was that as far as she knew, she herself had never instigated that . . . process. She had always been called, summoned really, by one or more of the guides. Dragged from sleep or into one of the scary blackouts without so much as a by-your-leave.

Or, as in the most recent case, by the voice in her mind she thought now had probably always been Missy.

Which meant she hadn't a clue how to, on her own and without prompting, fashion or open a door into that realm.

But she had to try. Because among the countless puzzles and questions of this day, one question stood out from the rest, haunting her.

She had to at least try to find the answer.

Quentin wouldn't approve, she knew that. And she also knew that his likely disapproval was worth paying attention to for the simple reason that he was far more experienced in psychic matters than she was—consciously, at any rate—and very likely knew when something paranormal shouldn't be attempted.

Which was why she hadn't told him she was going to try this.

She made herself comfortable on his bed, lying atop the turned-down covers, propped up with an extra pillow. She turned off all but the lamp on the nightstand, so that the room was only softly lighted.

Even as she closed her eyes and tried to relax, Diana was aware of the nagging notion that attempting this so near in time and place to a vicious murder was probably not the safest thing she could have done.

That didn't stop her either.

Not knowing how else to do it, she breathed steadily, evenly, and concentrated on trying to make herself boneless. Limp. One muscle at a time, limb by limb. Then, when she felt as relaxed as she was likely to become, she tried to visualize a door. Rather to her surprise, it was very easy to do, forming rapidly in her mind's eye as though it stood just before her.

And to her increasing uneasiness, the door was green.

Diana hesitated, but in the end her need to find the answer to the question haunting her was stronger, even, than her instincts for self-preservation. She reached out and grasped the doorknob, surprised to "feel" it as though it were actually real, and turned it.

She opened the door and stepped through into the gray time. A long corridor stretched before her, cold and gray and virtually featureless.

Diana hesitated again, still holding the door open as she half turned to gaze back through it. Eerily, she saw Quentin's bedroom, the lamp on the nightstand glowing warmly, the turned-back covers and banked pillows on the bed.

The empty bed.

"I'm here," she heard herself murmur, her voice as always hollow in the gray time. "I'm here physically."

She hadn't counted on that.

"This is not a good idea."

Startled, Diana turned quickly back toward the corridor, and the doorknob slipped from her hand. She found herself facing the little girl who had guided her down to the stables, Becca.

"You're not supposed to be here, not yet," Becca told her.

Diana glanced back over her shoulder to see the green door closed behind her. "As long as I remember where this door is, I can get back," she said.

Becca shook her head. "That's not the way things work here. The door won't be in the same place. The **place** won't be in the same place."

"I'm not in the mood for riddles, Becca."

The little girl heaved a sigh. "It's not a riddle, it's just the way things **are**. You'll remember if you think about it. You made the door, so you carry it with you. Sort of."

"Then I'll be able to find it if I need to leave in a hurry, won't I?"

"I hope so."

Diana tried to pretend to herself that the little chill she felt was entirely due to the usual coldness of the gray time rather than to the child's obvious doubt.

"Where's Missy?" she asked Becca.

Becca cocked her head to one side, as though listening to some distant sound. "You really shouldn't be here, Diana. Killing Ellie was just the start. It knows about you now. And it wants you."

"Why?" Diana asked, as steadily as she could manage.

"Because you're finding the secrets. You found Jeremy's bones. You found the trap door and the caves. You found the picture of you and Missy."

"But those are just—pieces of the puzzle."

"And you have almost all of them now. You'll

be able to help us stop it this time." Her certainty wavered. "I think."

That didn't reassure Diana very much. "Look, Becca, I need to talk to Missy."

"Missy isn't here anymore."

17

Diana felt a deeper chill. "What do you mean?"

"I mean she isn't here. When you opened the door the last time, when she held your hand, she left the gray time and returned with you."

"Why?"

"Something she needs to do, I expect."

Slowly, Diana said, "I didn't see her. When I was back with Quentin, I didn't see her."

"Sometimes, we don't want to be seen, even by mediums. Besides, I expect you were upset. Remembering about your mama and all."

"You know about that?"

Becca nodded. "Uh-huh. Missy told me."

"Do you know—" Diana steadied her voice. "Do you know why our mother was trapped on this side of the door?"

"That's why you crossed over, isn't it? And why you crossed over all the way, in the flesh. You tried too hard. Because it means so much to you. Because you have to know what happened to your mama."

"Answer me, Becca. Do you know what happened to her? Do you know where she is?"

Becca turned and began walking down the long corridor.

Immediately, Diana followed. "Becca—"

"Don't get too far from the door, Diana."

Diana hesitated, glanced back. But the green door was still there. She continued to follow the little girl. "I've followed you guides most of my life," she said, not without a touch of bitterness. "Always following, always doing whatever it was you needed me to do. Dammit, this time **I** need something. Why can't one of you help me for a change?"

"We've been helping you all along, Diana."

"Oh, sure. Leaving me up to my waist in a lake, or driving my father's car down a highway—"

"That wasn't us."

"What do you mean, it wasn't you? I blacked out, and—"

"The drugs were too strong. They pulled you back before you were supposed to go."

Diana didn't find that terribly reassuring. "So just because I came out of most blackouts safe at home doesn't mean that's where I was the whole time, I gather?"

"Well, it's very helpful for us to have someone who can cross over in the flesh," Becca said. "Most mediums can barely see or talk to us, much less walk with us."

"Speaking of which," Diana said, "where are we going?" The words were barely out of her mouth when she stopped abruptly, momentarily disoriented, because she and Becca were no longer in the long corridor. Instead, they were standing in the garden outside the conservatory.

They were still in the gray time, which meant the garden was as motionless as a photograph and looked blurred and one-dimensional and colorless, and the landscape's lighting did nothing to change any of that.

Becca, who had also stopped, turned to face her. "Since you're here, we have to take the chance. There's something you need to see."

"Oh, God, not again." Diana frowned at her. "I told you, I have a question of my own this time."

"Then maybe he can answer it for you."

"He? He, who?"

Becca nodded toward the conservatory. "In there."

Diana would have protested again, but in a blink her child guide was gone, and she found herself alone. "Dammit." With little choice in the matter, she went into the conservatory.

For some reason, she wasn't surprised to see that the artistic workshop had left evidence of its existence on this side of the door.

There were the paintings propped on easels— except that there seemed to be an awful lot of them, a forest of them. Diana picked her way through slowly, looking at each in turn, feeling her scalp crawl and tingle unpleasantly.

These weren't the paintings she remembered from the workshop. There had been violence in those, images from troubled minds, but . . . not like this.

One after another, these images spoke of abject terror. Faces twisted in hideous grimaces. Bodies contorted into violent poses. Explosions destroying. Weapons tearing flesh. Disease, starvation, torture.

And symbolic as well as literal images of fear. Darkness slashed through with lightning bolts. Spiders. Snakes. Creepy alleyways. Lonely, deserted country roads. A broken window. A fly caught in a web.

Diana paused at last before the painting of an image that was terrifyingly familiar. A dark, dark space, tiny, airless, perhaps a closet. And in the back corner, her arms wrapped tightly around her up-drawn legs, sat a little girl with long dark hair and a tearstained face.

"Amazing how easy it is to identify her, isn't it? That tiny figure in that small, dark corner. She could be anyone. But she could only be Missy."

Diana stepped quickly to the side so that she could see beyond the painting. "You? What the hell are you doing here?"

"Waiting for you," Beau said.

Nate knew he should go home to bed, get a fresh start in the morning—later in the morning—but he also knew he'd be too restless to sleep. There was paperwork awaiting him back at the station, but that held even less appeal, and he wasn't really surprised to find himself just casually wandering past Stephanie's slightly open office door.

She was sitting at her desk, frowning over what he felt was an uncharacteristically untidy jumble of papers spread out on the blotter.

"You're working late," he said from the doorway.

Stephanie looked up with a start, but then smiled. "Not exactly work. Or at least, not work I'm being paid to do. I wanted to keep looking through the old files, see if I could find something useful."

"I could have been anybody, you know," he told her, pushing the door the rest of the way open. "Sneaking up on you—" He broke off, rather sheepishly, because the door creaked loudly as it opened wide enough to admit him.

Stephanie grinned and moved a stack of papers to reveal a gleaming .45 automatic. "I'm fast, especially with the adrenaline rush. If I hadn't instantly recognized your voice, you would have been looking down the barrel of this before you could get anywhere near the desk."

Nate sat down in her visitor's chair. "Never mind fast—are you any good with that?"

"Yes. And I have a license for it. A license to carry it, for that matter." Soberly, she added, "I think our nighttime security is pretty good, especially with your people patrolling as well, but with a killer here somewhere, I'm taking no chances. Army brat, remember?"

"I remember. And I feel a bit better about you working late alone down here. But only a bit." He paused. "You do realize this killer is likely to be someone you know? Or at least that he'll wear a familiar face?"

"The thought had occurred. In a place like The Lodge, all dressed in its Victorian grandeur, it'd be easy to imagine that only the odd maniac wandering past could possibly have sullied our good name with something as distasteful as murder."

He lifted an eyebrow at her.

Descending to normality, Stephanie said, "Except that this place never really was unsullied, was it?"

"Not according to Quentin."

"And not according to what records I've gone over so far. Did you know that the first death recorded on these grounds happened while the place was being built?"

"Yeah, one of my people found mention of that in a historical database. Not so uncommon around construction sites, especially over a hundred years ago."

"Yeah. But this guy didn't fall from a scaffold or get crushed by falling stone, or anything like that. The local doctor at the time stated in writing that the victim was frightened to death."

"Frightened? Of what?"

"Nobody could say. They came to work early one morning, and there he was, just lying near the foreman's shack. No cuts, no bruises. Place wasn't far enough along to even have security out here, not that they needed much in those days. Bottom line, nobody saw anything."

"Frightened to death. Heart attack?" Nate guessed.

"The doc stated that his heart stopped—but that it wasn't diseased, wasn't enlarged, wasn't any of the things they believed in those days showed signs of trouble. And, apparently, he looked scared out of his mind. His face was frozen in an expression of absolute terror."

Nate was silent, frowning.

"That's not all," Stephanie continued. "Another half dozen men died during the construction of The Lodge and its stables. And all the deaths were...just a little bit strange. Sure-footed men falling. Skilled men having accidents with tools. Healthy men getting very sick very suddenly."

"What about after construction?"

"Well, then the records get just a bit murky." She shrugged, frowning a little herself. "I know enough about record-keeping to know that the entries I've found so far concerning illnesses, disappearances, and deaths here were noted with an absolute minimum of detail, almost casually."

"What are you saying?"

"I'm saying that from the get-go, any sort of bad news for The Lodge—especially of the death-on-the-grounds variety—was strongly downplayed."

"Wouldn't that be expected for a hotel?"

"To a certain extent, yeah. But your average hotel, when faced with the disappearance, death, or even murder of one of its guests, would have paperwork up the wazoo. Police reports, security reports, doctors' statements. Every piece of paper that could possibly be required to acquit the hotel and all its employees of any wrongdoing."

"Which The Lodge doesn't have."

"Like I said. If you ask me, somebody very early on made the decision of how bad news was to be handled. And whether it became habit or an ironclad rule, that's how it was done from that point onward."

"No paperwork."

"No paperwork, and only the bare mention of an occurrence. Name, date, not much more. Usually buried in accounts of the day-to-day running of the place."

Nate rested his forearm on her desk, fingers drumming absently. "I know how many deaths and disappearances we're talking about in the last twenty-five years, thanks to Quentin's obsession. What about before that? How many?"

"Oh, jeez, it'll be weeks before I can tell you that. I'm barely up to about 1925."

"Okay. How many up to 1925?"

Stephanie drew a breath. "Counting the deaths during construction, I have reported on the grounds of The Lodge more than a dozen deaths by 1925."

It took a minute, but Nate finally said, "Of those, how many were suspicious?"

"In my opinion? All of them, Nate. All of them."

"Are you dead?" Diana asked incredulously.

Beau smiled. "No."

She took a step closer, uncertain. "Are you a medium?"

"No."

Diana looked around her at the gray easels with their gray canvases daubed and stroked with varying shades of gray paint. She looked at the gray plants here and there in the conservatory, looked down at her own gray self and then up at him. Gray too. Everything was gray.

"Then I repeat. What the hell are you doing here?"

"I told you. Waiting for you."

"Beau, do you know where we **are**?"

"I think you call it the gray time."

"What do you call it?"

He looked around him, as though in mild curiosity, and said, "Your name fits. It's an interesting place. Or—time."

"Only the dead walk here."

"You walk here."

"I'm a medium." She stopped, startled, and Beau smiled again.

"Is that the first time you've said it?"

"I guess so. First time I meant it, anyway."

"It'll get easier," he told her. "Not so surprising. Even ordinary, after a while."

Diana shook her head. "Never mind that. I don't understand how you're here."

"It's a knack I have. My sister says I'm . . . very plugged in to the universe."

"Is that supposed to be an explanation?"

"Probably not. Diana, it doesn't really matter how I'm here. All that matters is that you see what I have to show you, and listen to what I have to tell you."

"You sure sound like a guide," she muttered.

"Sorry." He turned, beckoning her to follow, and led the way to the back corner where her easel was set up.

Her easel. Her sketchpad. Her drawing of Missy, there despite the fact that she knew it was in the tote bag in her cottage. But more astonishing, there was a brilliant scarlet slash across the sketch, glistening wetly and, in fact, still dripping onto some rags below the easel.

Scarlet. Not gray.

Like the green door, this was a color she could see.

"Why?" she asked, sure somehow that she wouldn't have to explain her question more fully.

"Signposts," he said. "The gray time has them as well. Things to pay attention to. Things to remember, so you can find your way. Only here they stand out a bit more."

Diana thought about that. "The green door I get; it's the way back. The way out. But this?"

Beau stepped back, gesturing for her to move closer to the easel.

She did so, looking at the sketch that certainly looked like the one she'd drawn. At the scarlet slash across Missy's delicate form. The scarlet that seemed to be . . . bleeding off the edge of the paper. Almost as if . . .

Diana took another step and bent slightly forward, looking more closely at the scarlet marring the sketch. It wasn't easy to see, because the scarlet (paint? blood?) had run, distorting the shape of the . . . letters?

"It wasn't clear at first," Beau said from behind her. "Just looked like a slash of color. Then, slowly, the letters began to appear. That's when I knew you needed to see this."

Absently, she said, "Why not show me on the other side of the door, outside the gray time? It's there too, isn't it?"

"It's there. Here. But it's only a slash of color, no letters. Someone suggested I take a look here in the gray time, in order to see what was really there."

"Someone?"

"Bishop."

Diana wasn't surprised. "I should have known you were a part of that team. He expected you'd see a warning, huh?"

"I think so. And said you needed to see it. He also said it would be tonight, which surprised me. After the day you've had, I didn't think you'd try this so soon."

Diana straightened with a sigh. "I don't suppose he offered any instructions for me?"

"No. Not something he often does in cases like this."

"What's really astonishing is that there **are** cases like this. All this time, I thought I was alone."

"You aren't."

"Yeah. I'm getting that. I just hope it isn't too late."

"If it helps," Beau said, "my window into the universe tells me that Quentin is your ace."

"I've sort of been getting that too." She drew a breath. "But he is not going to like what I have to do next."

"You know?"

Diana nodded. "I do now. Seeing this . . . I remember all the nightmares. All the messages

Missy has been trying to send me since I got here. Even before I got here. She's been preparing for this all this time. Knowing I'd come. Knowing Quentin would be here as well. She's been . . . very patient."

"Some things have to happen just the way they happen. In their own time."

"Ironic that I learn that in a place with **no** time."

"As long as you learn it."

With a sigh, Diana said, "Anybody ever tell you that you sound a lot like a fortune cookie?"

"It has a familiar ring."

"I'm not surprised. And I don't suppose you can answer the one question I came here this time to ask?"

"Sorry."

"That too will come only in its own time?"

"Yes. Until then, you have other things to worry about, Diana. You've already been here too long."

"I know." The cold had been seeping into her very bones, and she felt stiff, almost sluggish. Even her thoughts were beginning to drift.

"Go back. Now."

Diana looked around her, frowning, and said, "I'm a long way from the door."

"Diana—"

"A long way. And I think . . ."

Tha-thum.
Tha-thum.
"I think it's looking for me."

Beau came awake with the suddenness of one leaving a nightmare, which was pretty close to the truth. He had to move quickly, and yet his body felt stiff and cold, and as he got himself off his bed and started toward the door, he was abruptly aware of a deeper appreciation of the colorful, three-dimensional world around him.

Stupid thing for an artist to need a reminder of, but one visit to the gray time had certainly cured him of any tendency to take this warm and living world for granted.

Even his Hyacinth Room, which he'd thought a bit too fussy for his taste when he first arrived at The Lodge, looked only pleasant and comfortable as he more or less staggered through it to the door.

Christ, he felt as though he'd walked up a mountain. With a Volvo on his back. Pounding heart, shaking legs, weak as a kitten. In thirty-odd years of psychic experiences, some of them truly horrendous, he'd never emerged from anything that had drained him this much.

He wondered if Quentin had any idea of just how strong Diana really was.

He had to traverse a long corridor and climb one flight of stairs to get to Quentin's room, and by the time he reached the door he felt he was only just beginning to function normally. He was still cold, though. Chilled to the bone.

He braced himself with one hand on the doorjamb, deciding that "normal" was probably stretching things more than a bit. Before he could rap on the door it was jerked open, and Quentin stood there. He was fully dressed, wide-awake and tense, and spoke to Beau as though the conversation between them had already started.

"She's in the gray time."

"Yeah. And I'm not so sure she can find her way out of it alone."

"Jesus. Why the hell didn't you—"

"Nothing I could do. I was just doing a version of dream-walking, not there in the flesh. And it's definitely her realm, not mine."

Quentin didn't even question that. "Where was she? Relative to our side, I mean?"

"The conservatory. But I don't know if she's still there. If her instincts are good, she's looking for a place to hide. Whatever's been doing all the killing here—I think it's after her."

"I knew I shouldn't have left her alone. God-dammit, she can't fight this thing without help."

"I don't think she even knew it would happen tonight; she just went looking for the answer to a question. But she's been in the gray time too long, especially here, and it's weakened her. Believe me, I know." He still had one hand braced against the doorjamb for support.

Quentin seemed to notice the artist's appearance for the first time. "You don't look so good."

"I'll be fine. Go after Diana. Your cop pal is still here; I'll get him to roust his people."

"What good will that do? I'm not even sure I'll be able to see her this time—I sure as hell didn't see her leave, and I've been up and wide-awake."

"Ellie Weeks, like all the other victims, was killed by a flesh-and-blood murderer. Whatever's pulling the strings from the other side, that killer's on our side of the door—and if he's hunting Diana, he's visible."

Quentin stared at him for a moment, then went back inside his room long enough to get his gun. Tucking it inside the waistband of his jeans at the small of his back, he said, "And he's hunting Diana because only the mind of a powerful medium can give him something he's never had before."

Beau nodded. "A permanent way out, a means to live again in the flesh. And Diana knows it, thanks to a warning from Missy."

After working so hard, fighting her way out of the haze of medications and then struggling to come to terms with what she could do, hiding now was the last thing Diana would have chosen. But—

You have to. Don't let it find you. Not yet.

There was a plan and Diana understood it, if only in its bare outlines. What she understood even more, however, was that she was not strong enough to stand alone, not now, not on this side of the door. That would be a battle she'd lose.

Hide.

It was almost like her own heartbeat, that voice in her mind, as familiar as her own thoughts. And yet separate, distinctly apart. Something she'd heard, listened to, all her life.

Or tried to, through the medicated fog.

"Dad has a lot to answer for," she muttered, stumbling from the conservatory and toward the main building.

He was doing what he thought best.

"He was afraid. I get that."

He was trying to save your life. He'd lost me. And Mommy. He couldn't lose you too.

"There was a better way."

He didn't know that. He believed if you didn't know about me at all, it would hurt less

than knowing I'd lived, and was stolen away—and died.

"So he came down here and bought a cover-up, right? And then kept me medicated so I wouldn't remember, couldn't learn about my abilities, much less consciously control them."

It wasn't that deliberate. The doctors and medicines. He never understood what happened to Mommy, but he was afraid it would happen to you too. He did his best to keep that from happening, Diana.

"If you say so." Diana hesitated, sticking close to the shrubbery that half masked one of the service entrances. "Now where do I go? Dammit, never a guide around when I need one." She crossed her arms over her breasts and shivered. She was cold. And getting colder.

You know why.

"Yeah. Your plan. Why didn't you try it sooner?"

Couldn't. I didn't live to be strong enough.

"And I did?"

Yes. It'll take your strength. Plus the others. The ones who're ready to move on.

"Waiting all this time for me?"

Yes. Waiting for a chance. A chance to stop it.

"You keep saying 'it.' All of you do. But Samuel Barton was a man once upon a time."

It was never a man. Not really. It was always evil. And when they killed its flesh, they set it free. Helped it grow even more powerful.

"So it could possess anyone not strong enough to fight it off."

Yes, sometimes. But if they weren't strong enough to fight it off, they weren't strong enough to hold it for long. They ... burned out. And it was energy again, building up, looking for another host. A more permanent host.

"Me."

Once you discovered what you could do, once you began remembering and became aware, it was only a matter of time before it sensed your strength. Your abilities. But it happened much faster than we expected. I'm sorry, Diana.

"Maybe faster is better," Diana said, half to herself. "I've barely had time to think. Otherwise, all this would probably drive me back into a mental hospital."

No. That won't happen again. You're too strong now.

"I hope you're right." Diana looked around again, then slipped through the shrubbery and used the service entrance. Despite the blinking control pad indicating the presence of a security system, she simply turned the handle and opened the door.

Electronics didn't work in the gray time. Or maybe they just didn't exist. Diana had never known which.

Tha-thum.

"Oh, shit," she whispered.

Diana.

She realized she was pressed up against the icy wall just inside the door, palms flat on either side of her hips. She realized that her legs were about to buckle, that she was about to slide down the wall and end up in a heap on the floor, helpless.

Useless.

Diana! Don't let it make you afraid. That's how it catches us. That's how it wins.

"I can make a door," she whispered. "I can bring the door to me. I can—"

No. You can't open a door. Not here. Not alone.

She drew a breath, fighting to steady herself, trying to will the strength to return to her body. It was the hardest thing she'd ever done, and she wasn't at all sure she was successful, but she tried her best. "Where is it?"

Near. But you have a safe place. The green door, Diana. Find the green door.

"I made one before."

You have to find the one that exists on both sides. In both worlds. Find that green door, Diana.

"Why aren't you here to lead me?"

Because there's something I have to do on this side. But I'll help you. Just keep going.

The plan. Diana pushed herself away from the cold, cold wall and started down what looked like an endless, featureless corridor, searching for a green door.

18

He hadn't really expected to find her in the conservatory, but Quentin checked there first, just to be sure. No Diana, just a dozen easels holding sketchpads and canvases. He stood in the doorway and gazed out over the security-lit gardens, trying to quiet his mind and concentrate his senses, trying to reach out for her. To see farther than he could see. To hear farther than he could hear. To touch what was just beyond his reach.

All he could feel was his pounding heart.

"Is there something between us? You and me?"

He should have answered her. Should have

told her the truth, all of it. He had an aching sense that it would have made a difference now.

"Quentin, what the hell's going on?"

It was Nate, with Stephanie beside him, both of them holding guns and looking worried, and Quentin was conscious of a distant shock that they had approached without his awareness.

Where was the spider sense? Why couldn't he sense Diana in some way?

"Diana's missing," he said, offering the short and reasonable version.

"Shit," Nate said, stepping back outside and fumbling for his police radio.

Stephanie said, "Would she have come out here? This late?"

Another question he couldn't take the time to answer with the truth. Instead, as a memory jabbed him, he said quickly, "Stephanie, are there any green doors in The Lodge?"

"Green doors? No, I—wait." She frowned. "Yeah, there is one. I remember a note about it in my manager's file, something about that door being left its original color because it was virtually the only wooden structure to survive the fire."

"The North Wing fire?"

"Yeah. Apparently, one of the owners was superstitious about it."

He stared at her. "My room's in that wing. I don't remember ever seeing a green door."

"Well, you wouldn't have. It's at the end of a hallway with a funny corner, and it's all service areas now. Has been since the wing was rebuilt. Linen storage, an equipment room, supply closet. There's no window at the end of that hall, and it's the opposite end from the stairs, so you wouldn't be drawn in that direction."

"And it's the only green door in the building?"

"Far as I know." She was frowning at him.

Quentin wasn't surprised. He thought he probably looked a little wild. Or a lot wild. "Where is it?" he demanded. "How do I get there?"

"It's—North Wing, third floor. Turn left at the top of the central stairs, then all the way to the end."

Christ, he'd been closer to it when he had first realized Diana was gone. Quentin didn't wait to see if the others joined him. He just ran. He thought he heard Nate yelling something after him, something about one of his men reporting that Cullen Ruppe had been attacked, but all his energy was focused on finding Diana.

And it was when he was halfway up the dimly lit stairs that he was brought almost to his knees by the first real vision of his entire life.

For the very first time, he saw the future.

Diana thought it was going to take more strength than she had, but somehow she managed to follow Missy's directions. Turn. Take the stairs. Up another floor. Turn again.

She was getting colder and colder, so cold that she wondered why her breath wasn't misting the air before her. Except that was another thing that never happened in the gray time.

Tha-thum.

Tha-thum.

She tried to move faster, but her legs ached and it was difficult just to put one foot in front of the other. And that strange, hollow fluttering that seemed to be inside her. She wasn't sure if it was her own heart pounding or that other, more primitive sound.

Listen to me, Diana. The green door is just ahead. Just around that corner. I want you to open it. But don't go in.

"What?"

Quentin's coming. He'll be your lifeline.

"I've never needed a lifeline."

This time you will. And you can trust him. He won't let you go, you know that, don't you, Diana?

"Because you mattered so much to him," Diana said.

No. I'm his past. You're his future. That's why he won't let you go.

Diana wasn't sure she believed that, but she didn't question because she'd finally reached the end of the long hallway, and saw the odd turn at the end. The short hallway that ended in a green door.

Tha-thum.

Tha-thum.

She pushed herself those last few feet and grasped the old-fashioned door handle. "If I open this—"

You open two doors. In both worlds. Don't let go of the handle, Diana. Not until it's over.

"But—"

Reach for Quentin. And open the door.

Diana turned the handle and at the same moment reached back with her free hand. And reached out with more than flesh, more than will.

Almost immediately, there was a bright flash, and for an instant the gray time was gone. The door was a brighter green, and the embossed wallpaper of the short hallway showed its rich Victorian colors.

Then another flash, and this time she felt the warmth and strength of his hand gripping hers. Another flash, and she turned her head, saw him there.

And—

She was back. One hand holding the handle

of a slightly open green door. The other hand holding Quentin's.

"Diana—"

Tha-thum!

Tha-thum!

She caught a whiff of the unnervingly familiar stench, and before she could warn Quentin they both felt the heavy tread of surprisingly quick footsteps bearing down on them.

Don't touch the vessel, Diana.

To Quentin, she whispered, "Don't—"

"I know," he breathed in return. His fingers tightened around hers, and like her he pressed his back to the wall, leaving the hallway as open as possible in front of them as they both watched the corner.

She was already speaking as she came around it.

"There you are. I've been looking everywhere for you. This late, you should be in your bed. That's where I expected to find you."

It didn't take the strange light in her eyes or the weirdly pleasant smile to show that the creature who looked like Mrs. Kincaid was something other than sane.

The bloody butcher knife she carried was more than enough.

"I told Cullen," she went on as she stood in the short hallway with them. "I told him I wouldn't let him stop me. Wouldn't let any of you stop me. He tried, of course, just like he'd tried to warn Ellie. He really shouldn't have done that. Made me angry."

"You killed Ellie," Quentin said.

"Oh, that was just a favor for Mrs. Kincaid." It laughed. "She was pissed because she was pretty sure the girl had gotten herself knocked up by one of the guests. Can't have that, now, can we? Bound to cause trouble. So I took care of it."

Diana said, "Like you just tried to take care of Cullen?"

"I told him he should have stayed away. That he had no business coming back here. He's lucky I didn't take care of him years ago, when he figured out what was going on. But who was going to believe him? The cops? Of course not. Made 'em wonder about **him,** though. So he left."

"Why did he come back?" Quentin asked.

"Said a voice in his head told him to. Told him there'd be somebody here now who could stop me. That he could help. Funny as hell, isn't it? He's helping by bleeding all over himself."

Quentin said, "You're—Mrs. Kincaid is a medium. That's why you've been able to use her more than once."

Still holding the knife in a loose grip that wasn't at all casual, she—it—looked at him and smiled. "Why, yes. Always has been. But un-taught, and not very powerful. It was easy to get in, though. Easy to use her. I could never stay very long, of course. But long enough. Always long enough.

"And you never picked up on it, did you? All your visits over the years. Even way back, when you were just a kid. You didn't want to see the future, so you couldn't even see what was right in front of you, most of the time. Blind, in a way."

"I'm better now," Quentin said.

"Are you? Because of her, I suppose." She used the knife to indicate Diana. "I knew somebody was opening doors, but I wasn't sure who. Not until she started visiting the gray time."

"You were a killer once," Diana said. "A long, long time ago. You killed a lot of people."

"Why, yes, so I did. Still do, of course. Thanks to the bastards who killed me. I'd never felt rage until then. Never been so sure I wanted to go on living. So I did."

Quentin said, "In a manner of speaking. You existed, possessed weak minds and vulnerable bodies. That was why so many children died be-cause of you."

"You don't get it. The fun wasn't in killing the kids. The fun was in possessing their parents and forcing **them** to kill."

"Then Missy—"

"The one calling herself Laura Turner killed Missy. With a little help from me." The human face behind which a monster lurked twisted in a grimace. "Drove her mad. It does that sometimes, to the weak-minded. I had to get out of her fast. Couldn't control her after that."

"You—Mrs. Kincaid gave Laura an alibi."

"Well, of course. I didn't want anyone here at The Lodge under suspicion. This is my . . . home base, you might say. Besides, I wanted to use her again. But then she called the child's father, babbling out of her head about what she'd done and how she ought to be punished. I didn't wait for him to come do it, though. Took care of things myself."

"She hadn't left, had she?"

"No, but I made it look like she had." The thing inside the housekeeper shrugged.

Diana said, "And when he—when the child's father got here, he wanted it all to . . . go away."

"Guess he did. Because that's what happened. Which was fine with me."

Diana felt Quentin's fingers tighten on hers, and she knew he was aware of how much of her concentration was focused on that partially open door she was holding. It was taking all her strength and some of his as well; she could feel the pull on the other side, the natural force of something intended to be closed except in brief intervals.

The longer she held it partially open, the more force was being exerted in the effort to slam it shut.

It would require all that force, Diana knew. The only way to destroy the evil confronting them was to hurl its energy back through the gray time, through the limbo between worlds, and to what lay beyond. To carry it far beyond the physical world so that no doorway could ever allow it access again.

Diana was afraid she wouldn't be able to hold the door open long enough, even with Quentin's help, but then she saw Missy appear behind the creature, and the frail-looking child pushed its physical shell violently from behind, toward the doorway.

Using every ounce of strength she and Quentin could muster, Diana pulled the green door open all the way.

For just long enough.

In a moment out of time, Diana saw the ghosts of The Lodge, all of them, rushing past, helping to carry the creature and its shell through the doorway. The woman in Victorian dress, the nurse, the man in rough worker's clothing, the little boys—and then a blur of energy, of spirits, dozens of them, merging, meld-

ing, flowing through the doorway, all the door-
ways, raw power with absolute purpose reaching, grasping, drawing the black essence that was
all that was left of Samuel Barton out of the
human vessel containing it—

It seemed for that eternal instant that the energy pouring through the doorway would carry
Diana in as well, but Quentin didn't let go. Until
finally the last wisp rushed past and jerked the
door from her hand, slamming it closed.

"It's all right. It's just a door now."

Diana leaned weakly against Quentin as they
both looked at Missy.

A different Missy. Flesh, seemingly, rather
than spirit. Still thin and fragile, but smiling
now, no longer haunted.

Now, there's a thought. Diana almost
wanted to laugh.

Still without letting go of Diana's hand,
Quentin said tentatively, "Why can I see you?"

"Because Diana can. You two connected the
first time you touched." Her smile widened. "I
think some people call it fate." She held up one
hand, from which dangled a small locket.
"Maybe that's why the thing inside Mrs. Kincaid
took this from Ellie's body after it killed her. So
I could get it back."

Almost too tired to think, Diana began,
"Missy—"

"She's at peace, Diana. Mommy. She crossed over a long, long time ago, after she found me."

"That's why?"

"After I was abducted, she thought she could use her gifts to find me. But they were too strong for her. The door she made was only . . . one-way."

Softly, Quentin said, "And a body severed from its spirit doesn't live too long."

Missy nodded.

Diana had endless questions, but she knew there was little time left. So she asked the only thing that mattered, to her and to Quentin.

"Are you okay now?" she asked her sister.

"I'm okay now. It worked. The energy of everybody who was ready to cross over was enough to pull that evil out of the vessel holding it and through the gray time to the other side. It can't hurt anyone ever again."

Quentin glanced at Diana. "A basic law of physics. Energy can't be destroyed, only transformed."

Solemn, Missy said, "Yes, it's all about physics."

Again, Diana wanted to laugh. Instead, she said, "You do realize that once the sun comes up, I'm going to be convinced I dreamed all this?"

Missy looked at their clasped hands and smiled again. "I don't think so. I think that from now on, you won't have any trouble at all knowing what's real and what isn't." She stepped past them and opened the green door. There was an oddly blurred moment, and then they could see inside what appeared to be a pretty, old-fashioned bedroom.

"Missy—"

She looked at Quentin. "Thank you. For caring enough to keep coming back here all these years. It helped give me the strength to do what I had to. And it wasn't your fault, you know. It was never your fault. Something that old . . . that evil . . . You couldn't have known, and you couldn't have stopped it. And some things are meant to happen just the way they happen."

Diana would have said goodbye, wanted to, but Missy took the choice out of her hands by smiling sweetly at them both and stepping into the pretty bedroom. And closing the door behind her.

Quentin and Diana were left staring at each other, with barely a moment to adjust before Nate hustled around the corner, gun drawn.

"Jesus," he exclaimed, "are you two all right? Cullen said the Kincaid woman went nuts and tried to kill him. He's bleeding like a stuck pig. Where is she?"

Diana hesitated, then reached out and slowly opened the door. Inside, they all saw the orderly shelves of a linen closet with sheets and towels piled high. And in the center of the room, beside an empty laundry cart, lay the sprawled body of Virginia Kincaid, the bloody knife still clutched in her hand.

Nate went in cautiously, kicking the knife away before bending to check her pulse. "She's still alive," he said.

"Breathing, anyway," Quentin murmured.

"The doctors say she had a stroke," Nate told them much later that morning. "She's in a coma, and they don't know if she'll ever come out of it."

"I have a feeling," Diana said, "that she won't." She also had a feeling that much of Virginia Kincaid's spirit had been eroded over the years, and that the final release had been just that. A release from an evil and unrelenting hell.

Unaware of—or studiously ignoring—undercurrents, Nate added, "And Cullen Ruppe is out of danger, since they got the bleeding stopped. He claims not to know why she suddenly went after him. Ask me, the woman just went nuts. I think there's something wrong with the air in this place."

"Not anymore," Quentin said.

The cop eyed them both as they sat side by

side on the sofa across from his chair. "You two look pretty chipper, considering a very long night with no sleep."

"Lots of coffee," Diana said.

Nate grunted. "I've had gallons, and I'm still beat. And you'd never know it's Saturday, from all the stuff I'm supposed to be dealing with. Since the Kincaid woman confessed to you that she killed Ellie—the cell phone records show, by the way, that Ellie called an out-of-state number we've traced to a guest who stayed here a couple of months ago, and the doc confirms she was pregnant, so— What was I saying?"

"Since she confessed," Quentin prompted.

"Oh. Yeah. Since she confessed, that pretty well solves the murder. That spelunker team you told me about is coming to check out the caves, but it'll probably be next week before they get here. In the meantime, the forensic anthropological team arrives first thing in the morning, and I'm keeping someone posted in the tack room twenty-four/seven for the duration. The team will also take a look at the skeleton we found in the garden, though the DNA analysis confirms the remains of Jeremy Grant. Thanks for pushing that through so fast, by the way."

"No problem," Quentin said. "Somebody owed me a favor."

"Must have been a doozy. In the state labs, it can take months to get DNA results."

Without responding to that, Quentin merely said, "Has the boy's mother been notified?"

"Yeah. Closure for her."

"Sometimes," Quentin said, "that's what we need before we can put something behind us. And look ahead rather than back."

"The end of an obsession?" Nate asked curiously.

"You could say that."

Stephanie, coming into the lounge just then, said, "I still can't believe my housekeeper was a murderess. Except that part of me **can** believe it, which is creepy." She, also, looked rather bright-eyed for a night without sleep.

"Think of her as sick," Diana suggested. "Very, very sick."

"Lizzie Borden sick, yeah." Stephanie shivered. "I want to hire a new housekeeper. Soon."

Quentin looked at her. "One who won't write down secrets of the guests?"

"Exactly. Because I'm pretty sure she did. All on her own, though, not because she was paid to."

"That list you showed us of the managers who **were** paid to record all the secrets they knew of here—it ended with the manager who was here about five years ago?"

She nodded. "Neither of the two managers

prior to me was on that list. And neither am I, obviously. I didn't even know about it until I found it. And I wouldn't have recognized it for something suspicious if I hadn't been looking for just that. At first glance, it was just a list of bonuses paid to Management. Nothing unusual, on the face of it. It wasn't until I dug into separate salary records that I could be sure the **bonuses** were way out of line. Plus, I found the first of the account ledgers to cross-check, and so far at least a couple of those so-called bonuses were paid in cash and off the books."

"I'd call that suspicious," Nate said.

"And I wonder why it ended five years ago," Quentin said. "Stephanie, any idea who was keeping the list?"

She nodded promptly. "If I had to guess—and I do—it was probably Douglas Wallace. I think he instigated the so-called organization of the records in the basement just about five years ago, probably just because he's an anal neat freak. But then he found the sort of stuff he really didn't want to find, and started compiling that list.

"I double-checked some dates, and about the time Doug was going through old records in the basement, the last descendant of one of the original owners had just died."

Nate guessed, "You're saying the secret-keeping died with him?"

"Well, the official secret-keeping. And it makes sense. What probably started out as a pretty ruthless way to get some leverage when necessary back in the old days of robber barons just gradually became a practice nobody questioned and, finally, like a lot of old traditions, became unnecessary."

"We haven't found any recent dates," Diana noted. "Though, like you, I'm willing to bet we'll find a journal among Mrs. Kincaid's belongings. I'll bet she was keeper of the secrets in recent years."

"Maybe she didn't want to see the old tradition die," Stephanie offered. "She was like that, pretty much."

Diana didn't argue, since she had no way of knowing whether the housekeeper's own spirit had been capable of that or if it had been the controlling influence of Samuel Barton.

Stephanie shook her head. "I wonder if this place can ever be anything approaching normal."

"Maybe it can," Diana said. "Now."

"We'll see. Look, I don't know about you guys, but the mundane truth is that I'm starving, the cook does a wonderful brunch. How about a little good food to balance all that coffee?"

Nate got to his feet promptly. "You don't have to ask me twice."

As Diana and Quentin also rose, Stephanie said to them, "If anybody's interested, I think we'll be able to lay quite a few sins at the doors of The Lodge and the people who owned and ran this place over the years. Do you know, I found in one file a newspaper clipping about a man and his family who'd been killed in a car crash between here and Leisure about ten years ago. The article strongly implied that he'd been depressed and suicidal. And in the very same file was a notation from, I assume, the manager here at the time that a waiter had been fired sometime afterward for making up stories for reporters. The manager had also added another note that the surviving family members should be notified of the false newspaper article. But it was never done."

"How do you know?" Quentin asked.

"No copy of the letter in the file. And that particular manager seems to have been extremely meticulous about copying **everything.**"

"You," Nate informed her, "have too much time on your hands." He took one of them and led her, laughing, from the room.

Quentin was about to follow suit when the little girl they'd seen several times came into the lounge from the connecting library, carrying her dog.

Gravely, she said, "Bobby needs to know that."

"Needs to know what?" Diana asked.

"That Daddy wasn't trying to kill us." She held her dog, rubbing her chin absently in his silky fur. "See, my little brother Bobby wasn't with us. He'd been sick, so he stayed with Grandma while we came here. And when we left, well, it was raining. And foggy. And Daddy wasn't used to mountain roads. That was why."

Quentin was conscious only of shock, but this was clearly a familiar thing for Diana, who simply nodded and said, "We'll make sure Bobby knows the truth. What was your name?"

"Madison. And this is Angelo. He was with us that night. He goes everywhere with me. Everywhere."

"You can both go now," Diana said gently. "And be with your parents."

Madison sighed. "I thought they were here, you know. But... I was always good at imagining things. I guess I imagined them here. I miss them, though. Angelo and me, we're ready to go now. Thank you."

"You're welcome, Madison."

While they watched, the little girl carried her dog toward the doorway, fading into nothingness before reaching the hallway beyond.

"Jesus," Quentin said.

Diana looked up at him, smiling a little.

"Everything we went through last night, and you're shaken by one little girl and her dog?"

"Well...I've been seeing her. Clear as day." He frowned suddenly. "Since the morning we met."

"Guess Missy was right. We connected."

After a moment, Quentin reached for her hand and held it firmly. "I guess we did. How do you feel about that?"

"Hopeful."

"You'll go back to Virginia with me?"

"Well, I've got to meet Bishop."

"Diana."

Her smile widened. "I'll make you a deal. You help me convince my father that despite the secrets he kept for my own good, I'm a sane and rational woman, and—we'll go from there. Deal?"

"Deal," he replied, and kissed her.